1

Jade Foster could feel the familiar tension coiling in her stomach as she locked her front door, the key slippery in her fingers. She wiped her hands on her jeans, picked up the cellophane-wrapped bouquet of white roses and was just turning when she heard the sound of running footsteps on the dirt track that fronted her Wiltshire cottage, followed by a woman's breathless voice.

The woman appeared, grey haired and with a vibrant yellow straw bag flapping from one arm, panting heavily, in her front garden.

'Oh, I'm so glad I caught you,' she gasped. 'You are the animal rescue woman, aren't you, dear? They said in the pub I'd find you here. But you're going out?' She paused for breath and added in a bemused voice, 'You don't look a bit like I expected.'

Jade smiled and wondered what her visitor had expected. She was wearing jeans, which had started off black, but were now faded to grey, along with a cream tee-shirt – one of the few she owned that didn't have a flippant slogan on the back. She'd meant to be smarter to visit the cemetery. It seemed disrespectful to go in her scruffs. She'd clipped back her unruly brown hair and put on mascara, but she hadn't been able to find any more suitable clothes in her wardrobe. Probably because most of them were stuffed in the laundry basket and laundry was way down her priority list at the moment.

'I thought you'd be older,' her visitor gasped. 'And bigger – stronger – you know.'

'I'm stronger than I look,' Jade murmured, wondering what she was letting herself in for. Lots of people who turned up at Duck Pond Rescue seemed surprised when they saw her. She wasn't sure what she was supposed to look like. Evidently not tall and slightly built – she hadn't been called beanpole for nothing at school – and most people were amazed when she told them she was twenty-seven, not seventeen.

'Are you all right?' she asked gently, because the woman's face was scarlet with exertion and there were beads of sweat below the silver rims of her glasses. September had turned into an Indian summer. 'Where have you run from?'

'Oh, only a little way – my car's parked down on the main road. He flew straight at me, you see. I didn't have a hope of stopping.'

'A bird?' Jade said, concerned, because birds rarely survived run-ins with cars. 'Do you know what sort of bird he is?'

'Blooming great thing – I was lucky my window wasn't open, he'd have been in the car then and I'd probably have crashed it. I don't know what kind he is. I don't know anything about birds, see. He's not dead, though, he was fluttering about on the grass verge. I couldn't get anywhere near 'im. Tried to attack me, he did.' She was already backing away down the track. 'You will come, won't you?'

'Yes, of course I'll come. It was good of you to stop.' Jade caught up with her visitor, torn between not wanting to rush her – she was elderly and still out of breath – and worry about getting to the injured bird before a predator did. Mind you, not being able to get 'near 'im' sounded promising. The bird couldn't be too badly hurt if it was still trying to defend itself.

'I hope I'm not holding you up, dear. You were just on your way out, weren't you?'

'Yes, I was on my way to see someone, but we didn't have a set time.' Understatement, Jade thought, swallowing down a mixture of regret and relief that she had an excuse to put off the inevitable looming confrontation for a little longer. She grabbed a small animal transporter and a net from an outbuilding on her way past and followed the woman back along the lane.

She'd been expecting a buzzard – there were dozens in the Wiltshire countryside – but as they got closer to the stricken bird, she realised it was bigger than a buzzard. A lot bigger and not the right colour either. It had chestnut feathers and a pale-coloured head, almost white with a yellow hooked beak. Jade frowned, racking her brains.

She'd had a friend, Ellen, at vet school who was really into birds. They'd often spent nights chatting about wildlife and about how to recognise the different birds of prey. This bird had distinctive yellow legs and a yellow beak. Also a forked tail.

'I think it's a red kite,' she told her companion with growing excitement. 'I've never seen one this close. Until a few years ago, they were virtually extinct in England, but they're common now.'

'Mmm.' The woman eyed her anxiously. 'You watch yourself, dear. Mind his claws. Poor little lamb's none too happy – not that I can blame 'im for that.' She hung back.

Jade approached cautiously with the net.

'Poor little lamb' were the last words she'd have used to describe the kite. Proud and beautiful, certainly, but this bird of prey was far from a 'little lamb'. Jade felt a surge of admiration as the bird glared at her and tried to rise in flight, but only succeeded in toppling sideways onto the grass verge. Broken wing, Jade guessed; it was surprising it wasn't dead after tangling with a car. Its wingspan must have been a couple of metres. Netting it without injury to either of them was going to be tricky, if not impossible.

She contemplated heading to the Red Lion, which was a couple of miles back along the road, and enlisting some help. On the other hand, the pub would have been open since midday; it was now gone four. The last thing she needed was a crowd of rowdy onlookers who fancied themselves as bird experts following her down here.

Deciding to have a go on her own, she edged forward. If she could restrain the bird with the net, she might be able to get close enough to immobilise it without frightening it into hurting itself further or injuring her.

Luck was on Jade's side for once. When the bird felt the net, it flapped angrily, tried to back its way out and ended up trapped against the fence that edged the ochre-coloured ploughed fields beyond the road. Taking care to avoid the lethal talons and wickedly hooked beak, Jade tightened the net, and the bird, no longer trying to escape but shrieking furiously, let her get close enough to touch.

Sweat dripped into her eyes as she crouched on the grass verge and, talking softly all the time, let the bird get used to her presence. 'All right, my sweetie, I'm not going to hurt you. I just want to check out that wing. You are a beauty, aren't you?'

When a car door slammed close by, Jade assumed the woman had decided to wait in her car, but then she heard a voice. She glanced up and saw a man in jeans and a casual jacket heading her way.

Great, that was all she needed. An interfering passer-by.

'Can I help?' He paused a few feet away, which she supposed

was better than blundering in and frightening her prospective patient.

'I'm fine,' she muttered, wiping sweat out of her eyes. 'Don't make any sudden movements, I don't want it scared. And please don't come any closer.'

'I wasn't planning on it.' His voice was wry and now she could see him properly she had an impression of a strong, angular face, fair hair that was slightly too long and cool grey eyes.

'I thought you might have broken down,' he added, hunkering down on the grass verge, his movements slow and controlled. 'That's why I stopped.'

The bird fluttered, aware of his presence, and distracted, Jade nodded. 'You could help, if you don't mind. You could open the door on that cage for me and pass it over very slowly.'

'Sure.' He did as she said and inched the transporter across the grass towards her.

There was one sticky moment when she was edging the bird into it and the woman, who Jade had forgotten all about, clapped her hands in excitement and shouted out, 'Well done, dear! Good for you!'

The bird fluttered wildly and extricated a leg from the net and Jade was only just in time to snatch her fingers out of slicing distance of its talons. She drew the net gently back into place, latched the transporter with a sigh of relief, wiped her face once more with the back of her hand, and stood up slowly.

The man who'd stopped to help glanced at her. 'Nice work. What will you do now – take it to a vet?'

'No need, I can sort it out myself. I think the wing's broken, but it's not irreparable. It just needs strapping up for a while. If it survives the shock of all the human contact, it'll be fine. I trained as a vet,' she added, which was true. 'I run an animal rescue place now.' She'd expected raised eyebrows, which was how people usually reacted, but he just nodded thoughtfully.

'Good luck.'

'Thanks. And thanks for your help.'

'Pleasure.' He gave her a little nod and headed back to a white Toyota, which was parked behind the woman's car.

'He was a nice young man, wasn't he, dear? I'm Dorothy, by the way. Dot to my friends.' The woman's sunny smile told Jade that she was now included in Dot's circle of friends. 'I'll give you a lift back up the lane, shall I?'

'It's probably better if I walk,' Jade said. 'Less stressful for our friend here than going in a car. It's not far.'

'Well, if you're sure, dear.' Dot's voice was dubious. 'I think it's wonderful what you do. I'm so relieved, I can't tell you. I felt awful when I hit him. I wasn't going very fast. I never do around these country lanes.'

'It's all right,' Jade reassured her. 'There's not a lot you can do when they fly straight into you.' She wondered if she should ask Dot back for a brandy – she could have done with one herself. And then she remembered she had a prior engagement. She'd been putting it off all day; she was amazed she'd managed to forget about it.

'Well, I'd like to give you a donation, dear. It's the least I can do after putting you to all this trouble.'

Jade shook her head, fully taking in for the first time her companion's appearance. Grey hair, which was coiled in a tight bun, kind faded blue eyes, a face creased with years of worry and navy-blue trousers shiny with age. Living on a pension, Jade decided. 'No need for a donation. Thanks again for coming to find me. Lots of people wouldn't have stopped.'

She watched the woman drive away and then she lifted the transporter, which wasn't much heavier with the bird in situ than it had been when it was empty. She would settle her patient in more permanent accommodation and leave it alone for the night. Then she really should get going before dusk fell. She'd rather have dealt with a dozen birds of prey than go where she'd been heading before Dot had interrupted her, but there could be no more putting it off. Bracing her back slightly and feeling guilty that she even wanted to put it off, Jade quickened her step. It wasn't long before she could see light glinting off the duck pond that had given both the lane and her cottage its name, and the weeping willow that overhung it like some dark green sentinel came into view.

2

Having settled the bird and left it water, Jade locked up the converted pigsty, which she referred to lightly as 'the hospital block', and went to collect the white roses she'd abandoned by her front door. Then she strolled along the quiet roads past untidy hedges that spilled out like overgrown mops of hair, revelling in the peace and enjoying the clear honey-coloured light of the September evening.

Ten minutes later, she was letting herself through the lichen-covered gate of the churchyard, aware of the small wooden thud as it swung shut behind her. She walked slowly along the mossy cobbled path between the graves. It seemed rude to run through a cemetery, disrespectful somehow, and however much she longed for this visit to be over, she didn't want to offend anyone. These people, whose headstones rose higgledy-piggledy from the ground on either side of her, seemed almost like friends, their names were so familiar, and she'd often wondered about their lives.

There was a newish headstone, close to the path, which she

always noticed because it had been erected just after she'd started coming here.

Benjamin and Evie McTaggart
Together Again

From the dates, it looked as though Evie had died a few weeks after her husband. How sad. There was a pot of wilting yellow carnations, which seemed out of place somehow, more of a wedding flower.

Jade paused to trail her fingers over the twin cherubs on their final resting place. She knew she was putting off the moment of confrontation. Silly to still think of it as a confrontation, yet a year of coming here hadn't made things any more bearable than they'd been in the beginning.

Sighing, she continued on until she was in one of the most peaceful parts of the cemetery, shaded as it was by a giant oak. Its leaves were caught halfway between summer and autumn. Soon they would fall, but for now they shone gloriously orange in the liquid golden light that preceded sunset.

She halted, her heart pounding, by the gleaming milk-white headstone with its marble angel, wings folded peacefully and head bowed, eyes cast forever downwards.

Elizabeth Foster
16 September 1969–21 September 2023
Rest In Peace

Such a simple epitaph for such a complex woman, Jade had thought at the time, but she'd been unable to think of anything else to say. She'd always had trouble knowing what to say to her mother. And when she'd died so unexpectedly of a stroke just before her fifty-fourth birthday, it had suddenly been too late for words.

'Hi, Mum,' she whispered, pausing for a few moments and feeling a little shiver run across her bare arms. It still felt odd to be talking to a grave, as if her mother could somehow hear her from beneath six feet of soil. And why should she be listening in death, when she had never listened in life, Jade wondered as she knelt on the dusty ground.

She laid the white roses on the grave and stroked their petals, feeling their cool perfection beneath her fingertips. Silken and unscented, so perfect on the outside, but with something vital missing. Like Jade's childhood had been. She'd had everything she'd ever wanted in material terms. Her own pony, piano lessons, swimming lessons, ice skating lessons and a string of childminders to take the place of her mother, whose hotel business paid for it all. On the outside she'd had an idyllic rural upbringing, which she knew that her school friends, with the exception of her best friend, Sarah, who was far more perceptive than most, had envied madly. But she'd have swapped it all for the chance to have spent more time with her mother instead of being looked after by strangers.

She sat back on the warm ground and hugged her knees to her chest. The Arleston Court Hotel, her mother's flagship hotel, and also the one where they'd lived, had been a business, not a home. And the biggest regret of her life was that she'd never really known the woman who now lay beneath this Wiltshire soil, and now she never would.

'The sanctuary's coming along well,' she murmured. 'I rescued a red kite today, a bird of prey – beautiful...' She tailed off because even as she spoke, she could see the disappointment in her mother's dark eyes and hear her voice in her head, contemptuous and impatient. 'Oh, for heaven's sake, Jade. Most people grow out of wanting to save the world when they're about twelve.'

Guilt washed over her. It left a deep uneasiness in her, even now, knowing that her mother would have been furious that she'd sold the family business – the four hotels, including the flagship Arleston Court – and spent the money on buying a smallholding. This included an old cottage, with five acres of land, stables, and several farm buildings. It had been the perfect place to set up an animal rescue centre.

Jade knew Elizabeth would have scorned her plans, but she'd gone ahead and done it anyway, rebelling after her mother's death in a way she'd never dared to do while she was alive. She hadn't spent all of the money. She had a large chunk of it invested too, so maybe she'd inherited some of her mother's hardheaded business acumen after all.

Now, Jade swiped a stray tear from her eye, not sure whether the hard knot of grief in her chest was down to guilt, or pain because she'd never been allowed to get close to her mother. Never been allowed inside the barriers her mother had erected.

'Your father would have stayed if it wasn't for you,' she'd told Jade once. 'He never wanted kids. He had big plans. Thought kids would get in the way. Pity he didn't hang around to see how wrong he was.' She'd smiled at the young Jade as she'd spoken and with the benefit of hindsight Jade knew her words were intended to be a comfort, not a rejection. But it hadn't felt like that at the time. Her parents would have stayed together if it hadn't been for her. That still hurt. It hurt desperately. Especially as her mother had never married again but thrown herself into the business of building her hotel empire, dating periodically, but never getting close to anyone.

Jade let the tears fall for a while. She often cried here when she was alone, although strangely she'd shed no tears at the funeral. Perhaps she was still hoping for absolution, she thought, rising slowly to her feet, wanting desperately to be away from this place of shadows, which seemed to encapsulate all that had been wrong in her life for so long.

She hurried back through the churchyard, her vision so blurred with tears she didn't see the man until she'd collided with him.

'I'm so sorry,' she mumbled, glancing up into startled grey eyes that softened immediately as he looked at her.

'No problem. Hey, are you all right? No, you're not, are you?'

It was him, the man who'd stopped to help her earlier. Recognition softened his voice and Jade bit her lip, embarrassed to be caught crying. She wanted to run past, but he was blocking the path so she stayed where she was, trying to sniff inconspicuously and wishing he'd leave her alone.

He looked vaguely familiar. She'd thought so earlier, but now she was less distracted it was more apparent. Perhaps he worked in the village. Perhaps he was one of the business owners she'd approached about sponsorship for Duck Pond Rescue.

It was his eyes, she thought, frowning. His grey eyes were comfortingly familiar, yet she was almost sure they hadn't met before today.

'We must stop meeting like this,' she muttered, trying to bring some levity into the situation, but spoiling it when she had to swipe more tears from her face with the back of her hand because she hadn't brought a hanky.

'People will talk.' He finished the phrase for her, rummaged in his pocket and pulled out a mini pack of tissues. 'I'm not following you – in case you were wondering – I've been visiting my grandparents. They're in that plot over there.' He gestured with the tissues and then handed them to her. 'Here, have these.'

She took the pack, grateful he hadn't claimed to know how she felt or offered any of the usual platitudes. Practical help she could deal with. Anything else would have felt like an intrusion.

He waited while she blew her nose, not looking at her, but not looking embarrassed either, as if he was quite used to dealing with sobbing women. Even through her distress, she thought how kind he was. She racked her brain to work out why he was so familiar.

'What did you say your name was?' she asked when she was in control of herself again.

'I didn't. But it's Finn. Finn McTaggart. I'm not local, although I did spend quite a bit of time down here when I was younger – my grandparents retired here – but Dad and I still live in Nottingham. We're here to sort out their house and I thought I'd pop by, say hello to them. You know how it is.'

She nodded. 'I'm Jade Foster. I know your grandparents – well, what I mean is that I know their grave, I pass it every time I come. Yellow carnations. You didn't lose them long ago...' She stumbled to a halt, aware of how inane she must sound. He put the carnations there, of course, and she had just trampled like an idiot over his feelings.

'I've been visiting my mum,' she mumbled, feeling her face burn. 'It's a year today since...' She tailed off, unsure what else to say to him. It felt slightly surreal, standing in the swiftly gathering mosquito-edged dusk crying in front of a stranger. She clutched the pack of tissues, wondering whether she should offer them back. There were only a couple left. 'Well, thanks for these.'

'You're welcome.' His eyes were sympathetic. 'And believe me – it does get easier, Jade. I promise.'

'Right,' Jade said, touched by his kindness, but anxious to get away. She was beginning to feel supremely embarrassed that he'd seen her in such a state. He'd think she wasn't capable of looking after herself, let alone running an animal rescue. Annoyed with herself, she looked back into his eyes, her gaze steady.

'Well, thanks again,' she muttered, relieved when he moved out of her path. 'I'd better get going.'

3

Finn watched her hurry back along the moss-covered path and
reflected wryly that after two chance meetings he should have
taken the opportunity to ask for her number so he could see her
again. Except that at neither time would it have been appropriate.

Then he chided himself for assuming she'd be interested in
him – or even single. He'd thought she was lovely earlier, and she
was, even with her nose red from crying and the strands of her
long dark hair that had escaped from their clips in a scatter
around her face. Her eyes, almost black with pain, had looked
haunted, and even though everyone was vulnerable when they
were visiting their lost loved ones, he'd sensed she didn't usually
'do' vulnerability.

He'd had to fight back the urge to put his arms around her
slender shoulders and hold her tightly. He told himself he'd have
felt the same towards any woman so obviously in need of
comfort, but he suspected it wasn't true.

'Forget it,' he muttered crossly. Why on earth would she take a
second look at him? She'd barely taken a first look, he reminded
himself as he watched her fumbling with the latch on the gate

and tear up the road. She'd been too preoccupied with rescuing the bird and this time she'd been too blinded with grief to see where she was going, poor kid. She was young to have lost her mother. He hoped she had someone back home who was supporting her through it. Losing a parent was terribly tough. His mother wasn't dead, but he'd lost her just the same.

He waited until Jade was out of sight, sensing her need for distance, and then strolled back to his grandparents' cottage, which was less than a quarter of a mile from the cemetery.

He still thought of it as theirs, even though they'd left it to his father when they'd died within weeks of each other, eight months earlier.

'You took your time, lad, thought you'd got lost.' Ray greeted him from the front garden where he was puffing furiously on a roll-up, and Finn realised his father must feel the same. His grandmother had never let anyone smoke in the house.

'I bumped into a girl in the churchyard. I saw her earlier too,' he added, frowning, and deciding not to tell Ray about the bird rescue, as the only birds he was interested in came fully plucked, cooked and with gravy.

'Oh, aye – you were supposed to be sorting out graves, not chatting up women.'

Finn watched him draw on the thin roll-up so deeply that the burning end shot towards his fingers, and he had to drop it on the path.

'That stuff will kill you one day. I wish you'd pack it in.'

'Too late now. I reckon I've done all the damage I'm going to do.'

Finn doubted that very much, but his dad could be a stubborn old fool where his health was concerned.

'And I wasn't chatting her up. She was upset. She was visiting her mother's grave.'

'Ah,' Ray said, and promptly shut up.

One nil to me, Finn thought without much satisfaction as he went past his father and into the house. The mention of mothers worked every time. But he'd have given a lot for things to be different.

He was doing a Wordle on his phone when Ray came into the back room.

'Shall I do us some burnt sausage and chips again for tea or shall we risk the pub?'

'The pub, I think.' Finn glanced up. 'I could do with a pint of Guinness.'

And he could ask the landlord about Jade, too, he decided as they strolled down to the Red Lion. Mike would know who she was. He knew everything that was going on in the village and was an incorrigible gossip.

He looked pleased to see them, too, Finn saw as he pushed open the heavy oak door, lowering his head as they stepped into the dark beamed interior. They weren't here often enough to be classed as locals, but often enough for Mike to know what they drank.

'Usual, is it, gentlemen?' he queried, grinning through his salt-and-pepper beard and rubbing his hands together. He'd have looked more at home behind the bar of a seafaring pub strung with fish nets holding plastic lobsters, Finn had often thought. Captain Bird's Eye. Deciding against asking about the girl in the cemetery, he carried their pints to the table where his father sat. He didn't want it to get back to her he'd been asking, and it more than likely would if he said anything to Mike.

'Do you two want the wood burner lit?' Mike called after him. 'It's a bit chilly once the sun goes down, isn't it.'

'No, you're all right,' Ray said, rubbing his hands together as

Finn settled opposite him. 'We're from up north. We don't feel the cold. Not like you soft southerners.'

Finn didn't catch Mike's disparaging reply. This was a nice pub, he thought, trying to decide if it had changed since the last time they'd been down. No. The Red Lion probably hadn't changed much in the last couple of hundred years. It was a piece of old England, with its thick cob walls, ancient beams and big old inglenook fireplace. Their local, the Sheaf of Arrows, was more working man's club, with pitted tables lined by faded velveteen seats that you sank into when you sat down because the springs had long since gone. The walls were dotted with black and white pictures of football teams that no one had ever heard of. The walls of the Red Lion sported ancient hunting prints and a couple of faded water-colours. Above the bar hung a banner printed with the words:

A good wine should be drunk and not worshipped. A good landlord should be worshipped and not drunk.

'So, what's the verdict, son?' Ray asked, swigging his pint and interrupting Finn's musings. 'Do we let the place go to rack and ruin for lack of funds, or do we cut our losses and put it on the market?'

'It's yours. What do you want to do with it?' Finn asked, even though he had a pretty good idea he already knew. His father had never really taken to the countryside. He was much happier in his terraced two-up, two-down in Nottingham, steeped in traffic fumes and noise and surrounded by tarmac. He'd never been one for open spaces and 'wild animals', as he called them – which covered everything from rabbits to cows.

'I think we should get it on the market, lad. I could buy my place then. Might even get enough for you to put a deposit down on a little place yourself.'

'Yes,' Finn replied, without enthusiasm. As far as he could see, his grandparents had had the right idea. Who wanted to live in the city when they could be surrounded by clean air and rolling fields? Ever since they'd died and left his father the cottage, he'd harboured the faint hope he could somehow raise the funds to buy it and move down. He was sure he could get work locally – he could turn his hand to most things. And in his spare time he could paint pictures, a passion for as long as he could remember. His grandparents, particularly his grandmother, had encouraged his artistic endeavours. A couple of his early landscapes still hung in the cottage. Dad, who was more practical, a man's man, had never been as enamoured. 'You'll never earn a living with a paintbrush, lad. Not that kind of paintbrush, anyways.'

He was probably right. Finn knew it was a pipe dream, really. Cottages in the Arleston countryside, a stone's throw from the beautiful medieval city of Salisbury, even tiny cottages, which needed a lot of money spending on them, didn't come cheap. He knew his dad couldn't afford to sell it to him for much less than the market value. Not unless he wanted to spend the rest of his life scrimping and saving, which Finn was determined he wasn't going to do. Consequently, he hadn't ever raised the subject.

'Course – you've probably got better memories of the place than me, eh, lad?' Ray said slyly. 'Wild, drunken Christmas parties, if my memory serves me right.'

'I was young and foolish then.'

'Not that young. Twenty-five if my memory serves me...'

'Yeah. All right. But it was a one-off.' Finn frowned. 'Which is why Gran never forgot it.'

'She never forgot it because you were sick all the way up her stairs.' Ray drained his pint triumphantly, leaned forward and tapped his empty glass on the table. 'Want another one? It's my round.'

'I'll get them.' Finn escaped to the bar because that was one night he particularly didn't want to remember and certainly didn't want to discuss. He'd had the worst hangover of his life the following morning. Being sick all up the stairs hadn't been good – but it had been a fairly minor crime in the scheme of things.

The Christmas party had been held in someone's house on the outskirts of the village. He'd been drinking with a group of lads in the Red Lion and when the pub had closed they'd invited him along. The alcohol had flowed freely, and Finn had drunk far more than he was used to. He vaguely remembered leaving the party with a really pretty blonde, who'd been younger than him. He wished he could blank out the rest of the evening, but he couldn't. He'd hated himself for weeks afterwards. Not because the girl hadn't been willing – she'd been just as keen as he was to find a quiet spot where they could 'get to know each other better'. But he'd known they were both too drunk to have really known what they were doing. And it wasn't Finn's style to have one-night stands.

What had made it worse was that he'd had to leave for Nottingham the following morning, which meant he hadn't had time to see her again. What would he have said if he had, he wondered? 'Sorry' or 'Thanks' or maybe even 'What did you say your name was?' He doubted they'd have seen each other again. A few minutes of fumbled lovemaking in a freezing, muddy field wasn't the best start to a relationship.

He'd never seen her since, which he supposed wasn't all that surprising. Arleston wasn't a tiny village; there was no reason to bump into her even if she had been a local. Perhaps, like him, she'd been far from home and had simply done too much celebrating.

He sighed and headed back to their table with the drinks. Maybe his father had a point about it being best to cut all ties with the place. Nottingham was home. It was where his mates were, where his roots were, and very probably where his future lay. Moving to the countryside, swapping his job at the electrical engineers and trying to paint pictures for a living were all pipe dreams. Fleetingly he thought about Jade again and rationality kicked in. Another pipe dream. There were plenty of attractive women in Nottingham.

'I think you're right, Dad,' he said, clunking their pints onto the knotted wooden table and watching a thin trail of froth spill down one of the glasses. 'You should put it on the market – we don't get a lot of use out of it, do we? Do you want me to nip down the estate agents in the morning?'

'Aye, thanks, lad. You're better at all that malarkey than me.'

Ray's grey eyes lit briefly with warmth and Finn thought with a mixture of regret and relief that it was probably for the best.

4

Jade shielded her eyes against the afternoon sun and watched the two people she loved most in the world heading up the yard towards her. Sarah Tate, her best friend forever, and her son, Ben, who was five and a half, which wasn't much older than Sarah and Jade had been when they'd first met at school.

Ben was the image of his mother. It really hit her when she saw them side by side like this. He had the same honey-coloured hair with streaks that were bleached almost white from playing outside over the long summer holidays. A smattering of freckles curved across his cheekbones, and he had the same small nose as Sarah's and the same eyes. No, he didn't, she thought with a small frown. Ben's eyes weren't the same shape, and they were grey, not summer blue.

His shorts and tee-shirt were a lot grubbier than her friend's, too, she saw, smiling as they got closer. Then Ben spotted her standing by the kennels, dragged his hand from his mother's and came hurtling up the dusty concrete yard.

'Can I see Sacha's puppies, Auntie Jade? Have they grown any bigger? How's the little black one? I bet he's as fat as a piglet.' The words tumbled out in one long, unbroken line. 'Can I help give Sacha her dinner? Mum said you might let me if I was really good and quiet.'

It was impossible to imagine him being quiet for long. Jade smiled into his eyes, which were as wide and innocent as he could make them. 'Of course you can, sweetheart.' She bent to kiss his head, ignoring his screwed-up face as her lips brushed his hair. He was going through the 'kissing is for girls' stage, Sarah had told her last time they'd spoken.

'So how was school, Ben? Is it good to be back?'

'We did maths today. Boring. Double boring. Treble boring.' Ben spun out the words dramatically. 'I like art best. We did that yesterday. Mrs Benson said I'm really good. I did a picture of a horse like Wosanna with brown hair and a white patch on her head.'

'Did you now?' Jade said, straightening and looking across to where Rosanna grazed in the paddock, flicking away flies with her tail. 'I'd love to see that some time.'

Sarah caught up with her son, puffing in the heat of the day and flapping her pink tee-shirt with her hands to get some airflow.

'Still hard at it, I see.' She eyed the pot of wood-stainer at Jade's feet. 'Did you realise you've got that stuff in your hair?'

'It washes out.' Jade pulled a section of her long dark hair in front of her face to look and wrinkled her nose. 'Yuck. It doesn't make very good perfume, though. I should get this cut. It would be much more practical.'

'It wouldn't suit you.' Sarah grinned. 'So how's it going? You look as though you're getting somewhere at last.' She looked around the smallholding, narrowing her eyes approvingly. 'You've transformed this place. It almost looks like an animal sanctuary. Which reminds me. The woman across the road from me can't keep her dog any more because her grandchildren are asthmatic. Would she be able to bring it here? It's a cockerpoo, I think. It looks just like a rug on legs. You might have a job re-homing it.'

'There'll be someone out there who'll love him,' Jade said, feeling a stab of sadness, because she knew Sarah was right. When she'd been at vet school in Bristol, she'd helped out at a local dog's home and people did seem to go for looks, passing over the scruffier ones and the older dogs in their quest for cute. Still, at least she was in a position to do something about it now.

'And if I don't find him a home, he can stay here forever,' she added, touching Sarah's arm. 'That's why I started this place. It feels so good to actually be able to do something. When I worked at the vets, I used to feel so helpless when people brought their unwanted animals in for us to...' She didn't finish the sentence but spread her arms wide to encompass the kennels and fields.

She'd dreamed of being a vet, but the reality had put her off. There'd been a visit to a slaughterhouse as part of their training and, Jade, a lifelong vegetarian, had known she could no more witness an animal being slaughtered than she could fly to the moon.

'I've decided to call this place Duck Pond Rescue,' she told Sarah now. 'What do you think?'

Sarah clicked her tongue. 'Very apt as you live in Duck Pond Cottage, in Duck Pond Lane, and there's that flaming great overgrown pond across the road.'

'That pond's an iconic landmark, I'll have you know.'

Sarah rolled her eyes. 'If you say so. But Duck Pond Rescue isn't exactly original. Couldn't you have called it Paws and Claws or Heaven's End or something like that?'

'Too trite.' Jade knew she was an odd mixture. She couldn't do trite and corny any more than she could do death and destruction.

Sarah glanced around them. 'Why are there two lots of kennels?'

'This is the quarantine block. It's for when new dogs come in. You have to have somewhere to segregate them in case there's anything wrong with them. The block further down is the regular kennels and I've got the cattery sorted now, too. Someone bought a cat in last week. Poor little mite had hardly any fur left. He got trapped under the bonnet of a car and driven for miles before the owner realised he was there.'

'Is he all right?' Sarah gasped in horror. 'Did you sort him out?'

'It was touch and go, but yes, he'll be fine. I've called him Diesel because it seemed appropriate. I think I might keep him.'

'You'll be overrun at this rate. I thought the idea was to re-home them, not keep them.'

'I'll only keep the odd one. Did you see the chicken run I've just set up in the small field? I scrounged it from a farmer up the road, along with some of his ex-battery hens. I like chickens.'

'Ben saw it. I had to drag him out of it by his ankles. That's how he got so filthy. He's almost as crazy as you are about animals.'

Jade laughed. 'He'll clean up. I've got another bird he'd like to see. It's a red kite, a bird of prey. It ran into a woman's car out on the main road a couple of days ago and injured its wing.'

'So you're taking in wildlife as well. Isn't that the council's responsibility? I hope the woman left a donation.'

'She wanted to, but she didn't look like she could afford it, so I didn't let her.'

'You can't afford it either.' Sarah shook her head. 'Jade, you're way too soft. Your mum's money won't last forever.'

'It'll last a while and I've done well on the sponsorship lately.

I've got three businesses in the village, including the Red Lion and the vets, who've agreed to regular funding.'

Sarah didn't look that convinced, so Jade changed the subject. 'I've hardly seen you lately. I take it the romance is still going strong?'

Colour crept across Sarah's freckled cheekbones. 'You've been busy with this place. I didn't like to intrude while you were setting things up. But yes, it is. Callum's great. He adores Ben.'

'Good.' Jade glanced at her friend's face, which looked hotter than the sun warranted. 'So, when do I get to meet him? Or are you keeping him under wraps forever? I'm beginning to think there's something wrong with him. Or is it me you're ashamed of? Your crazy friend with the animal sanctuary.'

'Of course I'm not ashamed of you.' Sarah sounded genuinely affronted. 'I just didn't want to tempt fate. In case things didn't work out between us – you know.'

'Hmm.' There was probably an element of truth in that, although Jade had a feeling there was more to it. She suspected Sarah was being cagey about Callum for reasons that had nothing to do with tempting fate.

'You can come round for tea one night if you like.' Sarah picked a piece of straw out of Ben's hair. 'How about Friday? I'll get Callum to cook us something. He's utterly gorgeous, Jade, and he can cook too. Very important, as I can't. Did I tell you his dad's a chef?'

'Once or twice,' Jade quipped. She took a deep breath of the balmy Wiltshire air and turned her face up to the sun, which was still warm despite it being late afternoon. There was a part of her that still couldn't believe she was really here – doing what she'd wanted to do, all her life.

'So, what have you told Callum about Ben's father?' she asked casually when Ben was out of earshot, running ahead of them to the newly installed cattery. She stole a glance at Sarah's face and could tell by her fleeting look of panic she was right on target. That was why she hadn't been allowed to meet Callum yet – in case she inadvertently let something slip. Feeling a little put out that Sarah might not trust her, she added softly, 'I am on your side, you know. I'd back up whatever you said.'

'Yes, I know you would.' Sarah glanced at her son, who'd paused just ahead and was crouched in the dust, staring intently at something on the ground. She hesitated and then, aware that Jade wasn't going to let her get away with that, she added, 'To be honest, I haven't told Callum much. I just said that Ben's father was much older than me and did a runner before Ben was born.'

'But isn't it going to be difficult, Sarah, when he finds out the truth? It sounds to me as though you're pretty serious about this guy.'

'He won't find out. He can't. You're the only person who knows.' Sarah flicked back her shaggy blonde mane and gave Jade a sharp sideways glance. 'And you're not going to tell anyone, are you?'

'My lips are sealed.' Jade smiled to soften the seriousness of her voice, because it did worry her that Sarah was still living a lie. Not because she hadn't confessed to Callum – after all, they'd only been seeing each other a few weeks – but because Jade knew her friend had never faced the truth herself. She didn't want Ben's father in her life, and because of that she'd denied Ben the chance of ever knowing him either.

Jade and Sarah were the same age, twenty-seven, and they'd been best friends forever, but in many ways they were worlds apart. It bothered Jade a lot more than it seemed to bother Sarah that Ben was growing up without a dad. He was growing up without grandparents too because Sarah had fallen out with her adoptive parents a couple of years after he'd been born.

A deeply moral and traditional older couple, they hadn't liked the fact she'd refused to trace his father and was determined to bring him up alone, and in the end, Sarah, who was the most stubborn person Jade had ever met, had cut contact with them too.

Jade hoped Sarah would reconcile with them one day, but she knew what it was like to have parents who weren't on the same wavelength as you. She knew what it was like to grow up without a father too. But one day Ben might want to put a face to the man who'd helped to conceive him, and Jade was worried about how Sarah would cope when he did.

Although, to be fair, Jade had never tried to trace her own father. Some deep-down pride prevented her from chasing after a man who'd clearly never wanted to know her.

'Enough of my love life, how's yours?' Sarah asked, fanning her face with her hand and pausing to check on Ben, who was now heading purposefully across the small field towards the chickens. 'Is he all right in there, Jade?'

'Yes, he's fine. It doesn't matter if he lets them out. I'll deal with them later.'

'Has that hunky vet persuaded you to go out with him yet?'

'If you mean Aiden Southerland, no – and he's not interested in me.' Jade wasn't sure this was true. Aiden had said a couple of things lately that had made her wonder. But he'd certainly never asked her out.

'I'm too busy for a relationship, so it's immaterial. And I've had enough of vets,' she added with a small frown.

'Not all vets are like two-timing Antonio. Anyway, who said anything about a relationship? You could have some fun, couldn't you?'

'I am having fun, sorting this place out.'

'Jade, this is work, not fun.' Sarah screwed up her face in exasperation and put her hands on Jade's arms. 'I know you've had a rough time of it lately. And I know that's why you've buried yourself in deepest Wiltshire with a bunch of waifs and strays no one else wants. I'm not completely blind, you know.' Her blue eyes softened. 'But you can't hide yourself away forever, there's a world out there.'

'I'm not hiding,' Jade protested, gazing across the fields of long grass that surrounded her land. The grass, bleached yellow by the sun, flowed like a golden sea in the sultry breeze. 'I'm fine now. Truly I am.' She waved her hands in a careless gesture of dismissal, daring Sarah to argue with her. 'I'm over everything. Antonio, my old life, Mum. All the stuff in Bristol – well, it all seems like it happened to someone else. Really, I'm fine.' She rushed on before Sarah could contradict her. 'If Ben wants to feed Sacha's pups, I'm just about to do it. Do you want to give him a shout?'

Sarah shook her head in exasperation, and then put her fingers to her lips and gave an ear-splitting whistle.

Jade breathed a sigh of relief and hurried ahead of her to unlatch the metal gate that led down to the lower part of the sanctuary. She'd had two stone outbuildings turned into a reception and a feed storage area, and in the old pigsty 'hospital block', quiet and out of bounds to the public, she kept the smaller, more vulnerable animals until they were ready for re-homing. Dogs like Sacha and her litter of scraggy black Heinz 57 pups. Not that the fact they were scraggy bothered Jade.

Sometimes, she thought she cared about the ugly ones more than she cared about the sleek, expensive pedigrees that were guaranteed a loving home. They brought out all her protective instincts; she'd have kept them all if she'd had the money.

She tugged open the wooden door of the feed store, bashed her head on the low beam just inside, and swore under her breath. After years of living in houses with normal-height ceilings, she still hadn't got used to the low doorways of the farm buildings. Her cottage wasn't much better. When she'd first moved in six weeks ago, she'd banged her head so many times she'd found herself going around with a permanent stoop. She'd got used to the place now and only the odd doorway, like this one, still caught her out.

Standing for a moment in the dim coolness of old stone, she rubbed her head and then hauled down a sack of dog food ready for Ben to open. She wondered what Sarah would have said if she'd confessed the only man she'd felt completely comfortable around lately had been the one that she'd met in the cemetery. Despite the fact she'd spent most of their meeting blubbing.

She'd have bet money on it that he hadn't been comfortable, however chivalrously he'd behaved. She'd never met a man who'd been able to deal with a woman in tears. None of the vets in Bristol had been very good with tears, especially Antonio, who should have been used to it, considering how many hearts he broke.

Perhaps Sarah was right, perhaps she wasn't quite as recovered as she thought. Antonio had hurt her badly and she'd still been reeling from his betrayal when she'd lost her mother. Two devastating body blows in a matter of months. It was bound to take time to recover. But Duck Pond Rescue was going to help her, not hinder.

Hard work was a cure-all, her mother had often said. It cured everything from the pain of a broken love affair to the absolute full stop of bereavement. Jade had to admit her mother had been right about that. She was too busy to hurt most of the time. She reached up for the plastic scoop and one of the pristine stainless steel dog bowls from the shelf and put them on the floor beside the sack of food.

As for Sarah's throwaway line about hiding away from the world, that was rubbish. She shook her head impatiently in an attempt to banish the shiver of unease that always accompanied thoughts of her mother. The clang of the gate heralded Ben and Sarah's approach. Jade glanced up as they came into the feed room. Sarah might be partly right, she might not be 100 per cent recovered, but she was healing, not hiding. There was a massive difference.

5

Jade felt oddly nervous when she pulled up outside Sarah's little semi on Friday at six for their planned supper. She reached for the bottle of her friend's favourite red wine that was rolling about in the passenger foot-well and wondered what Callum would be like.

All Sarah had told her, other than that he could cook, was that they'd met through work. Callum sold marketing databases for big companies, which was the same field Sarah was in, except she wrote the software, rather than sold it.

He also loved travelling and had a camper van, which Jade had just parked behind outside Sarah's house. She glanced at its pristine paintwork as she climbed out of her Land Rover. That must have set him back a bit. It was almost new. Callum wasn't short of money then.

Edging past it, she breathed in the scent of the pink roses that clambered up the front of the house as she went round to the back door. It opened just before she got there.

Sarah was smiling, her face unusually shy, and behind her was Callum, who wasn't a bit like Jade had expected.

He towered over Sarah and had a good four inches on Jade. At least six foot three, he had flaming red hair and eyes the colour of amber and a gold hoop in one ear. He looked like a pirate from one of those swashbuckling films, and Jade had a brief, vivid image of him forcing people to walk the plank.

'It's great to meet you, Jade.' He held out a giant hand, and she felt her own hand disappearing within his firm grip. She had an impression of warmth and strength and gentleness. 'Sarah's told me so much about you.' His voice was soft, with a faint Scottish lilt, and there was shyness behind his smile.

Another contradiction, Jade thought a little breathlessly as the pirate image evaporated. 'All good, I hope?'

'Of course!' Sarah interrupted. 'Come on through, Ben can't wait to see you.'

Ben, in a Thomas the Tank Engine tee-shirt, was sitting on the floor, watching television, but he leapt up when he spotted Jade, hurtled across the room and wrapped his arms around her legs.

'Steady on, you'll have me over,' she said, hugging him. 'So how are you, young man?'

'Very well, thank you, lung lady.'

Jade giggled, as much at the seriousness in his grey eyes as his pronunciation. 'You're a bundle of trouble, you are.'

'You're a bundle of trouble!' Ben shrieked in delight.

'Don't call your Auntie Jade names,' Sarah chided. 'Or she might not want to stay.'

'I started it,' Jade said, smiling. 'Come and sit on my lap then, Ben. You're not too big for laps, are you?'

He shook his head, put his thumb in his mouth and clambered up, a little more reticently than usual, which she put down to the fact that Callum was there. The balance in the room had changed. But it was a nice change. Comfortable.

'We're doing a barbecue outside,' Ben told Jade.

'Callum's done us home-made burgers,' Sarah added. 'He's made veggie ones especially for you – and they'll be ready in about ten minutes.'

'Yeah, yeah, yeah,' Ben shouted. 'I'm gonna be a vegan-arian when I'm six.'

* * *

Much later that evening, when Ben was tucked up in bed, and Callum had left them to their girlie chat and headed home, Sarah and Jade lounged on the sofa.

'So, what do you think?' Sarah asked, putting her hands behind her head and leaning back with an expression of such utter satisfaction it was obvious the question was rhetorical.

'I think he's awful. Big-headed, boring, ugly. Can't cook either, can he?'

Sarah's eyes widened in shock. Jade giggled and poured some more wine into their glasses, from her position on the carpet beside the coffee table. 'God, you're so easy to wind up. I think he's great, you lucky cow. Has he got any brothers?'

'No, he's a one-off,' Sarah said proudly, and unnecessarily, because Jade couldn't imagine ever meeting anyone like Callum. When Sarah had told her he was a salesman, she'd conjured up a smooth-talking charmer, probably blond, because Sarah usually went for blonds. She hadn't been expecting a Scottish flame-haired giant of a man who could cook like a top chef, which apparently he'd learned in his father's Dundee restaurant.

'What?' Sarah asked, and Jade jumped.

'I was just thinking Callum's not your usual type. Why didn't he go into the family business?'

'Because he wanted to see the world – well, he wanted to see

England anyway.' Sarah giggled. 'What did you think of his tattoo? He had that done in London.'

Sarah had made Callum show her the wolf, which was emblazoned across his chest, halfway through their second bottle of wine, and he'd blushed scarlet as he'd undone his shirt buttons.

'The poor guy wanted the floor to swallow him up,' Jade chided gently. 'He's obviously not an exhibitionist like you. But seriously, Sarah, I'm so pleased for you. It's about time you met someone really nice.'

Sarah's blue eyes were as contented as a Cheshire cat's. 'You see, there are some good ones out there. You mustn't let one bad experience put you off men for life.'

'I wasn't planning to.' Jade felt warmed by the wine and Sarah's almost tangible happiness. 'I'm over Antonio now. Seriously – I can't imagine what I ever saw in him in the first place.'

An image of her ex-boyfriend flashed into her mind. Dark eyes he'd inherited from his Italian grandmother, a tangle of black hair, a sexy pouting mouth, which could transform instantly from sultry to sulky if he didn't get his own way, and a body that drew admiring glances on the beach.

It was hard to hold on to the image – dark eyes were fading to cool grey ones, and, disconcertingly, she saw Finn's face again. She hadn't told Sarah about their two chance meetings. Partly because she'd have had to confess she'd gone to pieces in front of a stranger, which would have meant admitting she wasn't as over everything as she wanted Sarah to think. Finn was an attractive stranger too; it was a shame he wasn't local. She'd half hoped she'd bump into him again. But she hadn't, which probably meant he was back in Nottingham. Pity.

She sighed and Sarah, who'd obviously misread her expression as regret that she and Antonio were finished, threw a cushion at her.

'The bloke was sex on legs. I could see exactly what you saw in him. And he was a complete two-timing bastard as well. I bet he's doing the dirty on that young receptionist by now. He's not the type who can stay faithful for more than a few months.'

'Six in my case.' Jade was surprised it didn't hurt any more. At the time it had been pretty painful. But then Antonio's betrayal had been overshadowed by her mother's sudden death.

'I'm surprised he hasn't been sniffing around here, now you're a rich heiress.'

'He wasn't exactly broke himself,' Jade chided, because whatever else Antonio had been, he'd never been a sponger. 'Besides, I can't see him leaving Bristol. He always hated the countryside. He hates the smell and he doesn't like animals much. Strange he ever decided to be a vet. He was quite good at it, too.'

'So, he was hardly a long-term option, was he? For a woman who prefers animals to people.'

For once, Jade was far too relaxed to rise to the bait. She yawned and stretched her arms above her head and then rubbed her eyes. 'I think it's time I curled up on your sofa bed. Some of us have to get up at the crack of dawn. I may only have a handful of animals at the moment, but they still need looking after.'

'You can help me finish this wine first,' Sarah pressed, refilling their glasses. 'I'm glad you're over Antonio. You can do far better.' She paused. 'Bugger, I've just remembered Callum made us a lemon meringue pie, too, because I told him it was your favourite. Shall we have some to mop up this alcohol? He'll be disappointed if we don't eat it.'

'I'll get it,' Jade offered, escaping to Sarah's tiny kitchen and poking about in the fridge, which was filled mainly with cans of beer. The pie, tucked away at the back, was a beauty, all white curly peaks topped with golden brown, and she felt her mouth water.

She cut them both a slice and as the lemon scent hit her nostrils, she was transported back to a long-ago day in her mother's kitchen.

She'd been about seven and had just come in from school when she'd discovered a whacking great lemon meringue pie cooling on the top shelf of the larder. She'd needed a chair to reach it and she'd struggled with her conscience because she knew it was for the guests' dessert and pinching a slice was going to end in trouble. Then again, the pie was massive. No one was going to miss a little slice. There'd be plenty left for the guests.

She'd reached up, pushed the giant-size coffee tin across, and, taking care not to knock the butter portions over, inched the plate towards her.

'Jade Foster, whatever do you think you're doing? Get out of there, this minute. Do you hear me?'

Jade had jumped violently and after that, everything seemed to happen in slow motion. Half on and half off the shelf, the plate tilted and then overbalanced and the lemon meringue pie slid between her hands and the whole lot went crashing onto the tiled floor.

Her mother was beside her in an instant. 'You naughty, naughty little girl! How many times have I told you to not to come in here and help yourself?' Jade felt her arm seized roughly and she was half lifted, half pulled from the chair, which also overbalanced. She scraped her knee on one of its wooden legs, felt the stinging hotness of the graze, and the hurt of her mother's digging fingers. Through a red haze of tears, she heard the angry voices.

'What's going on? Oh, good heavens, I am sorry, Elizabeth, I didn't realise she was in there.' That had been Brian, the chef, with his hideous red face and sharp eyes.

'It's not your fault. She knows she's not allowed. Bloody hell, look at this mess. Get a mop, can you. And you, my girl, can go straight to your room. Go on.'

'But... I only wanted... some pie... and, and...' Tears were getting in the way of her voice. She wasn't sure which was worse, the beautiful pie smashed to pieces on the larder floor, more lemony now it was broken, or people staring at her. Her mother's face was blotched and furious and her voice hot-edged with crossness.

'If I've told you once, I've told you a million times, you do not just help yourself to food. That's tonight's dessert you've ruined. What am I going to give the guests now?'

'I don't know.'

'No, I don't know either. Go on, get out of my sight and stop snivelling. Or I'll really give you something to cry about.'

Jade stopped crying and ran. The unfairness of it all was bubbling into her throat, but there was no arguing with her mother when she was in this mood. She didn't go to her room in the family annexe where she and Mum lived, though. She raced out of the door at the other end of the kitchen and through the games room, past the darts board and the pool table and out of the side door, which led on to the little yard where they grew runner beans and tomatoes.

Felix, her cat, was lying on an upturned milk crate, flicking his tail in the sun. She wrapped her arms around his neck and cried into his warm ginger fur. Someone would come in a minute and tell her off again, but she didn't care. She hated them both, Mum and Brian, but most of all she hated the guests.

'Bloody guests,' she sobbed, and Felix wriggled a bit, but he didn't move away. Felix was the only one who understood. No one else knew how she felt, what it was like to always come second to the guests. He began to purr and she buried her face in his soft body.

'Bloody guests, bloody guests, bloody guests,' she'd whispered, her voice matching the rhythm of his purrs. 'Bloody guests, bloody guests, bloody guests.'

* * *

'Jade, what are you doing? I thought you'd fallen asleep out there.' Sarah's voice jolted her back to the present.

'Sorry, I was daydreaming.'

'Hey, you're not upset because I mentioned Antonio, are you? That was a bit insensitive. I didn't mean to rub it in...'

'I wasn't thinking about him – and you haven't. Honestly.'

'Wow, that does look good, doesn't it? There's some squirty cream in the fridge, shall we have that too?'

'You're not supposed to have midnight feasts when you're our age.'

'I know. I'm going to be as fat as a pig soon. Callum loves making puddings.' Sarah squirted cream liberally over their plates and rolled her eyes in ecstasy. 'I definitely recommend a man who can cook. By the way, I thought I saw a face from the past the other day in the village.'

'Really? Who?'

'The man from the Christmas party.'

'What Christmas party?' Jade frowned, and then realisation slowly dawned. 'Are you talking about Ben's father – the one you...'

'Shagged in a field,' Sarah finished quietly, moving across to shut the kitchen door. 'Keep your voice down. Yes, I am, but that doesn't make him Ben's father.'

'Why didn't you say so before?' Jade gasped, coming very close to dropping this plate of lemon meringue pie as well. It must be the wine. She was too shocked to argue with Sarah's illogical statement. 'Where was he?'

'He was going into the Post Office in Arleston. It probably wasn't him. I don't think he lives round here or I'd have seen him before. It was probably just someone with the same colour hair. To be honest, I doubt I'd recognise him anyway, after all this time, even if I did bump into him. I think I'm a bit paranoid. I probably only thought I saw him because we were talking about him the other day.'

'Yes.' Jade swallowed a mouthful of lemon, which was exquisitely smooth – just the right balance between tangy and sweet. 'I'm sure that's it.'

'Have you seen that picture?' Sarah asked her, gesturing to the fridge door, where Ben's latest drawing was held up by two Thomas the Tank Engine fridge magnets.

Jade gazed at the stick family. It showed two women, one blonde, one dark, a child, and a man with a blob of vibrant red hair. They were standing outside a house with a big smiley yellow sun in the sky. Underneath the picture, scrawled in loopy, childish writing were the words 'My Family'. Jade felt a lump in her throat. She'd always thought of Ben as family, even though they weren't related. It was good to know he felt the same.

Sarah's eyes shadowed and she blinked a few times. 'I know you think I was wrong not telling Ben who his dad was, but you can see why I did it, can't you? It wasn't just for me. Ben's happy, too. He loves you and he loves Callum. And the past is done with. Finished. A closed chapter.' She underlined her words by drawing a swift line in the air with her hands.

Jade nodded slowly. They'd had dozens of arguments about this when Ben was a baby. It was one of the few things they'd ever totally disagreed on. But Jade understood her friend's decision, even if she didn't agree with it. Sarah had been dumped in a children's home when she was six months old. She'd subsequently been adopted by parents who loved her but Ben was the only biological family she'd ever had. Jade knew Sarah's reasons for not contacting his father stemmed mainly from fear. She'd been scared he might fight her for custody and, more worryingly, that he might win. She hadn't dared risk it.

And now, as Jade looked into Sarah's anxious eyes and then back at the picture, which summed up how Ben saw the world, she was almost certain that Sarah had been right. There was no guarantee Ben's father would have wanted a child. He certainly hadn't bothered to contact Sarah again. He could have made an effort, if she'd meant more to him than just a one-night stand.

'I'm so happy at the moment,' Sarah went on, blinking rapidly. 'I've never felt like this. I've never had a proper family before. I don't want anything to spoil it.'

'Nothing's going to spoil it,' Jade said firmly. She abandoned her pie and went to hug her friend. She hoped her words wouldn't come back to haunt her.

6
___

Five months later, on a freezing February morning, Jade stamped the heel of her boot against an ice-plated puddle in the yard and wished Aiden Southerland, her vet, would hurry up and get here. He wasn't usually late. Her opinion of him had gone up over the last few months. Unlike a couple of the vets she'd worked with in the city practice in Bristol, he seemed to care more about the welfare of his patients than how much revenue they brought in. He was always prepared to go the extra mile, coming out uncomplainingly at odd hours if she was worried about any of her animals and refusing to take extra payment.

Jade had a feeling Sarah had been right about Aiden being interested in her. Even though he still hadn't asked her out, she sensed he was building up to it, which was awkward because, much as she liked him, she didn't want anything other than a professional relationship.

So far, she'd managed to avoid the issue, but it was getting more difficult. As she waited for him to arrive, she tried to analyse her feelings. Aiden was attractive in a slightly old-fashioned, gentleman-farmer sort of way. He always wore a tweed jacket with leather patches on the elbows and green wellington boots, which never looked dirty; she'd no idea how he managed that when he spent so much time tramping around farmyards. He had neat brown hair, serious dark eyes, and a slightly intense gaze, which she found a bit unnerving. Yet there was no doubt he was kind and generous and shared her passion for animals, particularly dogs.

He let her have drugs at cost and regularly brought over batches of medicines that were close to their sell-by date, which he refused to let her pay for. They had masses in common, and, logically, she knew he'd be the perfect partner. Yet she couldn't summon any interest beyond friendship despite Sarah's regular jibes that she ought to get a life beyond the animals. Maybe it wasn't just Aiden. Maybe she just wasn't ready for a relationship.

The crunch of tyres on gravel heralded Aiden's arrival, and his sunshine-yellow jeep drew into the yard. Even that looked immaculate, she thought idly as she went to meet him. He must hose it down every night.

'Morning, Jade, sorry I'm late, I got a bit held up with a sow at Jackson's – cold one today, isn't it?' He rubbed his hands together as he spoke, his breath clouding the winter air, his rugged, outdoor face wreathed in smiles.

'You're not late.' She smiled back at him. 'And I'm probably worrying about nothing. But I thought it was better to be safe than sorry.'

'Always better to be safe than sorry.' He leaned into the jeep to get his case. 'And you know you're my favourite customer.'

'Right,' she said briskly, deciding it would be better not to say she was bound to be with all the work she put his way in case he contradicted her. 'Step this way and I'll show you your patient.'

The hospital block, warmed by a pair of Calor gas stoves, felt cosy and inviting after the bitterness of the February morning, and Jade hurried ahead of Aiden towards a pen inhabited by a thin lurcher bitch and her litter of pups.

'I'm just going to borrow one of your babies a second,' she murmured, stroking the bitch's soft head. Then very gently she leaned into the pen and scooped up the smallest pup, who was a miniature version of his mother, brindle stripes running through his pale gold fur.

* * *

Aiden frowned as he watched her bend over the pen. How could anyone who spent her life in sweatshirts and old jeans have such an instant and devastating effect on him?

Not that Jade could have the faintest idea of how he felt about her, or ever would, the way things were going. He'd been her vet for the last five months, give or take a week, and he'd been meaning to ask her out for most of that time. But he'd never quite found the courage to cross the bridge between professional and personal.

'This is the pup I'm worried about.' She straightened and handed him a scraggy lurcher pup. 'Whoever tied his mum up to the gate last week must have known she was about to whelp, but the poor love was far too thin. This little one only just made it. I've called him Tiny. He's got a slight infection and I'm worried.'

Aiden took the pup, which squeaked and snuffled blindly at his fingers. Forcing himself to concentrate, he examined it carefully.

'Yes, you're right. I'll give him something for that. He's a little dehydrated, too. Try and get more fluid into him and make sure he gets plenty of Mum.'

She nodded, her eyes anxious, and he placed the pup gently

back into the run. 'He's tougher than he looks, Jade. He's got this far, I'm sure he'll be fine.'

She looked at him and he was momentarily lost in her eyes. They changed colour according to her mood, going from soft brown to almost black. Today they were very dark.

'Thanks, Aiden. I'm so pleased. I know it sounds mad, since I'm not exactly short of dogs round here, but Tiny's a bit special. Probably because he kept me up all night when he arrived. Does that make sense?'

'Perfect sense.' He cleared his throat. 'How are the rest of the crew? Is there anything else you'd like me to take a look at while I'm here?'

'I had another horse come in the other day.' She frowned. A strand of dark hair had come loose from the band she tied it back with and Aiden ached to reach out and brush it back with his hand.

'A horse? That's unusual. Cruelty case, was it?'

'No. I was a bit surprised, actually. The owners were very keen to get rid of him and he's not just some shaggy pony. He's part thoroughbred. The last sort of horse you'd expect to end up in a place like this. Come on, I'll show you.'

They left the litter of puppies and went out into the small courtyard and on up towards the stables.

Aiden followed her, cursing his shyness, and wishing he had the nerve to ask her out to dinner.

As far as he could tell, she didn't wear make-up, but her skin always looked perfect, and the most she ever did with her shoulder-length dark hair was tie it back off her face. She had a strong face, an air of confidence that drew people to her, but there was a touch of aloofness too that said, 'don't take liberties, don't get too close'. Or maybe that was just his paranoia. He'd never had much confidence with women.

She was different around animals; softer. It was people she kept at arm's length; well, men anyway, Aiden thought. Or maybe it was just him.

He was no closer to working out what made Jade tick than he'd been on the first day he'd met her.

'I'm Jade Foster,' she'd said when she'd called into the practice at the tail end of the previous summer. 'I've just opened an animal rescue place up at Duck Pond Cottage. And I'd like to discuss your rates.'

Aiden's illusions about her being some romantic animal lover had swiftly dissolved as she'd negotiated payment periods and discounts with the skill of a drugs rep.

When she finally got up to go, she'd shaken his hand again. 'It's been a pleasure doing business with you, Mr Southerland.'

'Call me Aiden, please,' he'd said, but that was the closest he'd ever got to being personal with her. She was always pleasant, happy to talk about neutering programmes or treatments or her plans for the sanctuary, but on a personal level he was still at first base.

'Actually, Aiden, I've decided to get some help with the place,' Jade said conversationally as they walked up towards the stables in the fading light. 'Paid help, I mean. I've put a card up in the post office, and Mike, at the Red Lion, said he'll keep an eye out for me, too.'

He looked at her, startled. There were dozens of volunteers who came in on an ad hoc basis to walk the dogs and help out in reception, mostly mothers from the surrounding villages, nagged by their offspring and the lure of animals.

'I've got enough on my plate with the fund-raising and looking after this lot,' she went on. 'I can't keep up with the heavier jobs. Most of the fencing in this place is rotten and the guttering is coming off the older kennel block. With hindsight it was a mistake to buy second hand.' She sighed. 'Not to mention the drainage problem.'

'Maybe I could help you out with some of that,' he heard himself saying. 'It would be a pleasure.'

'That's very sweet of you, Aiden, but you haven't got time.'

He tried not to feel rebuffed. Changing tack, he said, 'Can you afford to employ someone then? I thought it was touch and go on the financial side.'

'I can afford someone for a while and I was thinking I could throw in somewhere to live. I've got a spare room.'

'Good idea,' Aiden said, although he wasn't sure it was. His heart was thumping uncomfortably. Did she mean to share her cottage with a stranger?

They went past the paddock railings, which looked pretty solid to him, and Jade switched on the stable lights. A chestnut horse stuck his head over the door of the middle stable and whinnied at them.

'This is Ashley,' Jade said, undoing a padlock before sliding back the bolt. 'He can undo them,' she explained, ushering Aiden into the stable ahead of her. 'So if I don't padlock him in, he lets himself out and causes chaos.'

'What sort of chaos?'

Perhaps he should ask her out now. If they were dating then he could offer to pay for someone to come in and do the jobs she'd mentioned. He'd offered to do this once before, but she'd turned him down flat. She might feel differently if they had more than a purely professional relationship. Spurred on by the consequences of not acting and with his heart pumping madly in his chest, he blurted, 'Jade, there's something I've been meaning to ask you.'

'I think the Hendersons may have got rid of him because he was – er – over-sexed.'

They spoke at the same time and he gestured for her to go first.

'He keeps chasing after Rosanna. He lets himself out, and then he lets her out and... Well... You don't need me to spell it out for you.' She hesitated. 'Rosanna's in season at the moment and she's a terrible flirt, but this horse is supposed to be a gelding. He looks like a gelding – well, he does to me. Does he look like one to you?'

Aiden looked at the horse's nether regions and agreed that he'd definitely been castrated.

'I've tried keeping them apart, but it's tricky because he can get out of anywhere. Dawn, my most prolific volunteer, caught them in the hay barn the other day. They'd bent the lid of one of the feed bins, but they certainly didn't have food on their minds. They...' She broke off and looked at him and he could feel her discomfort. 'I've got enough to do without dealing with over-sexed males,' she added briskly. 'Sorry, what was it you wanted to ask me?'

'Oh, it was nothing important.' Aiden avoided her eyes and glanced back at Ashley. There was an awkward pause.

'So what do you think his problem is?' Jade asked. 'Could it be hormonal?'

Aiden switched into professional mode.

'Sometimes you get what's called a rig. He might have been gelded when he was younger, but perhaps he had an unde-scended testicle. Then he'd look like a gelding, but he'd still have all the normal urges.'

'I see.' She looked interested and she was evidently completely unaware of the effect this conversation was having on him.

'There's a test that can be carried out. I'll look into it for you. I can speak to my Uncle Seth, he's more of an equine specialist than I am. He's a vet now but he used to be a jockey.' In an attempt to disguise his embarrassment, he knew he was talking far too quickly, but she didn't seem to notice.

'Thanks, Aiden, I'd really appreciate it. It's embarrassing having two horses – well – mounting each other in the field when there are people walking about with kids. Talking of kids, I've got to pick Ben up from school. I'm babysitting for Sarah tonight. So I'm going to have to love you and leave you.'

They came out of the stable together and he watched her hurry away from him, her hips swinging tantalisingly. He'd have to ask her out soon. Either that or suggest she found herself another vet. There were only so many cold showers a man could take.

'We're going to the Red Lion for tea,' she called back over her shoulder. 'I want to see if Mike's found me a handyman yet and I promised Ben a pizza as it's Friday and there's no school tomorrow. Pop by if you've got any news about Ashley. It's quite urgent.'

'I'll give my uncle a call today. Why don't I swing by and give you and Ben a lift to the Red Lion?' he said before he had time to think about her refusing. 'Then I can update you. And it'll save you driving.'

'OK, great, thanks. About six. That should see me done here.' She gave him another quick smile and then she was gone, driving out of the front gate in her Land Rover in a spray of gravel.

Aiden had an urge to punch the air but restrained himself. It was hardly a date. She'd have Ben with her and much as he liked the youngster, he'd far rather have taken Jade out on her own. Still, it was a start.

Maybe he could raise the idea of a proper date while they were there. Yes, good plan. Tonight he would ask her out, come what may. If she hadn't liked him, she wouldn't have suggested he join them, would she?

7

'Long time no see,' Mike said as he pulled Finn a pint of Guinness and put it on the bar to settle. 'I thought you must have taken your patronage elsewhere.'

Finn shook his head. 'My father's got a cottage in the village – the last time we were here was at the end of last summer. We were in a lot then, but we've not had the chance to get down since. I'm only here now because we've just sold the place.'

The landlord's face cleared and he clicked his fingers in the air. 'Of course. It's Finn, isn't it? Good to see you again. Did you get a good price?'

Finn told him, knowing he could probably find out anyway, and the big man nodded seriously. 'Mmm, not bad. Not bad at all. So how long are you planning on staying? Just until the deal goes through?'

'Maybe a bit longer. I'm between jobs at the moment.' 'Between jobs' sounded better than admitting he'd just been made redundant, along with several of his colleagues, after a management buyout.

'What sort of work do you do?'

'I'm an engineer by trade – lately I've been working at a switch-making company in Nottingham. But I can turn my hand to most things. I can do maintenance, plumbing, electrical work.' He hesitated, not sure whether to divulge the rest of his plans, but Mike looked interested, so he cleared his throat and carried on.

'I can paint a bit, too. I thought I might do some painting while I'm here.'

'Houses, you mean?'

'No, I'm an artist.' The words felt strange. Probably because it was the first time he'd ever said them. He wasn't sure if he even meant them, but they were out now, and he was Mike's only customer so it wasn't as if there were any witnesses. 'I do landscapes mostly – watercolours.'

'Are you any good?'

Finn sipped his pint for Dutch courage. 'I've got some framed canvases at the cottage – local views. My grandparents liked them, but as we're selling the place, they'll probably end up at Oxfam.'

'Tell you what, why don't I have a look? That sort of thing can go down well with the tourists. If I like them, you can put a couple on the walls, stick a price on. I'd have to take commission, of course – if any were sold.'

'Why not?' Finn said, smiling nervously and wondering what on earth he'd let himself in for. 'Yeah – go on then – I'll pop a couple in the car next time I'm in.'

A few more customers began to drift in: an old boy in a flat cap, with a border collie at his heels; then a couple of teenagers, busy scrolling on their mobiles.

The pub was cosy. The woodburning stove kicked out warmth, and burning logs spat out red hot sparks as logs shifted within it. Peace personified.

Finn was on his second pint, still sitting at the bar, when the door opened and a couple came in with a child. The woman was Jade, he realised with a jolt.

It was true what he'd told Mike: he was here to sort out the house sale to save his father the hassle, and he liked the idea of spending some time painting – the scenery was beautiful in this part of the world. But he couldn't deny that the possibility of bumping into Jade again had been appealing, too.

He just hadn't expected it to happen so soon.

Finn put down his pint and tried not to stare. She probably wouldn't remember him, anyway. He picked up a paper that was lying on the bar and withdrew to a table in the window, where he could watch the trio without being obvious. Perhaps the guy was her boyfriend; husband, even.

He watched as the man, a burly, stocky guy wearing a tweed jacket that made him look like a gentleman farmer, took Jade's coat and draped it awkwardly over the back of her chair. Then he fussed around her, his hands fluttering, as if he wanted to touch but wasn't quite sure of his welcome.

Business acquaintances, Finn decided, or casual friends, at most. The body language was wrong for them to be anything more. He'd have laid bets on it that the boy wasn't hers either. Well, not if looks were anything to go by. Jade had dark hair and the child was fair and they had different-shaped faces, different colouring altogether.

He went back to his newspaper, feeling a surge of disappointment. He'd wanted to bump into her, but these circumstances were no more ideal than when they'd met before.

The idea of Mike selling his paintings also seemed suddenly ludicrous. He'd spouted off about being an artist, and it was true that he'd drawn and painted since he was a child. But he'd never been professionally trained, unless you counted the odd evening class, where he'd always felt out of place, being the only man.

Going to art college hadn't been an option. He hadn't even bothered suggesting it to Ray, knowing what his reaction would be. 'Don't be so bloody soft, lad, art's not going to pay the bills.'

Finn felt a surge of affection for his father despite their differences. Had there still been working mines in his hometown when he'd left school, Ray would have had him down one at the first opportunity.

He supposed he should head back to the cottage. He had the last of the packing up to do, but it was still early and he didn't relish the prospect of spending the next twelve hours alone. Not that this place was exactly buzzing. Jade and her companion had ordered pizzas, which had just arrived, and the boy was tearing open sachets of tomato ketchup and squirting patterns on to his. The smell of food had Finn's stomach rumbling and he realised he hadn't eaten all day. Maybe he should order something.

Packing up the last of his grandfather's suits for the charity shop had been sadder than he'd anticipated – the end of an era. It was a pity Ray had decided to sell up, but Finn could see the sense in it. Ray would put the money to good use.

The next time he looked up, they'd finished eating and Jade was chatting to the landlord. Every so often they glanced in his direction and he had the odd feeling they were talking about him. He was being paranoid. Why would they be?

He stared out at the velvet blackness beyond the dark woodframed windows and decided to forget ordering food and head back. If the truth be told, he was just as alone here as he'd be at the cottage.

He took his empty glass back to the bar, confident now that Jade hadn't recognised him, and was about to head for the door when Mike called, 'Hey, Finn. You got a sec? Jade here has a proposition for you.'

Finn jumped out of his skin. He really had to get a grip. He turned slowly.

'What sort of proposition?' He met Jade's direct gaze.

'Hello, Finn. I thought it might be you, but I wasn't sure until Mike told me your name. We met last year,' she explained, turning to her companion, who looked none too happy about the turn events were taking.

'Back in September,' Finn murmured. 'Yes, I remember. How are you?'

'I'm fine, thanks.' There was a flash of embarrassment in her eyes and he knew she was remembering the circumstances of their meeting.

'You were right,' she added, a faint flush colouring her cheeks. 'It does get easier.'

Finn nodded, aware the man was watching, his gaze cool. The little lad was fiddling with a beer mat, bending one corner of it backwards and forwards. Close up, Finn was even more certain they weren't related – although he supposed the child could be adopted. No, that was unlikely – she was too young to have decided to adopt a child.

Realising that Jade was still speaking to him, he looked back into her face.

'I've a job I think might interest you, Finn. Why don't you join us and we can have a chat?'

He was about to say he wasn't looking for a job, but then he caught the enthusiasm on Mike's face and, realising he'd misinterpreted his 'between jobs' as meaning 'looking for a job', he nodded slowly.

'This is Ben, my godson,' she went on, warmth threading through her voice as she glanced towards the boy, who gave Finn a gap-toothed grin. 'And Aiden Southerland, my vet, and friend.'

Finn heard the edge of awkwardness in the word 'friend' and

felt a little stab of relief. That was good news. There was nothing established there, then – at least not as far as Jade was concerned.

Ben, obviously anxious to get back into the limelight again, drew his plate towards the edge of the table and began to fiddle with his knife and fork.

Out of the corner of his eye, Finn saw the plate begin to tip towards the boy's lap. He'd always had lightning reflexes. Before anyone else could move, he reached across in front of Aiden, who was sitting next to Ben, and caught the plate just before it tipped completely and deposited its cargo of ketchup-soaked pizza into the child's lap.

Unfortunately, he wasn't quite quick enough to prevent the sauce-smeared knife from landing in Aiden's lap, pointy end down.

'Bugger,' Aiden muttered, leaping out of his chair like a scalded cat and glaring at Finn as the knife clattered to the wooden floor.

'Sorry.' Finn held up his hands in contrition, aware that Jade was frowning at Aiden, presumably because she didn't approve of him swearing in front of her godson, who looked thrilled at the fuss he'd caused.

'Mum tells me off if I say naughty words.' Ben was giggling.

'I should think so, too.' There was mild reproof in Jade's voice. Finn could see she was trying not to smile, but Aiden looked mortified.

'Sorry,' Finn murmured as Aiden dabbed at the red smear on his hitherto immaculate trousers with a green paper napkin.

'It's fine. No worries. At least I caught it. What's everyone drinking?' Aiden was clearly eager to get back into Jade's good books, and Finn found himself being pressed into another pint of Guinness.

'Do you like animals?' Jade asked while Aiden was at the bar.

'We used to have a dog,' he said, puzzled. 'My father reckons they're less trouble than people. They're always pleased to see you and they stay loyal.'

She nodded in approval and went on without preamble. 'I think I told you I run an animal rescue home last time we met. I'm looking for someone to help out.'

'I see.' Finn was slightly thrown. Had he and Mike even had the same conversation? 'Do you mean you need someone to look after the animals? I've no experience with livestock.'

'No, don't worry. Nothing like that. I do all that side. It's the place itself I need help with. Mike was saying you're looking for work and can turn your hand to most things, maintenance wise.'

'That's right.' He rested his chin on his hand and was pleased when she unconsciously mirrored the gesture.

'So you could do things like fix dodgy electricity supplies? There's a bit of fencing too. Drainage, guttering – that sort of thing.'

'Doesn't sound too complicated.'

'She hasn't told you the best bit yet.' Aiden was back. He put their drinks on the table, and although his voice was light, his body language told Finn a different story. Aiden couldn't wait to get rid of him. He'd have thought he was interrupting a romantic date, had it not been for Ben's presence.

'What's the best bit?'

'You'll be working all hours and earning a pittance.'

'Oh, don't put him off, Aiden.'

'He hasn't,' Finn said, raising his eyebrows. 'I'm used to that.' This wasn't quite true, but there was no way he was letting Jade get away without at least arranging another meeting. Not that she seemed in any hurry to get away.

'Aiden's right. I'm afraid I can't afford to pay you much. We're a charity, you see. I could throw in accommodation, though. Mike said you've just sold a cottage – so you're going to need some-where to live.'

Finn saw Aiden give her a sharp look and he realised his earlier suspicions had been right on target. They weren't a couple, but Aiden certainly wanted them to be, and he didn't want another bloke muscling in.

He sipped his pint and decided, for once, to throw caution to the wind. If fate decreed that the woman he'd had trouble getting off his mind in the last few months should offer him a job, he certainly wasn't going to turn her down out of hand.

'Maybe if I came and had a look round and you showed me what you need doing. Would tomorrow morning work?'

'That would be wonderful.' Jade's face lit up, and Finn found himself thinking he'd have worked for nothing if she smiled at him like that every day. No wonder Aiden was smitten.

'You could see Candy's pups.' Ben had been busy with another beer mat, but now he pushed the torn-up pieces into a little pile on the table and rested his chin on his hands. 'And Auntie Jade's got a sick buzzard. And chickens. Millions of smelly chickens.'

'Sounds wonderful,' Finn said, turning towards the boy. He liked kids and this one was a right live wire. He stood up. 'Can I get anyone another drink?'

Jade shook her head. 'Thanks, but I need to get this little man home to bed.' She got gracefully to her feet and offered Finn her hand. 'I'll see you tomorrow then, Finn. About ten?'

Her fingers felt cool and surprisingly smooth, considering her job. Nice nails – short, and painted with some clear shiny varnish. There was no sign of a wedding ring. 'I'll look forward to it,' he said, acutely aware that beside her Aiden didn't look quite so thrilled. Finn wondered if she could feel the atmosphere. There was no sign of it in her face. So was she oblivious to the way Aiden felt about her, or just playing it cool?

It would be an interesting meeting tomorrow, he thought, hoping Aiden didn't have any say in whether he got the job or not. Not that he actually needed the job – but he'd like to get to know Jade better.

His memory hadn't let him down. She was maybe a touch thinner than he remembered, but she was still just as attractive, and there was a very slight air of aloofness about her that made him want to know what went on behind those dark eyes. Why on earth had a woman like Jade Foster decided to bury herself in the wilds of Wiltshire looking after a bunch of animals that no one else wanted? Finn was intrigued. And he hadn't been intrigued by a woman for a very long time.

8

Sarah arrived to collect Ben just after nine the next morning and Jade told her about her prospective employee as they stood outside reception.

'It sounds to me like you fancy the bloke,' Sarah said, putting her head on one side. 'How old is he and what does he look like?'

'Thirtyish, I'd guess. I didn't really notice what he looked like,' Jade lied. 'And of course I don't fancy him. I just need some help. It's not fair to keep asking Callum when I can't manage.'

'Callum doesn't mind. And you know Ben loves it here. He'd far rather be with you, getting filthy, than at home doing boring stuff.'

'It's the animals he likes, not me,' Jade protested, ruffling Ben's fair hair and brushing some flecks of dried mud off his back. She didn't know how he got so dirty; perhaps it was because he was closer to the ground than they were. 'Isn't that right, young man?'

Ben gave her the full benefit of his gap-toothed smile and shook his head emphatically.

Jade laughed. 'You're a right smoothie, you are. So are you

telling me you'd still come and stay with me if I didn't have all my waifs and strays?'

'Course, Auntie Jade.' Ben widened his eyes. 'Anyway, I'm a big help, aren't I?'

'A big help' was his latest catchphrase, which Aiden had started off when Ben had helped him catch a litter of puppies that he needed to vaccinate.

'A big pest, more like,' Sarah muttered. 'Talking of which, are you still sure you don't mind having him next week?'

'Of course I'm sure.' This was true, but Jade was also terrified at the prospect of being responsible for Ben for a whole week, especially as it was half term. Not that she had any intention of telling Sarah this because she knew how torn her friend was. Callum's father was ill and Callum's mother had asked if he could possibly go up and cover his shifts in the restaurant for a while. It was getting really expensive to pay for cover.

'Callum still feels guilty about abandoning the family business,' Sarah had explained, 'so he's keen to go, and it would give me the chance to meet his parents, seeing as things are getting serious with us two. But Ben's adamant he won't come with us.'

'I'm looking forward to having him all to myself,' Jade reassured her. 'He'll have a lot more fun here than traipsing up to Scotland in that campervan.'

'Yes, that's what he said. I'm going to miss him, though,' she added, with an ache of longing in her voice. 'It's going to be really strange being childless for that long.'

'You can Zoom call him every day,' Jade said. 'And he can tell you what he's been up to, can't you, Ben?'

But Ben wasn't listening any more. He was in reception, trying to tempt a dove perched on the corner of Jade's filing cabinet to land on his hand.

'Dawn's coming in every day next week, too,' Jade went on.

'And with a bit of luck I'll have a full-time handyman then as well.'

'What time is he coming – this handyman chap? Maybe I should hang around and help you interview him.'

'No, thank you. I'm quite capable of interviewing him myself.' Jade knew Sarah wouldn't be able to resist teasing Finn about sharing the cottage and she didn't want him frightened off.

They went eventually and Jade breathed a sigh of relief. Finn probably wouldn't take the job anyway. Not when he found out what she could afford to pay him. And even if he did, he wouldn't stay long, she decided as she looked around the yard. He'd just stay until he got a better offer and then he'd be off again; but having someone around, even for a short while, would be a great help. She'd made light of it to Aiden, but it did worry her that the place needed so much maintenance and she didn't have time to do anything about it.

* * *

Finn's white Toyota drew into the yard just before ten and from the reception window Jade saw Finn get out and stand in the muddy yard, looking around appraisingly. He'd probably only turned up because he didn't have anything better to do. In half an hour he'd be gone, shaking his head as he drove away, his impression of her as a batty animal lover entrenched. A tale to tell in bars across the country. No, she mustn't pre-empt. He might be desperate enough to work for her. She took a deep breath and switched on the answer machine and fixed what she hoped was a welcoming expression on her face.

As she went out to meet him, Jade tried to imagine what Duck Pond Rescue must look like to a stranger. After all the rain they'd had lately, tracks of mud ran round the yard, and the outbuildings, although in better shape than they'd been when she'd moved in, thanks to her prowess with a paintbrush, and some help from Callum, still looked dismal and run down. No one in their right mind would want to work here.

'I'm afraid you're not seeing it at its best.' She glanced at his unsmiling face, which told her nothing. His eyes were thoughtful. He was either very good at hiding his feelings or simply indifferent. She hoped it wasn't the latter. But at least he didn't look horrified, which was a good start.

'Shall we just walk round and you can see what you'd be letting yourself in for?'

'Sure.'

She took him through the gate that led up past the cattery and the horses' paddock and on towards the kennels. This part of the sanctuary was on higher ground and wasn't as muddy as the reception end. Above their heads, a weak spring sun was trying to push through the clouds.

'There's a lot to be done,' Finn remarked as they went past the tatty pink caravan where she kept bedding for the dogs. 'That's not the accommodation you're offering, is it?'

She glanced at him sharply, before realising there was humour in his grey eyes. She was about to make an appropriate retort when Diesel, who had the uninterrupted run of the place, strolled around the side of the caravan, almost at their feet, with a large wriggling mouse in his mouth.

Jade gasped and Finn looked at her. Swiftly, before she could react, he picked up Diesel by the scruff of his black neck. The cat was so surprised he dropped the mouse and it scurried away across the yard.

Diesel yowled in disgust and Jade burst out laughing. 'You've just made an enemy for life. You realise that?'

'By the look on your face, I figured that mouse must be one of the residents,' Finn said, still holding the struggling Diesel in his arms.

'Not that I know of. But I'm glad you stopped him. Diesel's a cold-hearted monster. He's always murdering things and I'd rather he did it out of my sight. This is an animal sanctuary, after all.'

As she spoke, Diesel gave another frantic wriggle, scratched Finn's hand and leapt to freedom.

Finn looked so affronted that Jade started to laugh again. Then she remembered she was trying to get him to work for her and said solicitously, 'He hasn't hurt you, has he?'

'It'll heal.' Finn glanced at her. Then his grey eyes warmed. It was in that moment that Jade knew it was going to be all right. He was going to take the job.

* * *

Twenty minutes later, she was proved right when he agreed to do a week's trial – to see if it suited them both – starting the following Saturday.

Jade had to restrain herself from jumping up and down in excitement as he drove away. At least until he was out of sight anyway. Fortunately, the blast of her mobile diverted her. It was Aiden.

'Hi, Jade. My Uncle Seth just got back to me about the test for Ashley. We can arrange it no problem, but it'll take some time to get the results. In the meantime, he's suggested moving Rosanna to another stables while she's in season.'

'I'm not sure I can afford to put her at livery, Aiden.'

'No need. Uncle Seth's got links with another animal sanctuary in the New Forest. They're called Puddleduck Pets and the owner, Maggie Crowther, is happy to take her. Apparently she has a lone mare at the moment who'd enjoy the company.'

'Really? That's wonderful.'

'Isn't it? I think the duck connection helped. Apparently when Seth spoke to her she said, and I quote, "If we were towns, we'd be twinned with each other, wouldn't we? How could I possibly refuse a request from a spiritual twin?"'

'That's amazing. Thank you so much. Did they say when they could take her?'

'Today if that's convenient for you. I can give you a hand this afternoon if you like? I'll be finished by lunchtime. And I know where the place is.'

'Aiden, thank you. That would be brilliant.'

'About two thirty?'

'Perfect.'

Aiden disconnected, and Jade walked back to reception with a smile on her face. Underneath that slightly awkward exterior, there was no doubt that Aiden had a very good heart.

9

Finn drove back to the cottage, deep in thought. It wasn't like him to make impulsive decisions where women were concerned. Not since things had gone so badly wrong with Shona, the last woman he'd been involved with. That impulse had cost him dearly.

Shona had been his best friend's wife. Make that former best friend. Andy was great except when he drank, after which he had a complete personality change. Unfortunately, he'd drunk more and more the last few years.

Shona had thrown him out when he'd got handy with his fists once too often. In Finn's opinion, *once* was too often, but Shona had put up with a lot until the day had come when she'd decided enough was enough.

After Andy had gone, Finn, who'd once been close friends with them both, but had now vowed to have nothing more to do with his former best friend, had tried to support her. In the beginning he'd just been a shoulder to cry on. But his feelings had grown deeper and when it seemed that Andy was completely out of the picture, things had developed between them and they'd become a couple. But then just six months later, Andy had reappeared, begging Shona to take him back and promising that he'd joined AA and was a reformed character.

Finn had doubted very much that he was. Andy had made plenty of promises before that he'd swiftly broken again, but Shona had believed him and so Finn had stepped back with a very heavy heart. He knew he'd always be concerned about her welfare. Shona was a beautiful person, inside and out, and Finn had loved her unconditionally, but he knew it was her decision, not his. He still worried about her welfare, but at least Ray had promised to keep a discreet eye on things.

Ray would let him know if Shona needed him. That would have to be good enough for now.

Finn frowned, snapping his thoughts back to the present. Charging in without thinking about the consequences always led to trouble. Was that what he was doing now?

By the time he'd got back to the cottage, he'd convinced himself he wasn't. Taking the job was sensible. It meant he could stay here longer than he'd planned and maybe give the painting a real go, too. Besides, he was hardly overloaded with options. If a job fell into his lap, he'd be a fool not to take it. It was only a temporary position; Jade had made that clear.

It would be interesting living in her house and although she hadn't offered him much money, free lodgings were a bonus. Finn had never needed much money.

He wandered around the empty rooms of his grandparents' cottage. Two or three more trips to the charity shop and one more trip to the tip should do it. The contracts had been exchanged and the completion date was next Friday.

He'd agreed to start at Duck Pond Rescue the following Saturday, so he'd have a full week to finish the last bits of clearing up at the cottage and to paint. He had a feeling he wouldn't have an awful lot of spare time once he'd started working for Jade. He glanced at the faded oblong squares on the walls where the paintings had once hung and remembered he'd promised to show Mike his work. Deciding he might as well have lunch at the Red Lion, he packed the canvases into the car.

* * *

'Bit of a result that, eh, Finn?' Mike grinned at him across the bar. 'Bet you didn't expect to find a job and a place to live so soon – eh?'

'Thanks very much for the introduction.'

'She's a sweetie, Jade Foster. She's had a tough time of it lately. She lost her mother last year. Think it did something to her, that. She was all set on some high-flying veterinary career in Bristol.'

He paused, a frown crinkling his forehead. 'She grew up round here, but she wasn't like the rest of the kids. She left as soon as she got the chance. Must have been difficult coming back and I must say I was surprised when she set up that animal rescue place. I've heard a few mutterings lately that the place is going to rack and ruin, becoming an eyesore. But that'll change now you're here. Mind you, you'll have your work cut out.'

'Reckon I will.' Finn sipped the half pint of Guinness Mike had put in front of him.

'So what's Aiden like? Are they...?'

'Good lord, no.' Mike guffawed and slapped a hand down on the bar. 'That's not to say Aiden wouldn't like them to be.' He rested his elbows on the bar and lowered his voice with the air of one sharing a confidence. 'For someone who has his hands up cow's whatsits half his life, he's bloody uptight. He was married once, but she left him for the best man a week after the wedding. Poor fellow's never got over it.'

'Right,' Finn said, feeling a little sorry for Aiden and deciding to be very careful what he said to Mike in future.

'Jade's attractive, though, isn't she?' Mike probed, his eyes glinting at the prospect of gossip.

'She's not my type,' Finn lied smoothly. 'Besides, I don't believe in mixing business with pleasure. Always ends in tears.'

* * *

Finn was just leaving the pub when Mike called after him. 'Hold on a tick. Weren't you going to show me some paintings?'

He hesitated. Last night, fortified with Guinness, it had seemed a good idea, but now, in the cold light of day, he felt a bit vulnerable. He'd never shown his work to a stranger before.

'I'll come and have a quick shufty,' Mike continued. 'You're not rushing off, are you?'

He couldn't refuse without seeming rude. What was the worst that could happen? Mike could say they were no good, which would only confirm his own suspicions. Painting was an odd thing, Finn mused. When he'd just finished a canvas, he was usually pleased with it. Still caught up in the fire of creation. It was only later, when he'd had time to study it and see all the imperfections, that the self-doubt would creep in.

A few moments later, they were standing in the car park beneath a sky that looked heavy with rain. Hoping it would hold off, Finn hauled the two biggest canvases off the back seat and propped them up against the tyres of the Toyota. One of them was of Stonehenge, the stones dark and brooding against a winter sky, and the other was of Bournemouth beach, which Finn had visited often with his grandparents. In the foreground, a small girl was building a sandcastle with a red plastic spade. The wind swept back her hair so you could see the intense concentration on her face. Behind her, the sea was a moody grey.

Mike studied the paintings without speaking and Finn could feel his stomach turning over. He wiped his hands on his jeans and felt sick. He'd just taken a few steps away from the car, deciding he could stand the suspense no longer, when Mike said, 'They're bloody brilliant, these are. Give us a hand to cart them inside and I'll find a place to put them up later.'

'Do you think they might sell, then?' Finn asked cautiously.

'Don't know about that – depends on how flush the tourists are. But it's worth a try.'

Finn nodded, feeling deflated.

'Twenty-five per cent commission if they do,' Mike said as they walked back towards the pub with the canvases.

'All right.' They shook hands on the deal and Finn went back to the cottage.

The winds of change were blowing. He wasn't sure whether he was excited about this new direction his life was taking or nervous. He guessed he'd find out soon enough.

* * *

Puddleduck Pets was impressive, Jade thought as Aiden drove the horsebox into the middle of a spotless yard later that afternoon.

They'd driven past some sort of posh estate next door, with a life-size bronze of a stag high up on an archway over the entrance, and a gatehouse. Puddleduck Pets itself was a patchwork of neat fields leading down to the road and a gorgeous farmhouse. There was even a vet in situ called Puddleduck Vets. Wow, what a great idea to have a vet on site.

Aiden pulled up carefully and turned off the engine. Jade gathered up the bags she'd brought with them, but before she could jump down from the cab, Aiden had run round to open the door.

She thanked him but he was already going across to two women who'd been watching their arrival. As she got there, she heard him say, 'Hi, which one of you young ladies would be Maggie?'

It was the older woman, Jade saw as she caught up with him.

'I'm Jade from Duck Pond Rescue, and this is Aiden. I'm so grateful to you.' She looked straight at Maggie, who was a lot older than her companion. She must have been in her seventies, but she had a vibrant energy about her. The younger woman, who'd introduced herself as Phoebe, looked as though she might be related. They had the same hazel eyes and lovely auras.

'This is such a massive help,' Jade said, gathering herself. 'I've brought over a bag of Rosanna's food and there's some hay in the horsebox, and there are also some other things in this bag.' She held it out. 'Chocolate cookies from the farm shop near us, and a bottle of wine. They're for you, not Rosanna. A little thank you. I hope that's OK?'

They were both smiling. Jade felt herself relax, which was rare around people she didn't know. Or any people, come to that, she sometimes thought. She'd always been much happier in the company of animals.

They chatted for a while about Seth's connection with Aiden and the joys and difficulties of taking in animals no one else wanted.

But Jade was relieved when they could finish doing the social bits and got down to the business of unboxing Rosanna.

As she watched the bay mare look happily around at her new temporary home, she felt Maggie's eyes on her.

'We'll take good care of her, don't worry.'

On her other side, Aiden touched her arm. 'She'll be fine, Jade.'

'Thank you,' Jade told them both, wishing she didn't feel so emotional. It was weird how much goodbyes affected her. Even ones that were just temporary. Maybe because there had been so many of them lately. She swallowed hard. OK, so maybe Sarah had a point about her hiding away from the world at Duck Pond Rescue along with a bunch of animals that gave you nothing but unconditional love.

10

'So, where is he?' Sarah asked Jade as she struggled into Duck Pond Cottage the following Friday evening with a small suitcase and a selection of bulging bags, which she plonked on the wooden floor of the hall.

'If you mean my new employee, he's not starting until tomorrow. He's an artist. He's been doing some sketching this week, apparently.'

'Should get on well with Ben, then.' Sarah grinned. 'I'll just get the rest of his stuff.'

'More stuff?' Jade said in alarm. 'What on earth is it all?'

'Clothes, school stuff, just in case we get delayed and have to stay an extra day, and that carrier bag is mostly stuffed with dog treats. He's been saving his breakfast sausages. I did tell him you fed them.'

Jade shook her head in amazement. 'It's a good job I cleared out the spare room. What time are you off?'

'We're planning to get going at 6 a.m. tomorrow. Callum's loading up the camper van now.' Sarah paced across the office and looked out at the darkening sky. 'It's set to get really cold again, according to the weather forecast. I hope we don't drive into too much snow. I'm glad you've got some help. I don't feel so bad about you looking after Ben.'

'Stop it, Sarah. You know I love having him. Where is he, anyway?'

'He went to see Candy's pups. He doesn't seem a bit bothered about me going. I'm going to miss him like hell, it's the first time we've ever been apart.'

'I expect he's more bothered than he's letting on,' Jade said, hearing the wistful note in Sarah's voice. 'But it's good really, isn't it – that he feels secure enough to want to stay here without you?'

'Yes, I suppose so.' Jade saw the shine of tears in her eyes.

'Oh, Sarah, come here.' She hugged her friend tightly, breathing in the scent of apple shampoo mixed with the wild musk scent she always wore. 'I won't let anything happen to him. He'll be fine.'

'I know he will. I'm sorry. I'm being silly.'

Sarah sniffed and Jade said softly, 'Come on, I'll take his stuff inside and you go and see what he's doing. A week will be gone in no time. And when you get back you can meet my new employee. Maybe we could all go out together. I'll ask Aiden, too.'

'What's his name anyway, this wonder guy?' Sarah asked at the same moment that Ben reappeared with a grimy face and eyes that were suspiciously glittery.

'Darling, what's wrong?' Sarah gasped as she and Jade both looked at him in alarm.

'Diesel scratched me.' There was a distinct wobble in his voice as he sniffed and rolled up his sleeve to show them the thin red weal on his arm.

Jade swallowed hard and wondered again if this was going to

work. Yesterday she and Dawn, who was sensible and middle-aged and had several grandchildren of her own, had gone round the entire sanctuary and 'Ben proofed' everything. There were padlocks on all the animal pens apart from the chickens, Jade's medical supplies were out of reach as well as under lock and key, and Jade was certain that the fencing around the paddocks was childproof.

But Diesel was a law unto himself. Jade wondered if perhaps she should confine him to the cattery.

'I was only cuddling him,' Ben mumbled. 'Not tight, Auntie Jade, honest, I wasn't.'

'He's a grumpy old sod,' Jade said, realising belatedly she shouldn't have said 'sod'. 'Let's get you some antiseptic cream and a plaster. You can cuddle Mickey in a minute. He likes a nice cuddle.'

Ben stuck his thumb in his mouth and looked around for Jade's dog, who was the only animal, apart from Diesel, who had the run of the place. Mickey was the 'rug on legs' that Sarah's neighbour had eventually given up because of her asthmatic grandchildren and Jade had decided with slightly irrational logic that the best way to avoid anyone rejecting him was to keep him herself.

Ben's arm now sorted out, Jade chewed her lip as she watched Sarah kiss his fair head and wished she didn't feel quite so terrified at the prospect of being solely responsible for him.

Not that she was going to admit this to her best friend. She knew how much this trip meant to her. It wasn't just about meeting Callum's parents, it was about giving Callum moral support. Sarah knew he was really worried about his dad, who had a recently diagnosed heart condition and had been told by his doctor to take things easy.

The Scotland trip wasn't a holiday. Both Callum and Sarah would be working in between helping his parents. Luckily both of them could work remotely.

Thankfully Ben seemed to have forgotten about his sore arm now it sported a plaster and was now happily cuddling Mickey, who adored kids.

'Let's go and wave Mummy off,' Jade said, holding out her hand.

Ben nodded cheerfully as they went and did just that. Kids were so amazingly resilient, Jade thought as he skipped happily ahead of her into the cottage. She wished she could be more like that.

* * *

'I'm not trying to interfere, Jade, but don't you think you ought to be more cautious? At least get some references. You don't know anything about the guy.'

'I doubt he's an axe murderer, Aiden,' she said, glancing at the vet's concerned face. He was obviously uneasy and she wasn't sure whether to be touched or irritated by his questions.

It was now Saturday morning and Ben was 'helping' Dawn clean out the chicken run, while she and Aiden were standing in the hospital block beside the dog pen. Aiden had declared that Tiny was coming along nicely, but didn't seem to be in any hurry to go. 'I didn't say I thought he was dangerous. I just think you ought to be careful. Not rush into anything. Especially as he's going to be living in your house.'

'I've already employed him. In fact, he should be here any minute.'

'I see... I'm sorry. I'll shut up.'

'It's fine. I appreciate you looking out for me. But don't worry. He's hardly going to pinch the silver, because I haven't got any. In fact, I've got nothing worth the trouble of carrying out the front door.'

He put up his hands in a gesture of defeat and she regretted her sharpness.

'Sorry. I know you're only trying to help.' She touched his arm lightly. 'But Finn's accepted the job despite the fact I'm paying him next to nothing, and to be honest, Aiden, I can't afford to be too choosy. He seems nice enough.'

'You will be careful, though, won't you? You'll let me know if he gives you any trouble.'

'He didn't strike me as being that kind of guy. Anyway, I'm a big girl. I can look after myself.' She hoped that would be enough of a hint, but it seemed to go straight over Aiden's head.

'I know that. I just meant you can't tell much about people, not from first impressions. He could be anyone.'

There was a cough from behind them. Jade spun round to see Finn standing there. She wondered how much of their conversation he'd heard.

'Er, I didn't realise you were here.' She glanced at Aiden, who seemed to have developed an all-consuming interest in something in Candy's pen.

Embarrassed, she fished a key out of her pocket and gave it to Finn. 'Please go and get settled in and make yourself at home. Help yourself to coffee, whatever. I'll be over in a minute.'

When he'd gone, she turned back to Aiden. 'Blimey, I hope he didn't hear that. It wasn't a great welcome for him, was it?'

Aiden nodded, biting his lip. 'Apologies. You're right. We should give the bloke a chance.'

* * *

Finn went across to the cottage. So, he'd been right about Aiden. The guy obviously wasn't at all happy about his presence. He wiped his feet on the doormat, which had a picture of a collie dog and the word 'Welcome' in black beneath it. Feeling like an intruder, he stepped inside. The place smelt faintly of dogs. He glanced around; he hadn't seen one when Jade had shown him round. The hallway had two doors leading off it, both of which were open.

The left-hand one led into a lounge, which Jade had shown him, but he hadn't really looked at it properly. Now he stood in the doorway, his gaze travelling over a brown patterned sofa and a matching armchair, both of which had seen better days. There was a bookcase stuffed with books, and a coffee table scattered with papers. In the corner was a plastic dog basket with a tartan blanket in it. Behind the chair was an open fireplace, which looked like it had been recently used.

The other door led through to a tiny kitchen. He saw a pile of washing-up in the sink as he went past. He continued on up the uncarpeted stairs. On the first floor were two bedrooms, Jade's and the spare, which she'd explained that Ben was staying in while his mum and dad were away.

'You can have it when he goes home – if you're still here then,' she'd joked, but he'd said no, the attic room, which was at the top of a further winding staircase, would suit him fine.

He carried on up and pushed open the door to his room.

Light flooded through a large, oblong skylight, casting golden pools across the little single bed. There was a small wardrobe and a washbasin with two white towels folded on the rail. Jade might not bother with the rest of the house, but this room was spotless, so she wasn't that oblivious, Finn thought, smiling as he dumped his stuff on the bed. There was a radiator behind the bed, which was on, he discovered, when he touched it.

He glanced out of the window and saw Aiden and Jade coming out of the hospital block. Perhaps he'd unpack first and sort out a few things. He could catch up with Jade later when Aiden wasn't around.

11

'Sorry, I haven't had a chance to see much of you,' Jade called as Finn came down the attic stairs later that evening.

'It's all right. I know you're busy.'

She was standing in the open doorway of Ben's bedroom, and when he reached her he could see that the boy was in bed. By the look of it there was a dog in there, too – although it was hard to tell it was a dog and not a hearth rug until it scrabbled a paw out of the covers.

Jade followed his gaze and smiled.

'Mickey's not supposed to be up here, but he's keeping Ben company until he falls asleep.'

'So I see,' Finn said softly, wondering if Ben was missing his mum. 'Mickey looks more fun than a bedtime story.'

'I have those too,' Ben told him, sitting up gleefully. 'Auntie Jade's a betterer reader than Mum. We had a long story, didn't we, Auntie Jade?'

'Yes and it's definitely bedtime so I think you should snuggle back down.' Jade's voice was gentle and Finn felt the edge of a memory, a long-ago painful memory of his own mother, and the awful, aching emptiness he'd felt when she'd gone. He swallowed. 'Sweet dreams then, mate,' he said, stepping past Jade and going downstairs.

He heard her say, 'Don't leave the light on too long, sweetheart. I'll leave this open in case Mickey wants to come down.'

Then she followed Finn downstairs and into the warmth of the little back room. An Ed Sheeran track was playing – so she was a romantic at heart, then – and an open fire was snapping and crackling in the grate.

'Wow, I haven't seen one of those for years,' he murmured, breathing in the scent of woodsmoke and stepping across the room to warm his hands. 'Dad used to have a real fire when I was small, but then he got a grant from the local authority and had central heating put in.'

'Not the same, is it?' she said, looking at him with pleasure and gesturing for him to sit on the chair beside it.

'Ben's a nice kiddie. Do you often look after him?'

'Not as often as I'd like to. Callum's father's not well and they've gone to help out. His parents have a restaurant in Dundee. Also there's a chance they might be longer than a week, and they didn't want him to miss any school. Besides, it's a pretty long haul for a six-year-old.'

'Yes,' Finn murmured, watching her face, which was animated when she talked about Ben. There was so much he wanted to ask her, like why she ran this place all alone and why she didn't have any children of her own, when she so obviously loved them. It was an odd life for a young, attractive woman.

'I was brought up round here,' she said, pre-empting him. 'My mother owned four hotels. She wanted me to go into business with her – run one of the hotels – but I'm afraid I disappointed her. All I ever wanted was to work with animals. So I persuaded her to let me go to vet school in Bristol.'

He wondered if she still felt guilty about that; it was never easy to go against your parents' wishes. He'd never gone against Ray's, but then despite the fact that Ray wasn't very good at anything touchy-feely, Finn had always known his father loved him, in his gruff, no-nonsense way. There was something in Jade's voice that told him she'd had a very different relationship with her mother.

'I should think it's very hard work being a vet,' he prompted, resting his elbows on his knees and leaning forward.

'Yes.' There was a hint of sadness in her eyes. 'But I never got that far. Mum had a stroke, you see, and I came back to look after her. Then she had another stroke – a fatal one this time. It was a huge shock. By the time I'd sorted everything out, I'd realised my life had moved on – I decided not to continue with studying.'

Finn nodded slowly, remembering the first time he'd seen her at the cemetery. She'd been pretty cut up then, a year after she'd lost her mother. There was a part of her that was still grieving. He could see it in her eyes.

'Was your dad involved in the business as well?'

'No, Dad left when I was small. I don't remember him.'

Her face was shadowed now, as though she was looking inside herself, at something she'd rather not see.

'That must have been tough,' he said quietly, wondering if he should change the subject. He didn't want to push her. It was obvious Jade was deeply troubled about something in her past.

Then she turned back to him and said in a voice that was a little too bright, 'Anyway, Finn, we're here to talk about you, not me. What's your background? Do both your parents live in Nottingham?'

Thrown at this swift change of subject, he hesitated. In some ways his background mirrored hers. Only it had been his mother who'd left. Finn could barely remember her. She'd left when he was six years old and he'd had nightmares about it for years. Ray had provided for him materially, but he'd never been an emotional man. Finn had spent many a childhood illness longing for the touch of his mother's hand, gentle on his forehead, the scent of her hair as she leaned over him in bed. Now and again he still had nightmares, waking up drenched in sweat and feeling an overwhelming sense of loss.

He coughed. He hated talking about his mother, but he felt obliged to say something.

'My parents split up when I was young, too. My mum was from Belfast, hence my name, and she went back when they separated. I haven't seen her since and neither has Dad.'

Jade nodded, and he thought with a stab of irony that it was a shame that the first thing they should find common ground on was painful memories.

'You don't have any other relatives in Nottingham? No other ties?'

'I was living with someone for a while,' he said, guessing this was what she wanted to know. 'But things didn't work out.'

He didn't elaborate. That was all he planned to tell her about Shona. To say anything else would have been tantamount to telling her what an idiot he was with women.

'Then I got made redundant at the end of January. I was lucky. I had a reasonable pay-off, and Dad needed someone to sort out the cottage, so I thought I'd take some time out. Plan what to do next with my life. Besides which, I've always liked it down here. I used to stay with my grandparents a lot when I was younger.'

There was a small pause and then the lounge door swung open and Mickey appeared with something white and lacy dangling from his mouth. Before either Finn or Jade could move, the dog trotted across to him and deposited what turned out to be a bra in his lap.

'Oh, I'm so sorry.' Jade was out of her chair, her face aflame with embarrassment. 'He must have been in the washing basket again. He's a terrible thief.'

Finn handed the bra to her, feeling almost as embarrassed as she was and deciding he didn't know her well enough to make some light-hearted remark about women's underwear. 'No worries. Er – I've a reference here from my previous employer. I can't give you any references on the house-sharing front, but I'm fully housetrained...'

'Thanks.' Jade stuffed the envelope and the bra into the pocket of her fleece without looking at him and he knew she was aware of what he hadn't said: *Despite what your vet may think of me.*

She got up and went across the room and proceeded to remove half a dozen items of clothing, mostly socks from what he could see, from the dog basket.

'You'll have to keep your door shut, or everything will end up in his basket – or in the garden if you're unlucky, down some hole he's dug.'

Finn smiled, relieved they were off the subject of anything too personal. He listened while she outlined the routines of the sanctuary and how she saw him fitting into things.

'Sounds fine,' he said, yawning. 'I guess I'd better turn in if I'm going to be any use to you tomorrow.'

* * *

He lay in the unfamiliar room looking at the scattering of stars beyond the skylight and thought about his grandparents' cottage. It felt odd that it now belonged to new owners. A young couple who'd modernise it and repaint, wiping away all traces of the past.

Finn had salvaged one or two things. A flat cap that had belonged to his granddad and a blue and white silk scarf that had belonged to Gran, both items that held the scents of their previous owners. Finn had held them to his face and breathed them in and then wrapped them away in a box under his bed, hoping that might preserve the scent. He'd also kept an album of old photographs, some of them black and white, stretching back to the sixties. His grandparents' wedding photo was amongst them.

It wasn't much for a lifetime of possessions. A life that had been very well lived. But being in Arleston still, even if it was temporarily, made Finn feel closer to them than if he'd said goodbye to the village for good.

12

'Auntie Jade, Diesel's got a mousey,' Ben yelled from the direction of the chicken run. 'Quick, come and see.'

With visions of Ben getting upset if Diesel did his usual decapitating trick, Jade hurried across to the child, who was standing on top of the chicken run, waving his arms about. It was fun having Ben around, but it was also exhausting. There was a part of her that would be heartily relieved when half term was over. Hopefully Sarah would be back by then, but if she wasn't, at least Ben would be at school. Trying to make sure he stayed out of trouble, was safe and kept reasonably clean was a Herculean task. She'd abandoned the reasonably clean bit after the first couple of days and just piled all his clothes into the washing machine every night.

'Look, Auntie Jade, he's very naughty.'

Ben pointed and Jade realised with a jolt of horror that Ben hadn't said mousey, he'd said Masie, which was the name of one of the ex-battery hens. Diesel was inside the chicken run, black tail swishing furiously – although when she got closer she could see that he hadn't got Masie at all. It was more the other way round. The hens had surrounded the black cat and had edged him into a corner and every so often one of them darted in for an experimental peck.

'How did he get in there?' she gasped, swinging open the latch on the front of the run and trying to avoid the big cat's flailing claws as he fled past her, pursued by several hens.

'He wanted to go in,' Ben said, widening his eyes innocently. 'He was scratching on the door.'

'So, you let him in. Oh, Ben, sweetie, I don't think that was a very good idea. He could have hurt them.'

Although, right now, she had to admit the opposite was probably more likely. Diesel gave one last affronted yowl of annoyance, hurtled away from his pursuers, and shot up the tree and on to the stable block roof, where he sat glaring at her accusingly.

Jade caught hold of Ben's hand. 'How about we go and take a dog out together.'

'I'm bored of dogs. Can we go and see the buzzard? I want to paint him for school.'

'How about painting some puppies? Bertie Buzzard's still not feeling too well – it's probably best if we leave him in peace and quiet today.'

The pups were in reception where she could keep an eye on Ben and also answer the phone. Dawn had been doing it while she tore round in circles trying to keep Ben out of trouble, and she was feeling guilty because Dawn – like everyone else who helped her out apart from Finn – was an unpaid volunteer.

* * *

'He's not doing my blood pressure any good at all,' she told Finn later that night when Ben was safely tucked up in bed, having just had a long Zoom call with his mum, which happened every night. 'I don't know how full-time mums cope.'

'Me neither.' Finn raised his eyebrows and smiled at her from the armchair by the fire where he was looking at something on his phone. 'Kids that age are hard work.'

He sounded as though he was speaking from experience and Jade glanced at him curiously, but before she could pursue this, the smoke alarm went off in the kitchen and she remembered the tripe she'd put on for the dogs.

'What the hell is that stink?' Finn said, coming in behind her. 'Ughh, I don't know how you can go near that stuff, it's disgusting.'

'I'm cooking it, not eating it,' she said crossly, rescuing the smouldering pan from the cooker and dumping it in the sink.

'Burning it, more like.' Finn shook his head in disbelief and opened several windows, fanning away the fumes from the smoke alarm. By the time peace had been resumed, Jade had forgotten his throwaway comment and she didn't remember it until the next morning when she moved a pile of paperwork off the kitchen table and knocked Finn's wallet on the floor.

He must have left it there last night, she realised as a handful of pound coins, a mixture of business cards and some credit cards slid out of various compartments. She knelt to pick them up. A couple of credit cards, a kidney donor card and a business card from a shop called Gedling Artwork. She was gathering up the pound coins when she found the photograph lying face down on the floor near the fridge.

It was a passport-sized photo of a child, a little boy with brown hair and blue eyes who didn't look much older than Ben.

Jade felt her heart thud uncomfortably. Finn hadn't mentioned any younger relatives – not that there was any reason he should, she supposed. She stared hard at the photo. The boy looked nothing like Finn, but that didn't mean they weren't related. Perhaps he was a nephew, although hadn't Finn said he didn't have any brothers or sisters? Well, whoever he was, Finn must be fond of him to carry his photo in his wallet. She slid it back, hoping she'd put it in the right place. She didn't want him to think she'd been nosing through his things. Despite Aiden's clumsy warnings, she liked Finn. She certainly wasn't going to pry into his private life, however curious she was. Jade put the photo out of her head, which actually wasn't difficult, as worrying about Ben took up most of her thoughts.

She was counting down the hours to the end of half term. It was looking likely that Sarah and Callum might stay in Dundee an extra few days. But at least Ben would be back at school. There was just today and the weekend to get through.

* * *

Jade broke the ice on the water trough the next morning and watched Ashley grazing with a sense of relief. He was much calmer now Rosanna was off his radar. Aiden had done the blood test to see if he was a rig, and they were waiting for the results. She had a few calls to make but she didn't want to get too distracted because of Ben.

'Ben can come and give me a hand if you need to make some phone calls,' Finn offered when he found out what she was worrying about. 'I'm replacing the rotten fencing in the top field – it's nice and mucky, he'll love it, and I'll make sure he doesn't come to any harm.'

'All right, thanks,' she said, after a moment's hesitation. Ben liked Finn and Finn was brilliant with him, endlessly patient with Ben's endless questions about painting. She trusted Finn instinctively – she had since the moment she'd met him, she realised, remembering when he'd stopped to help with the red kite.

The proud predator had healed beautifully and Jade had released it in a field close to where she'd found it. She still saw it occasionally, circling high above the smallholding. It warmed her heart.

Later that morning when she was about to go and check in on Ben and Finn, Aiden's jeep drew into the yard. Hoping for some news on Ashley, she went to greet him.

'Hi, Aiden.'

'Morning. I'm afraid this isn't a social call.' He inclined his head towards his vehicle. 'Sorry to spring this on you, but I thought you might be able to squeeze in a little one.'

'Always room for a little one,' Jade quipped, looking into his kind brown eyes. 'What have you got?'

'Jack Russell. Or to be more accurate, Jack Russell – ish.'

They went out into the yard and Aiden opened up the back. In the dog transporter Jade could see the outline of a little dog, mostly white.

'Hello, sweetie,' she murmured, holding out her hand.

The dog lunged at the bars, and Jade glanced at Aiden.

'Prosecution case. Sorry.'

The bitch stared at them, her lip curled in warning. Jade stared back, taking in the skeletal rib cage, the dark circular marks on the dirty coat. 'What happened to her?'

'You don't want to know. But she won't be going back. She's still young. I think she'll settle down in time. They have an enormous capacity for forgiveness, don't they?'

Jade swallowed. This was the worst part of her job and she didn't think she'd ever harden up. She didn't know how Aiden coped. If she'd met the little dog's owners, then prosecution or not, she knew she wouldn't have been responsible for her actions.

She gestured for him to bring the transporter to the kennels and they walked up the yard in silence.

Diesel was sitting on top of the chicken run.

'I thought you'd gone off chickens since your close encounter,' she said, pausing to stroke the big black cat.

He arched his back and spat at her and she withdrew her fingers just in time. 'There's gratitude for you. Tell me why I'm doing this again, Aiden.'

'Because you couldn't bear to do anything else,' he murmured, and she glanced at him in surprise.

'Is it that obvious?'

'It is to me.'

'The only reason I keep Diesel is because no one else would put up with him,' she said, which wasn't true, but was preferable to having Aiden think she was soft.

He gave her a disbelieving look and they carried on up the yard. By the kennels, a group of volunteer dog walkers were talking to some prospective owners. Some of them came from miles around to walk the dogs. Without their help, life would be much harder. And they were all here for the love of it. She gestured Aiden towards the quarantine block and went across to thank them, which she knew she didn't do nearly enough.

'No probs, love,' said one of the younger mums, who usually came in at school holiday time. 'Wears my kids out a treat, coming here. Don't hear a peep out of them when we get home. How you doing with Ben?'

'I think he's wearing me out more than I'm wearing him out,' Jade confessed, and they all laughed.

She caught up with Aiden at the quarantine block, which was empty, opened up a run at the very end because she had a feeling this little dog ought to be kept as far away as possible from the general public, and tossed a handful of doggie treats towards the inner sleeping compartment. Aiden unlatched the front of the transporter and put it inside the door.

'How's it going, Jade? New employee settled in all right?'

'I don't see that much of him.' This wasn't true either, but she didn't want to start Aiden off on another lecture about the recklessness of sharing her cottage with a stranger.

'Do the RSPCA know you brought her to me?' she asked as the Jack Russell, deciding it was worth the risk for a biscuit, crept out on her stomach.

'No.' His face shadowed and he didn't elaborate. They both knew where the dog was supposed to be. In a black bag by now, having been painlessly destroyed at Aiden's surgery – maybe the only pain-free thing that would have happened to her in her short life, Jade thought with a shiver.

Aiden edged the transporter back out again, but the dog ignored them. She was wolfing down another biscuit. They left her to it and went out into the brightness of the day.

'I'll pop in Monday lunchtime when she's had a chance to settle and see how she is,' Aiden said. 'She's not going to be easy, that one, and you've got enough on your plate.'

13

The Jack Russell not being easy was the understatement of the year, Jade thought as she filled up her water bowl from the safe side of the wire netting on Monday morning. She'd nicknamed her Fang because she tried to bite everyone who went near, which was a pain as it meant Jade had to see to the little dog herself. She couldn't risk anyone getting bitten.

At least Ben was back at school now, and there were only two more days until Sarah and Callum were back.

'How's she doing?' Aiden asked when he turned up at lunchtime as promised. 'Is she settling?'

'A little,' Jade lied, not wanting him to feel bad that he'd lumbered her with a dog that was three times as much work as the rest. 'Come and see. I was just about to check how she's doing.'

As they reached her kennel, Fang snarled and hurled herself against the wire.

'I could come in a couple of times a week, try and socialise her a bit,' Aiden said, stamping his feet and rubbing his hands together. 'Brrr, it's a cold one today.'

'Come in whenever you like. You can go in there now if you like, but put some gauntlets on if you're planning on touching her. Or you won't have any fingers left.'

'I've got a couple of calls, but I'll pop in on my way back,' Aiden said, glancing at his watch. 'I've got a few minutes now, though. Why don't I take her for a stroll? I'm sure you've got plenty of things you could be doing.'

'Thanks. I will need to go and pick up Ben shortly, as it happens.' Jade left him to it.

* * *

By the time she got back with Ben, Aiden had gone again. But at least he'd saved her a job by walking Fang.

Ben declared he wanted to paint a picture of the puppies, so Jade set him up at a table in reception, which was the warmest place, while she did some admin.

Ben was bored after ten minutes. 'Is it all right if I take a kennel dog out, Auntie Jade? I've finished my picture.'

'You can take Mickey.'

'We've been out already, but he doesn't like the frost on his paws. It makes him go all skiddy.'

'OK then, but not on your own. I'll come with you if you hold on a minute.' As she spoke, the landline rang and she picked it up, aware of Ben's disappointed gaze.

* * *

Ben went outside and cracked the ice on some puddles with the heel of his trainer while he waited, but by the look on Jade's face, it was going to be a long phone call. When he glanced back through the reception window, she shrugged her shoulders and mouthed 'sorry' and then carried on talking.

He put his hands in his pockets. He'd taken a couple of left-over sausages out of the fridge, which he was going to feed to whichever dog he took out. Jade was pretty cool most of the time, but she could be a bit of a fusser, like his mum. He didn't need her to tell him which dog to walk. It was easy enough to work out. He wandered up to the yard and found Finn up a ladder. 'Hiya, mate.' Finn always called him 'mate' and it made him feel really grown up as he echoed the words back at him.

Finn stopped what he was doing and came down a couple of steps. 'Hello there. How's it going?'

'OK. Need any help?'

'Not just at the moment,' Finn said, smiling. 'Maybe later if you've got some time spare?'

'Might have.' Ben scuffed his feet and blew on his hands, which were starting to go numb. He liked Finn. He didn't speak down to him or treat him like a kid and he'd said his painting of Diesel was really good.

'See you later, then,' he said, nodding seriously and heading up the yard. He stopped at the chicken run, tore off a chunk of sausage and stuffed it through the wire. One of the birds came across, pecked at it, then dropped it again. Ben glanced back down the yard. Jade wasn't coming and he was sure a minute had passed. Lots of minutes, probably. It wouldn't hurt to just nip up and have a quick look at the dogs. He mooched up and down outside the kennels, trying to decide which one to take first.

He was still undecided when he saw someone coming out of the quarantine block. That was where Fang, the new dog, was. Jade had told him not to go near Fang, but it couldn't hurt just to look.

He glanced back over his shoulder, but there was still no sign of Jade. Shoving his hands deeper into his pockets, he carried on through the last gate. There was a big notice on the door that said 'NO Adsomething' in spiky capital letters. Ben gave up trying to work out what it said, unbolted the door and stepped inside. There was a hot, crunchy feeling in his stomach as he headed up the walkway past the dogs' sleeping areas. Dogs smelt a lot better than chickens, he thought, peering into the first few runs, which were empty. At the end he found the run with Fang in. She was in her basket, curled up. A white roly-poly ball of a dog on a blanket, except that when she heard him, she stood up and he could see her ribs jutting through her coat. Her coat was a mess, Ben thought, crouching down for a better look. In some places the fur was missing altogether. He wondered if she was cold.

'Poor little sweetie.' He put his fingers through the wire door. She looked at him. She had a brown patch over one eye and pricky-up ears.

'Come on then, girl.' He wriggled his fingers and looked at the bolt that held the gate in place. 'You wouldn't bite me, would you?'

She gave a low growl and lifted her lip at him to show white teeth.

'Don't be scared. I'm not going to hurt you.'

He gave the bolt an experimental tug and it shifted easily. He pulled it right back and opened the gate enough to squeeze through. 'Look,' he said, putting his hand in his pocket and retrieving one of the sausages. 'Come and see what I've got here for you.'

* * *

Aiden drove to his next call, deep in thought. He wished he'd said more to Jade. Tried harder to talk her out of sharing her house with a complete stranger. Except that it had already been too late by then, he thought, switching on the demister to clear the windscreen, and wishing it was as easy to clear his mind of Jade.

It was his own fault for being such a coward. He'd told himself that he hadn't asked Jade out before because he didn't want to affect their working relationship, but deep down he knew he'd been kidding himself. There was only one reason he hadn't asked Jade out. And that was Anita.

He'd steered clear of women since his disastrous marriage, although there were plenty in the village who'd made it clear they wouldn't mind a liaison. They stood in his surgery, fluttering their eyelashes over heavily made-up faces, and 'accidentally on purpose' brushing his fingers while he examined their fat Labradors and their bad-tempered Persian cats.

He wasn't interested in any of them. Anita had put him off predatory women forever. Besides, he'd convinced himself he was happy with his life as it was. He loved his work, which he was good at, and he spent most of his spare time gardening. The house he'd shared briefly with Anita was a touch small, but it was fine for him and it had one amazing saving grace: French windows led out to a hundred-foot back garden, which stretched down to a stream, beyond which there was nothing but fields. Aiden tended the garden with the same careful precision with which he spayed cats and de-scaled canine teeth, and it was beautiful. Full of sweet-scented wild roses and climbing plants on artfully positioned trellises so that the garden was sectioned off into little private corners. This year's plan for it included the creation of a jasmine-scented bower. There would be a bench, where you could sit and sip wine on long summer evenings. Lately, he'd harboured the odd fantasy that one day he'd sit there with Jade, his arm draped casually along the back of the bench behind her.

He sighed. There was no sense in beating himself up about it. Suggesting that he call in regularly to socialise Fang had been a stroke of genius. And if Jade had suspected that his motives weren't entirely altruistic, she hadn't said anything.

At least it meant that he could keep a weather eye on that Finn chap. Jade might think he was the best thing since sliced bread, but Aiden had serious doubts. He wouldn't have been at all surprised if Finn were on the run from something or someone. Blokes like him didn't jack in well-paid jobs without good reason. The guy was definitely not all he seemed. Someone had to keep an eye out for her and Ben. They could get into all sorts of trouble.

* * *

Jade suddenly remembered she was supposed to be getting a dog out for Ben, who, to her alarm, seemed to have disappeared. Grabbing her coat, she hurried up the yard and found Finn up a ladder.

'You haven't seen Ben, have you?' she called up to him.

He climbed down, with difficulty, because his hands were full of bits of broken plastic guttering, and stood next to her. 'He was around a little while ago. Said he was going to give me a hand later.'

'Let me know if he's a pest and I'll find him something else to do.'

'He's not a pest.'

As he spoke, the phone began to ring again and Jade sighed.

'Damn, I promised I'd get a dog out for him.' She glanced up towards the kennels, her face anxious. 'I hope he hasn't gone by himself.'

'I'll go and check if you want to get the phone.'

She nodded and ran back down the yard. 'Tell Ben I'll be two ticks,' she shouted back over her shoulder. 'He's probably in the chicken run.'

* * *

Ben wasn't in the chicken run, so Finn walked on towards the kennels, setting the dogs off barking as he passed the first block. The kennels were full, Jade had told him yesterday when she'd pointed out some guttering that needed doing, except for the very end section.

'It's where we put the newcomers,' she'd said. 'We use it as a quarantine block, or, in her case' – she'd pointed out Fang – 'if they're not too good, temperament wise. We don't want to take any risks.'

As they'd passed, Fang had hurled herself at the wire door of her run and Finn had stepped back, alarmed.

'She's a cruelty case,' Jade had told him, her face darkening. She'd pointed out the circular marks on Fang's coat.

'Cigarette burns?' He'd been horrified.

Jade nodded. 'She'll settle down. But, in the meantime, I don't want any unsuspecting members of the public wandering up here. If she bites someone, I'll have to have her destroyed. And it hardly seems fair, does it? After what our kind has done to her.'

Finn went past the main block. There was no sign of Ben and he was about to turn back when he noticed, with a jolt of unease, that the door of the quarantine block was open. Surely Ben wouldn't have gone in there. Yesterday the door had been padlocked and bolted, but it wasn't now. It wasn't shut at all, Finn realised as it swung open beneath his touch.

'Ben,' he called, stepping into the run and closing the door behind him.

There was no answer. He made his way past the first few kennels, which were empty, and then he came to Fang's run. Through the wire mesh of the door, he could see Ben sitting on the floor holding something out towards the small dog.

'Come on, girl,' he was saying. 'Don't be scared now. Come and have a bit of sausage.'

Finn sucked in his breath. He knew very little about dogs, but this one didn't look happy. She'd backed away from Ben, almost into a corner. Her ears were flat against her head and her eyes were wary. As he hesitated, the door clanged at the other end of the run. In the same instant, Ben, who hadn't noticed he was no longer alone, began to edge towards the cornered dog.

14

Aware that Ben was in grave danger, Finn shoved back the door, which Ben hadn't re-bolted, and scooped the boy up in his arms. Fang snarled at him, but he swung away from her, kicking the door back in her face as she launched herself through the air. With Ben still in his arms, he slammed the bolt back into place. He wasn't sure whether it was his own frantic heartbeat he could hear or Ben's as, on the other side of the mesh, the little dog bounced up and down, barking furiously.

'Finn, what's going on?' He heard Jade's voice at the end of the run. Ben was big for his age and too heavy to hold for long. Finn put him gently on the floor, feeling the adrenaline pumping round his body, but for a few moments he was too breathless to speak.

'I said, what's going on?' Jade shouted, and Finn could hear the panic in her voice as she hurried towards them.

Ben had begun to cry. 'I wasn't doing nothing. I wasn't hurting her.'

'It's all right.' Finn knelt on the concrete floor beside him, feeling the dampness creep through the knees of his jeans. 'It's OK. You're not in trouble.'

'Oh, yes, he is,' Jade contradicted, reaching them and crouching down beside the boy. 'Ben, you're a naughty, naughty boy. What have I said about coming in here?'

'Didn't do nothing,' Ben yelled, and behind them Fang's barks grew ever more frantic.

Finn stood up, realising Jade was close to tears too. 'It's OK. He's fine. No harm done.'

She didn't look at him, just hugged the sobbing child, and he suppressed the urge to put his arms around both of them and hold them tightly. He was still a stranger, and he knew she hated appearing vulnerable in front of anyone. For reasons he hadn't yet fathomed, she'd spent a lifetime building walls. He knew because he'd done exactly the same thing himself.

He was tempted to tell her it was Aiden, not her, who'd left the kennel door unlocked, but, satisfying as it would have been, it wouldn't have helped, so he kept quiet and escaped from the all-pervading smell of dogs out into the bitter winter air.

* * *

Jade was only vaguely aware that Finn had gone. She hugged Ben to her. 'It's all right,' she soothed. 'It's all right. I'm sorry I shouted at you. I was scared, love. Scared you were going to get hurt. I'm sorry.'

She held him in her arms until gradually his crying stopped. She'd never shouted at him before and she felt terrible. Especially as she knew she'd only shouted because she felt guilty. She'd promised Sarah she'd look after him and she'd let him walk straight into danger. She should have remembered he wanted her to walk a dog. She should have made it more difficult for him to get into this block. She shouldn't have kept Fang in the first place. God knows what the little dog would have done if Finn hadn't pulled Ben out when he did.

'I only wanted to give her a sausage,' Ben mumbled, and Jade saw he was still clutching something.

'But you know what I told you about Fang, don't you, darling?' She tipped his face so that he was looking up at her with his huge, tear-washed eyes.

'You said some horrible people hurt her and now she doesn't like people any more.'

That was exactly what she'd told him, she remembered, blinking a few times.

'But I wasn't going to hurt her. I just wanted to show her that not all people are horrible.'

Jade swallowed. Telling him the truth, or at least a watered-down version of it, had seemed a good idea. But how the heck did she explain that Fang couldn't tell the difference between horrible and nice? That Fang would have bitten him anyway. She shuddered and glanced into the kennel. The dog was quiet enough now. But Ben had been in here, she'd seen Finn grab him and then kick the door back in Fang's face. What if he hadn't reacted so quickly? Things might have turned out so differently.

'Come on, sweetheart. Let's go outside now.'

'What about Fang's sausage?' Ben muttered, uncurling his fingers and showing her the squashed brown lump.

'We'll leave it here for her to have later. Come on now.' She held his hand and they went outside again into the clear, sharp air.

* * *

Finn kept out of Jade's way for the rest of the day. Or maybe she was keeping out of his, he wasn't sure. When he finally went into the cottage, there was no sign of her and he went straight to his room, exhausted. Starting work at dawn and being out in the fresh air was very different from doing nine to five in a warm building.

He flopped on to the bed and promptly fell asleep. When he woke up, the room was dark and he felt stiff and cold. For a moment, he couldn't think where he was. He rolled over, used to a double bed, and found himself on the floor. Cursing, he got up and switched on the light and reality came flooding back. He felt as though he'd been asleep for hours, but it wasn't that late. Only just gone eight-thirty. Blinking, he stood still for a couple of moments to clear his head.

'Are you all right up there, Finn?' Jade's voice came from the bottom of the staircase.

'I'm fine,' he called, going out on to the landing so he could see her. 'Is it OK if I have a bath?'

'Help yourself. Water's hot.'

As he came down from his attic room with a towel and a change of clothes, Jade said, 'Sorry, I haven't had a chance to see much of you.'

'It's all right. I know you're busy.'

When he got downstairs, feeling slightly more human after his bath, she was sitting at the table in the back room, surrounded by dozens of pieces of paper.

'Still at it?'

'Yes. Ben's only just gone to bed so I couldn't do it earlier. There's a lasagne in the oven if you want some.' She paused. 'I had no idea there'd be so much paperwork when I started this place. I'm just catching up with some invoices. Most of my suppliers are great; they know I'm running a charity. Aiden's wonderful; he lets me have all the drugs at cost and doesn't charge too much for his labour, either.'

Finn was pretty sure the vet would have liked to negotiate payment in kind if he'd thought he could get away with it, but he said nothing.

'The pet food supplier's the worst,' Jade went on. 'If I'm a day or two over, Reg Arnold sends me these reminders with "Over-due" stamped all over them in red. Bloody cheek. He's a horrible little man.'

'Can't you use someone else?'

'I could, but he's closest and he's cheap. Besides, I might find I've jumped out of the frying pan into the fire. I'm a bit of a believer in better the devil you know.'

She paused and glanced up at him, her dark eyes troubled, and he knew she was wittering on to avoid the subject that was uppermost in her mind. 'Thanks for what you did earlier, Finn. I feel terrible about that. I'd never have forgiven myself if anything had happened to Ben.'

'Nothing did,' he pointed out gently.

'Yes, that's what Sarah said when I told her.' She pressed her fingers to her forehead and he wondered if the pain was physical or emotional – probably a bit of both. 'But that's thanks to you, not me. If you hadn't been there... oh, God. I'm tempted to keep him locked in his bedroom until she comes back. At least he'd be safe.'

'When is she back?' Finn sat on the sofa opposite her.

'The end of this week. They extended it because Callum's dad took a turn for the worse. But they're definitely back Saturday.'

'I'll get a proper lock system sorted out for the quarantine kennels.' It was the only thing he could think of to say that would make her feel better without dumping on Aiden. 'I'll get on to it first thing tomorrow.'

'That would be great. Thanks.' She went back to her paperwork and he decided it would be best if he left her to it. He might not be comfortable about snitching on Aiden, but he would definitely say something to the vet next time he saw him.

15

A couple of days later, when Finn had got up before anyone else, which meant before six in this house, there was an ear-splitting scream from upstairs. Jumping and spilling hot tea over his hands in the process, he abandoned the mug and took the stairs two at a time. He found Jade dancing around on the landing, a white bath towel clutched around her and her face flushed from the shower.

Behind her, the bathroom door was open and steam was rolling out into the chilly air, but Jade seemed oblivious to this. She was jumping about on the bare floorboards as if they were scalding the soles of her feet.

'What's the matter?' he said, trying not to look too interested as she lost part of the towel completely and he was treated to a view of one breast, jiggling tantalisingly as she jumped up and down.

'Don't just bloody stand there staring! Do something. Catch it.'

'Catch what?' Finn asked, completely at a loss. He took a couple of anxious steps towards her. She'd got herself covered up again, but she was still dancing around like a cat on hot bricks. Then Ben's bedroom door opened and he came out yawning. Ben didn't seem at all disturbed by Jade's antics. He was scanning the floor, which, like the stairs, was uncarpeted. Then, to Finn's utter amazement, Ben launched himself into the air and landed with both slippered feet on the same spot of floorboard.

'Got it,' he yelled triumphantly, straightening up and inspecting the sole of his slipper. 'Yuk, that was a biggie.'

'I said catch it, not kill it.' Jade glared at him and pulled her towel tightly around herself, as if suddenly aware of her state of undress.

'She's scared of spiders,' Ben told Finn. 'Have you finished, Auntie Jade, 'cause I need a wee.'

'Nearly.' She did actually look quite embarrassed, Finn thought as with another cautious look at the squashed black object on the floorboards she fled back into the bathroom.

'Once when she was staying with me and Mum, a spider fell on her head when she was in the bath,' Ben told Finn gleefully. 'She didn't have a towel. She runned all round the house with no clothes on. It was gross.' He screwed up his face and Finn suppressed a smile.

'Women, eh?' He shook his head and Ben shook his too and they exchanged a man-to-man look. Ben scraped the rest of the spider off his slipper and poked it down a gap between the floorboards, then banged on the bathroom door. 'Hurry up. I'm wetting myself.'

Finn went downstairs. Gross was the last word he'd have used to describe Jade charging around with no clothes on. In fact, after what he'd just seen, the image was very appealing. He gave himself a mental shake. The more he got to know her, the more he liked her. He didn't want to blow it by making unwanted advances. He sensed that she would have to make the first move.

* * *

To Jade's intense relief, there were no more dramas in the next day or two, or at least none she couldn't cope with. Ben was happily back at school, secure in the knowledge that Sarah and Callum were coming home at the end of the week.

'Even if Callum's dad wasn't better, we'd have come back,' Sarah had told Jade. 'I can't believe how much I'm missing Ben.'

Jade hadn't told her that Ben was as happy as Larry, pottering around with her and Finn.

Jade re-homed four dogs and took in three more. When she phoned Maggie at Puddleduck Farm, she was told that Rosanna had settled in well and Maggie was happy to keep her as long as was needed.

Best of all, Ben didn't mention Fang again, although he took great delight in teasing Jade about what he called her spider dance.

'They can't hurt, you know,' he said at every opportunity, but particularly when Finn was around. 'They're only tinsy winsy little things.'

'Actually, they bite,' Finn said in her defence, and she'd given him a grateful look.

Ben was OK, that was the main thing, and she was pleased that Aiden needed so little prompting to agree to come in and socialise Fang as often as he could. Finn had fixed a padlock to the kennel door and given Aiden the spare key to it.

'I'll come in every night and take her out from now on,' the vet had told Jade. 'That should speed things up.'

'Well, if you're sure. Don't get yourself bitten.'

'I'll be fine. Besides, she didn't actually bite anyone, did she? Don't suppose she would have done. Finn was probably over-reacting.'

She'd glared at him and he'd changed the subject hastily.

Fortunately, Aiden's strategy seemed to be working. By the middle of the week, Fang no longer tried to attack anyone who walked past her kennel, although Jade still didn't let anyone else in with her. It would be a long time before she'd risk that.

Finn seemed to have settled in. She'd started off by telling him what needed doing, but soon realised this wasn't necessary, so she left him to get on with it. She tended to lock the main gates to the public at about six, but she often had paperwork to do at the end of the day, which she only took into the house if it got too cold in reception. Finn's days were governed by the light, or the lack of it. He spent the occasional evening at the Red Lion, which was within walking distance of Duck Pond Cottage, but he never came back roaring drunk. As Sarah had predicted, Ben and Finn were getting on well, their mutual interest in art drawing them together.

Jade was still curious about the photo that Finn carried around with him, but she put it to the back of her mind. She didn't want to pry into his personal life, although from the way he was with Ben, she guessed he'd been close to a child once.

'Perhaps he's got one hidden away somewhere?' Sarah suggested during one of her nightly calls.

'Maybe,' Jade said, hoping he hadn't. She knew he must have some baggage – you couldn't get past thirty without it – but she hoped it wasn't a child. She didn't like the idea of him having a child he no longer saw. It didn't fit with her impression of him, which was what, exactly, she mused as she was pinning one of Ben's paintings up on the wall of reception one morning after dropping him off at school.

A cough behind her made her turn and Finn came into the room with what looked like another of Ben's paintings in his hands.

'Have you seen this, Jade?' His face was serious as he laid the painting on the reception table and she looked at it, realising she hadn't, and feeling a twinge of jealousy that Ben had shown Finn before he'd shown her.

The picture was of a small white dog with a patch over one eye, crudely done, but unmistakably Fang. The dog was in a kennel. Above it, Ben had painted blue sky and a big yellow sun, but the kennel itself was dark. The dog was crying giant tears that had made a large blue puddle at her feet.

'Ben said she's sad because everyone hates her,' Finn said quietly.

'I didn't realise he was still thinking about her.' Jade could feel coldness spreading through her. 'When did he do this?'

'Last night, I think. Jade, to be honest, it's probably a good thing. It could be his way of dealing with it. Getting it out of his system. Painting can be very cathartic.'

She frowned. 'Do you think so?'

'Yes, and I should know. I've been doing it for long enough.'

Jade wondered if he meant painting as a catharsis or just painting. She couldn't imagine Finn needing to paint to get something out of his system. He always seemed so comfortable with himself. He was one of the few men she'd met who exuded calm. She glanced at him, dying to ask what he meant, but not sure if this would be misconstrued as prying.

He smiled as if he knew what she was thinking and went on in a voice that was lighter. 'Ben's going to be really good one day. Look how he's used different blues for the tears in the dog's eyes, and the tears on the ground, and another shade for the sky. Most kids would use the same colour. Blue's blue, but he hasn't done that.' As he spoke, he pointed to the various bits of the picture, his grey eyes lit with enthusiasm.

Jade stared at him, realising that in the last few careless

sentences he'd told her more about himself than he had since he'd been here. She'd never seen him look so animated.

They were standing so close their arms were touching and suddenly she was very aware of him. The fresh outdoor scent of him, his hands smoothing out the painting on the desk. She hadn't noticed his hands before. Strong hands, with long fingers, which were grubby at the moment from whatever he'd been doing outside. She felt breathless. Involuntarily, she stepped away from him. She couldn't remember the last time she'd felt like this. What was she feeling, anyway? Attraction? Lust? Yes, definitely both of those. She felt as though she could rip all her clothes off, and his, and make love to him, right here on the wooden floor.

Shocked at herself, she tried to concentrate on what Finn was saying.

'He should be taught. Properly, I mean. He has a natural talent that should be developed.' He glanced at her and she felt heat in her face, but Finn didn't seem to notice. He was too caught up in enthusiasm for Ben's painting. 'Do you think his mum would mind if I taught him properly? In my spare time, I mean. I don't want to affect his schoolwork or anything.'

'I don't suppose she'd mind at all. I'll ask her when I speak to her later.' To Jade's surprise, her voice came out quite normally. 'Thanks – I – er – just need to get something from the house.'

Outside, she took deep gulps of fresh air and wished her heart would slow down a bit. Fancying Finn McTaggart was a bad idea. A very bad idea. He'd not said anything about getting himself another job, but they'd agreed this was a temporary arrangement for both of them. It was only a matter of time.

Besides, he was too much of a free spirit to stay in one place for long. When she'd first met him, she'd thought him self-contained to the point of coolness. But every now and then it was as though he allowed his guard to drop and she saw great chinks of warmth in him. When he'd been talking about Ben's painting, there had been real passion in those grey eyes of his.

'Hi, Jade.' Dawn was just getting out of her car in the yard. 'What's the matter? You look all hot and bothered.'

'I've just been talking to Finn about Ben's painting. He's got hidden talents.' She hadn't meant to say that at all. She'd meant to say, 'Finn's said Ben's got hidden talents,' but somehow it had come out wrong.

'I wouldn't say they're that hidden,' Dawn said, grinning. 'If I were twenty years younger, I'd be making a play for him myself.' She arched her eyebrows, gave her blonde perm a little pat and glanced through the reception windows to where Finn was still standing by the desk. 'What's he been doing to you in there?'

'Nothing,' Jade said, escaping to the cottage before she could dig herself in any deeper.

16

Several miles away, Aiden was sitting in his car eating a ham and pickle roll and thinking about Jade. He couldn't believe he still hadn't plucked up the courage to ask her out. He was there most evenings. He'd felt certain that if he saw Jade so often, it'd be easy. He could just slip it into conversation.

'Jade, do you fancy dinner some time? Only there's this new Italian I've had recommended. I thought we could give it a try.' Or, 'Jade, how about we go into Salisbury and catch a film one night?'

He didn't even know what type of films she liked, he thought gloomily, tearing the cellophane off another roll and frowning as a lump of pickle fell onto his lap. Somehow, every time he got Jade alone, all his carefully rehearsed lines seemed to freeze in his throat. Finn being around didn't help. If Jade did turn him down, the last thing Aiden wanted was an audience.

Aiden was still smarting over the bloke's accusation that he'd left Fang's door open. Finn had cornered him about it a couple of days ago.

'All locked up in there, mate?' he'd murmured as Aiden came

out of the quarantine block, having just settled Fang for the night. 'We don't want any more nasty incidents, do we?'

'Are you trying to say something?' Aiden snapped, the tone of Finn's voice putting him instantly on the defensive.

'Jade's worried about that dog biting someone, which isn't surprising after the fiasco with Ben. I was just checking you'd locked the door.' The words 'this time' were never actually said, but they hung in the air between them.

'I'm very well aware of Jade's security arrangements, thank you.' Aiden had known he sounded pompous and defensive, but was too cross to care. How dare Finn accuse him of not being careful? He'd only been here five minutes and already he was throwing his weight around.

'I'm sure you are, but someone left that door unlocked.'

'Well, it wasn't me,' Aiden had said, bristling with anger. He was sure – well, almost sure – that he hadn't left the quarantine door unlocked, ever.

No doubt Finn had told Jade he was to blame too, although she'd been nice enough not to say anything about it.

Aiden tore his thoughts away from Finn before he got wound up all over again, ate the rest of the roll, and glanced at his watch. Ten past two. He'd best get on to his next call, which he wasn't looking forward to. He was doing a home visit to euthanise an elderly cat, which had kidney failure and no quality of life left.

Aiden hated this part of his job. Mrs Heath was sensible and kind and would offer him cups of tea and home-made cherry cake, even while she was blinking back tears. And he'd have to stand and make polite conversation in her front room, made empty without the presence of Tiger, who'd been her only companion since her husband had passed away.

Maybe after this call he'd do something positive and phone and book a table at the new Italian place. It would also take his mind off Mrs Heath and her loneliness and, if he booked the table for tonight, he'd have to ask Jade to go with him. They'd need to take Ben, of course, but that was OK. Ben liked pizza. It crossed his mind that it might be too late for Ben on a school night, although Jade didn't seem to mind taking Ben to the Red Lion. Maybe Finn would babysit. Aiden dismissed this possible setback for now.

He loved Italian food. He could almost smell the garlic. He imagined himself pouring Jade a glass of red wine. She'd catch his eyes across the candlelight and say, 'This is nice. We ought to do it more often, Aiden.'

'Yes, we should,' he'd reply, and he'd touch her hand ever so casually. It was a pleasing picture and one that warmed him all the way to Mrs Heath's pretty house.

* * *

At Duck Pond Rescue, Jade, Ben and Finn were in the caravan looking at some of Ben's paintings. Ben was standing by the window. When they'd first come in, Finn had turfed Diesel off the seat, so they could sit down. Diesel had stalked outside in disgust. Ben wished he could go outside too. The caravan was musty and too small for the three of them, but Jade said she could keep an eye on things from here without too many distractions.

Ben watched Diesel cross the yard, carefully avoiding the puddles, and jump up onto the roof of the chicken run. The black cat didn't seem very interested in the chickens. He was watching a couple of magpies in the field next door. As if suddenly aware of the danger, one of the magpies rose up in the air, its wings flapping against the white sky.

Ben wished he could be a bird, flapping his wings in the sky. Since the trouble with Fang, he hadn't been allowed to wander around on his own as he usually did. Jade kept turning up to check what he was doing. He glanced back at the table where she was chatting to Finn. He didn't know whether to feel pleased or embarrassed at all the fuss they were making over his pictures. He knew his paintings were good. Or at least some of them were. He could tell which ones were the best because of the little shivery feeling he got in his stomach when he finished them. If you didn't get the feeling, then the painting was rubbish. Simple. He'd tried to explain it once to Miss Benson, his art teacher, but she'd just looked stern and told him he must never tell people something he'd done was good, but must wait for them to tell him.

He'd tried to explain it to his mum once, too. 'All your paintings are wonderful, Ben,' she'd said.

'No, they're not.' He'd pressed his mouth into a straight line. 'Some of them are rubbish.'

'Don't be silly. They're all lovely.' He'd given up then. He didn't have the words to tell her properly about the shivery feeling. But he knew, as he watched Finn smoothing out the pieces of paper, that he would understand. Definitely.

'Which are your favourites, then?' Finn asked him now.

Ben pointed to a picture in the top right-hand corner of the table. It showed a tree bent over in the wind, with a lightning bolt in the dark sky behind it. Then he pointed to a small one of the chickens in their run. He'd spent ages getting the colours right for their feathers. 'Those two are best, I think.'

Finn grinned in delight. 'He's right, you know. Those two are the best. Are either of his parents creative? It quite often runs in families.'

Jade frowned. 'I don't think Sarah's ever tried to paint. I'm not sure about his dad.'

Ben wondered if he should mention his real dad had gone

away before he was born, but something stopped him. They never talked about his dad. There weren't even any photos of him in their house. And Mum didn't like talking about him either; she always changed the subject when he asked.

He stared out of the window. 'Can I go and see Candy's puppies?' he asked, without much hope, because Jade had been funny about him going near any dogs except Mickey lately.

'We'll go in a minute,' she said. 'Finn's got some paintings in the Red Lion, Ben.'

'Mike reckons he can sell them,' Finn said, and he had a funny, jokey sound to his voice and Ben knew suddenly that Finn wasn't sure if his own paintings were any good.

'I'd love to see them,' Jade added. 'Perhaps we could all go up tonight. It'll save me cooking. Do you fancy that, Ben?'

Ben sighed. Grown-ups spent far too much time talking, and for some reason they seemed to be even worse when they were in pubs. Although sometimes talking could be good, because it meant he could slip off. He looked at Finn. He was pretty sure Finn would let him try his beer when Jade wasn't looking. And he'd be able to stay up later if they went to the pub.

'OK,' he said, shoving his hands in his pockets.

Jade turned back to Finn. 'Shall I ask Aiden if he wants to come as well? He's bound to be in soon.'

'If you like.' Finn didn't sound bothered one way or the other. Ben didn't blame him. He wasn't over fussed on Aiden either – he was always in a rush.

'So, can we go and see Candy's puppies now?' he begged.

* * *

Aiden was whistling as he pulled into the entrance of Duck Pond Rescue, just after five. It was all arranged. He'd booked a table at

Da Vinci's for seven. That should give Jade enough time to finish up here and get changed.

He could see her through the reception window as he locked the jeep door. She was talking to a young couple, but she still glanced out and waved. Aiden waved back. He'd pop up and see Fang while she was busy. Then he'd come back and casually mention the Italian. His heart pounded as he walked up the yard. It had been a good idea booking a table. He couldn't chicken out now and change his mind.

On the way, he bumped into Dawn and Ben. They had Candy on a lead and were heading for the dog-walk field. That was good. Since the incident with Fang, Jade had been over cautious about Ben and dogs. Not that he blamed her. It could so easily have been a disaster. Aiden had discovered yesterday that he hadn't been to blame for leaving the door unlocked. Dawn had confided it had been one of the young volunteers, but Aiden had kept this information to himself. Apparently the youngster felt bad enough already. It was better if everyone thought it was him. He had broad shoulders.

'She's looking well,' he said, bending to stroke the lurcher's pretty golden head. 'How are the pups?'

'They're really cute,' Ben told him. 'They're all playing now and Tiny's put on loads of weight.'

Aiden already knew this, but he nodded seriously. 'Has he now?'

'We're going to the Red Lion later to see Finn's paintings,' Ben added. 'Auntie Jade's going to ask you to come too.'

Aiden felt his heart sinking. It had to be Finn, didn't it? Throwing a spanner in the works. 'What paintings would these be?'

'Pictures of fields,' Ben said. 'And he's done some of people. He showed me one of Big Lil from the pub.'

'Jade's looking forward to it,' Dawn added. 'She said there's no end to Finn's talents.'

'Did she?' Aiden stopped stroking Candy's head and straightened up. It didn't matter, he could still ask her. Surely she'd rather go for a meal with him than to the pub? But what if she said no? He knew he wouldn't ask her and as he walked up towards Fang's kennel, he felt as though all the sun had gone out of the afternoon.

On the way, he passed Finn carrying some tools. 'All right, mate?' Finn said pleasantly.

Aiden couldn't bring himself to even speak.

17

Jade was beginning to wish she hadn't suggested coming to the Red Lion. She was tired and tense, and the couple of glasses of wine she'd drunk too quickly, in an effort to relax her, were making her light-headed. Finn and Ben were talking about painting, their heads close together.

Aiden was sitting beside her. He'd hardly said a word since they'd arrived. Deciding she'd better make an effort to be sociable, she glanced at him. 'Are you OK? You seem a bit quiet.'

'I'm fine,' he said, not sounding it.

'So, what have you been up to today? Anything exciting?'

'I had to euthanise a cat. Belonged to an old lady who only lost her husband three months ago.'

'Oh, Aiden, that's awful. No wonder you look so fed up.' Instinctively she reached for his hand. 'Was she all right, poor soul?'

'Yes, she was gracious and dignified and a great deal braver than I'd have been.'

'Euthanasia's one of the worst parts of the job – even when you know it's for the best.' She squeezed his fingers.

She'd witnessed it enough times at the vets in Bristol where she'd done a placement, and it had never got any easier. Trying to console someone who'd just lost a much-loved pet was heart-breaking.

'Thanks, Jade.' His eyes lightened a fraction and she was glad she'd said something.

'Anyone fancy another drink?' Finn asked.

Jade withdrew her hand from Aiden's, aware that Finn had registered the movement. 'I'm all right, thanks.'

'Oh, go on, have another one,' Aiden pressed, shifting his chair a little closer so that his knee brushed hers. 'You hardly ever get the chance to let your hair down and you're not driving.'

Suddenly Jade felt reckless. 'Yes, why not.'

Another glass of wine wasn't going to make much difference. It was still early and poor Aiden wouldn't want to go back to his empty house just yet. Not after the day he'd had.

She watched Finn go up to the bar, feeling a pang of emotion she couldn't identify.

'You don't find the cottage too cramped with him there?' Aiden asked, and she saw he'd followed her gaze and there were frown lines crinkling his forehead.

'No, I don't.' She was relieved to see Finn on his way back with the drinks because Aiden wouldn't be able to pursue this conversation in front of him.

'One for the boss.' Finn leaned across to put the glass in front of her.

'Thanks.' She looked up at him and felt a little jolt. Then, aware of Aiden's scrutiny, she hastily looked away.

Finn sat beside Ben again, and Aiden said in a voice only loud enough for Jade to hear, 'They get on well, don't they? Got kids of his own, has he?'

'No, I don't think he has.'

'Bit of a dark horse, really.'

'It's his business,' Jade said, and then, anxious to change the subject, she said the first thing that came into her mind.

'Did we ever get the blood test results for Ashley? To check whether he's got an undescended testicle or not – I'd be interested to know.'

She wasn't aware her voice had been rising, but both Finn and Ben glanced across with identical expressions of surprise and she found herself thinking they were very alike. They could be mistaken for father and son. They had the same colouring, the same grey eyes too.

'I think the blood test came back negative, Jade. Sorry, I should have updated you. My Uncle Seth said that's a good result, although it doesn't help your problem. He seemed to think it could be more of a behavioural issue, possibly due to a late castration.'

'Thanks.' Jade took another sip of wine, wishing she hadn't started this.

'Can we go in a minute?' Ben asked when she was halfway through it.

'Of course we can, darling.' Jade's head ached from trying to work out if the atmosphere around the table was real or imagined. Going home suddenly seemed like a very good idea. She gulped back the rest of her wine.

'I'll give you a lift, Jade,' Aiden offered.

'What?' She stared at him.

'A lift... home...' He left spaces between the words as if they were speaking a different language.

'It would make more sense if I took them,' Finn interrupted. 'It'd save you going out of your way, Aiden.'

He stretched, seemingly oblivious to the annoyance in Aiden's eyes.

For a moment, there was a tight, awkward silence between them and then Jade rushed on. 'It's nice of you, Aiden, but Finn's right, it would make more sense...' She let her words hang in the air like a question.

'Right,' Aiden said.

He really didn't have any choice, Jade thought as he turned back to her, blocking the others out with his body.

'I'll see you tomorrow.' Then, with a nod at Finn, he called good night to Mike, who was serving, and left. He looked defeated and Jade felt guilty. Aiden was a nice guy. So was Finn, and yet when the two of them were together, the tension was palpable.

'Ready then?' Finn said, and Jade nodded. His face was blank, but she had no doubt he was aware of what had just gone on.

As they got into his car, Ben said, 'Aiden wasn't in a very good mood, was he? What was the matter with him, Auntie Jade?'

'He'd had a bad day, love, I think.' She avoided Finn's eyes and climbed into the front seat of the car. They drove back in silence. Jade rested her head against the coolness of the glass window and wished she didn't feel so dizzy.

Finn pulled up outside the cottage and Jade got out of the car, swaying a little as the chill evening air hit her, amplifying the effects of the wine. He stood next to her as she fumbled with her key in the front door, his proximity making her even more nervous.

'Shall I do that?' he said at last, not waiting for a reply, but taking the key from her. The brush of his fingers sent electricity sweeping through her and she snatched away her hand. He opened the door and she stumbled through it.

'Are you OK, Jade?'

'I'm fine,' she said, realising with sudden, intense embarrassment, that she wasn't fine at all. She was drunk and she was going to be sick. She made a dash for the bathroom and got there just in time. Afterwards, she sat on the edge of the bath, mortified.

About ten minutes later, there was a knock on the door. 'Er, Jade, are you going to be much longer? Only I'm crossing my legs out here and Ben wants to clean his teeth.'

When she went out, feeling deeply ashamed of herself, Finn was standing with one hand on the banisters.

Beside him, Ben looked interested. 'You're a bit white, Auntie Jade. Have you been sick?'

'No, of course not.' She lurched past them, feeling weak and dizzy. 'I'm just going to get a glass of water.'

'Make it a pint. And have a painkiller with it,' Finn called after her. 'That always does the trick for me.'

'I'm fine now,' she called back, ignoring the amusement in his voice. 'I'm just not used to drinking.'

All the same, once she'd tucked Ben up in bed, she did go back downstairs to get a pint of water. At least she didn't feel sick any more.

She switched off the light and lay in the darkness and a few minutes later she heard Finn's footsteps go past her door and up the top stairs to his room.

She lay thinking about him in the tiny bed upstairs, until eventually she fell into a restless sleep filled with dreams of Finn McTaggart leaning over her and saying, 'The best thing for hang-overs is to take off all your clothes. Trust me, I used to be a vet, you know.' Then his grey eyes slowly changed into Antonio's mocking dark ones and Jade woke up, bathed from head to foot in sweat.

* * *

Rather to her surprise, she didn't have a hangover the next day, although whether this was due to Finn's hangover cure or the fact she'd thrown up last night, Jade wasn't sure.

It was a surprise, however, to find out about Aiden's thwarted plans to take her to the Italian, which Mike took great delight in telling her about when she dropped off his order of free-range eggs.

'Poor chap was quite put out,' Mike said, leaning on the bar and grinning. 'He doesn't like Finn much, does he?'

'What's it got to do with Finn? He didn't know Aiden was planning to take me out. Neither did I, come to that. Why on earth didn't he say?'

'Oh, you know what Aiden's like. He might be a good vet, but he's a dead loss where women are concerned.' Mike frowned. 'Now let me see, I think Aiden's exact words were, "If it wasn't for that bloody bloke, Jade and I could have been having a nice meal."' He straightened the beer towel on the bar and looked pleased with himself. 'Da Vinci's, apparently. That trendy new place in Salisbury. He'd got it all set up. Taxis there and back, so you wouldn't have to drive.'

Jade stared at him in shock. 'But he knows I'm looking after Ben. What did he think I was going to do with him?'

'Ask Finn to babysit, I expect,' Mike went on slyly. 'Would you have gone then? If you'd known.'

'I don't know,' Jade said, aware that whatever she told him would be swiftly relayed to the entire village, with one or two embellishments of his own.

'He's quite a catch,' Mike said. 'Good looking. Bit of money. Be handy too, wouldn't it? Having a vet about the place. That's one of your biggest bills.'

'Oh, stop it, Mike. That's no reason to go out with someone.'

'The answer would have been no, then, would it? Poor Aiden.'

'The answer is none of your business,' Jade said, softening her words with a smile. 'And don't you dare tell him you've told me. He'd be mortified.'

'Mum's the word.' Mike tapped his nose. Then he leaned forward and picked a bit of straw off her coat. 'What about your new employee, then, Jade? What would you say if Finn asked you out to a posh Italian?'

Completely unprepared for the question, Jade could feel heat rising in her face.

'Thought so,' Mike said, banging his hand on the bar in triumph so that several beer mats jumped an inch into the air. 'Strikes me that Aiden wasn't so wrong about Finn mucking up his plans, after all.'

18

On Friday, the day before Sarah and Callum were due back, Ben went to his friend, Darren's, straight from school for tea and a stopover.

Jade had called Sarah earlier to check this was OK.

'Yes, it's fine, he's done it before, although sometimes he gets homesick around bedtime and wants to come back. Are you OK with that?'

'Of course. I'll go and pick him up if that happens.'

'Thanks.' Sarah's sigh came down the phone. 'Ben might not be homesick, but I definitely am. I can't wait to see him. We're setting off about 4 p.m. so we can break up the drive – we'll stop over in a layby Callum knows just before Liverpool – so we shouldn't be too late back tomorrow. What time did you say you'd get him from Darren's in the morning?'

'Elevenish.'

'Perfect. We can collect him. We'll stop off at yours to get his stuff. It's on the way to Darren's.'

* * *

That evening, Jade, feeling at a loose end, strolled up towards the quarantine kennels. It was gone six and Aiden hadn't turned up to take out Fang. She decided to put the little Jack Russell in the dog-walk field for a run about. Then, restless to do something, she started to hose down the block.

A few minutes after she'd started, she heard the door clang at the other end. 'Watch the floor,' she called, glancing up, expecting to see Aiden, but it was Finn. 'It's slippery,' she mouthed over the noise of the water as he came along the run.

'What?'

'The floor.' She gestured impatiently, and at the same moment felt her trainer skid beneath her. There was a second when she thought she would save herself, then a horrible stomach-wrenching instant when she knew she wouldn't. Her feet were sliding from beneath her and she was falling backwards. Her head hit the concrete and she was aware of flashing lights, then of not being able to breathe, then more slowly of pain and of wetness seeping through her sweatshirt.

'Jade, are you OK? No – stupid question. You went down with a hell of a bang.' Slowly, she became aware that Finn was crouching beside her in the run.

She struggled to sit up and he put his hand on her arm. 'Give it a minute.' There was concern in his eyes. 'You hit your head, didn't you? What else hurts?'

'My back. I've grazed it.' She glanced at the sharp edge of the drain that ran down the edge of the block. 'And I'm getting soaking wet.' She attempted to smile, but judging by the expression on his face, she wasn't making a very good job of it.

'Take it slowly,' he said. 'Lean on me.' He put his arm around her, supporting her.

She stood up, wincing. 'Thanks. I'm all right. Can you turn off the hose? I feel such a fool.'

'It's like a skating rink in here.'

'That's what I was trying to tell you.' Sickness was rising in her throat and she hesitated, then leaned forward, gripping hold of the wire netting, until the waves of dizziness passed.

'Just hold on a minute, Jade.' She was aware of him close behind her. 'How are you feeling?'

'Dizzy, but that's probably just shock. And I feel like I've scraped several layers of skin off my back.' She screwed up her face. She couldn't allow herself to be sick so soon after last night's performance.

'Take deep breaths.'

She did as he said, but only because she didn't have much choice. Tears weren't far away. If she'd been alone she'd have let them out, or at least done a great deal of swearing, but she didn't dare open her mouth in case she humiliated herself further.

'Now, slowly. Lean on me.'

'I've got – to get Fang – lock up.' The words were coming out in gasps.

'I can do that.' He looked at her. 'Hold my arm.'

She did as he said. Why did he have to be so damn calm and rational? Too bloody rational. He never seemed to get ruffled about anything. It was unnerving. And she knew it wasn't just his calmness that was unnerving. It was his proximity. But she felt too shaken up to do anything but lean on his arm as he led her along the ice rink floor, because if she didn't, she knew she would fall over and she was so, so scared of falling again.

Finn opened the door at the end of the run and they went out into the evening sunlight.

'You're as white as a ghost, Jade.'

'I'm fine.'

'Go and get showered off. I'll get Fang in and lock up.'

'Careful she doesn't go for you.'

'Relax, Jade. I can handle a stroppy little dog.'

In the end, she had to let him go because he was right. She felt awful and sick and all she wanted to do was sit down. She limped down the yard, aware of him watching her. Hating her vulnerability. But it was all right when she got into the cottage. All right to breathe again in the cool, welcoming dimness. She went upstairs to the bathroom, where she stripped off and inspected the damage.

A jagged graze ran from her shoulder blades down her back to her hip and a purplish bruise was already forming at the base of her spine. Her shoulders ached where she'd wrenched them trying to stop herself falling. Tomorrow, the whole lot would stiffen up and she would hurt like hell. She stepped into the shower, wincing as the water hit her skin. She forced herself to stay under the spray as long as possible. It wasn't enough. She could see in the mirror that the edges of the graze were still bleeding, but it would have to do for now. She patted herself dry as gently as she could. Putting on a bra was out of the question. She pulled on an old white tee-shirt, which was the softest thing she could find, and some leggings, and went downstairs.

Finn was in the lounge and he glanced up as she came in. 'Are you all right? Did you cut yourself?'

She shook her head. 'Just a bit of a graze on my back. I'll survive. Did you get Fang?'

'Yes, she's fine. She's improved a lot.'

'Thanks to Aiden,' she murmured.

He acknowledged this with a nod. 'And you feel all right in yourself? You hit your head pretty hard.'

'I'm fine, Finn, stop fussing.'

'Sorry. I was a first-aider at my last job. Old habits die hard. You could probably do with a stiff drink. Good for shock, but I couldn't find any. Second thoughts, you shouldn't have alcohol if you've hit your head.'

'I think I've had enough alcohol lately,' she said, bending to pick up one of her boots that Mickey must have stolen from their place by the back door.

Finn rested his chin in his hands and looked at her. 'There's blood coming through your tee-shirt, Jade. You ought to let someone have a look at it. I'll do it if you like. Or would you rather I ran you down to A&E?'

His grey eyes held hers and she sighed. 'Yes, I suppose you're right. I don't want it getting infected.'

'So do you trust me to do it? Or do you want to sit in A&E for a few hours?'

Her hesitation stretched out between them. 'I need to be here in case Ben decides he doesn't want to stay at Darren's. There's a first-aid kit in the kitchen cupboard. I'll get it in a minute.'

'I'll get it.'

The thought of him touching her made her come out in goose bumps. Not because she was attracted to him, she told herself, but because he was a stranger. But the thought of going to A&E was infinitely worse. She'd had enough of hospitals to last her a lifetime. She hadn't been in one since she'd lost her mother and she still had nightmares about that last, awful day.

When Finn came back, he was carrying the first-aid kit, a packet of cotton wool swabs and some antiseptic.

'I don't think you're supposed to put this on neat. Have you got a little bowl I can dilute some in?'

'There's one under the kitchen sink.'

A few moments later, he was back again.

'Actually, I think I'm fine,' she said again, her mouth dry. 'I'm as tough as old boots. I'm sure it's clean enough.'

'It won't take me a minute to check.' His voice was quietly

reasonable. 'And it's better to be safe than sorry.' He started to dilute the antiseptic and lined up a row of cotton wool swabs on the coffee table. Then he came across and knelt by the sofa where she sat. 'Don't look so worried. I was doing this sort of thing at work for ten years.'

'Dangerous place to work, was it?'

'You'd be amazed at the situations people got themselves into. Where did you hit your head? Can I see?'

She indicated the spot and he parted her hair with gentle fingers. 'You seem to have got away with that. Let's have a look at your back. It would be easiest if you lay on your front. You'll need to roll your top up.'

She did as he said, conscious she wasn't wearing a bra, tucking her elbows in tight to her breasts.

'It's a nasty graze, that. Can I roll this up a bit higher? Unless you want to take it right off.'

She glanced sideways at him, echoes of her dream merging with reality. He grinned. 'I'm joking about taking it off, but I will need to push it up a bit higher to get to the top of the graze. And I'm afraid you'll have to slip these down a bit, too. Don't worry, I can't see a thing.'

The humour in his voice relaxed her and she let him roll the tee-shirt up past her shoulder blades and slip the waistband of her leggings down a couple of inches.

'I'll just clean it up and then you can see how it is tomorrow. This might sting a bit.'

He was right. It did sting. She clamped her teeth together as he dabbed at the graze, but his fingers were gentle. As he worked, he asked her about the phone calls she'd taken that day and how the fund-raising was going, and she answered his questions, surprised. He wasn't much of a one for small talk. After a while, she realised he was trying to take her mind off what he was doing, and she was grateful.

'That's better,' he said at last. 'At least it's stopped bleeding and it's clean now. Dog kennels aren't the most hygienic of places to lie down in.'

'Thank you, Dr McTaggart.' She pulled her top down and sat up. 'From drain unblocker to first-aider, is there no end to your talents?'

'No need to take the mickey.'

'I'm not.' She touched his hand. 'Thanks.'

For a moment there was a softness in his eyes and she thought he was going to say something else. Then he blinked a couple of times and it passed and she wondered if it had ever been there at all.

'I've got some calls to make,' he said, and got up and went out into the hall.

Jade stayed where she was on the sofa, feeling more stirred up than she had in years. She didn't just want to go to bed with him, she realised, she wanted to get to know him. To discover everything about him: where he'd gone to school, who his friends were, what his deepest fears were, what he loved, what made him angry and what made him sad.

Startled by the force of her feelings, she giggled into the empty room and suddenly she felt afraid. It was the knock on the head, she told herself. Delayed shock. Sarah would laugh. Or maybe Sarah would understand. Maybe this was how she felt about Callum. She would ask her tomorrow.

19

'Hi, Jade, just to let you know our ETA's ten thirty at yours.'

Sarah sounded relaxed and happy and Jade breathed a sigh of relief as she pressed her mobile to her ear and glanced out of the reception window at the icy blue sky. March was as cold as February had been. Although there were definite signs of spring in the air.

The sun was out today, she could feel its warmth through the glass. Daffodils had sprung up around the duck pond and there were primroses and musky wood anemones everywhere.

'Is Ben still at Darren's?' Sarah asked, bringing her back to the present.

'Yes. I spoke to Darren's dad last night and apparently they were watching *Wonka*.'

Sarah laughed. 'Bless them. Ben's seen that film at least four times already.'

'So was Callum OK with leaving his parents to fend for themselves?'

'Yes. Although it's been manic. His parents are lovely, by the way. His dad looks just like him – but with more grey. I told them all about Ben and they can't wait to meet him.'

'Brilliant. Are you sure you don't want me to get him from Darren's in case you get held up?'

'No, it's fine. We'll nip in and get his stuff en route and then go and get him. I can't wait to see him. I know we've chatted on Zoom every night, but it's not the same. How's your handyman getting on?'

'He's great. I don't know how I ever managed without him.' She gave Sarah a list of what Finn had done so far, which included renewing all the guttering on the outbuildings, repairing a section of rotten fence, although there was a lot more to be done, and sorting out a downpipe on the quarantine kennels. She paused for breath when she heard Sarah sigh.

'What? What have I said?'

'I've never heard you so excited about a bloke.'

'He's not a bloke, he's an employee.'

'He's a bloke as well, though, isn't he? Even you must have noticed that. So, what's he like to live with? Does he bring you tea in bed?'

'No, he does not, he's never set foot in my bedroom.' Not that the thought was unappealing, she realised, feeling her face colour. Good job they were on the phone.

'I bet you that's only because Ben's been around,' Sarah said archly. 'It's like having a chaperone, isn't it?'

'Actually Ben gets on very well with him. They've been talking about painting – he's offered to give Ben lessons if you agree. I think he's going to ask you.'

'Loves kiddies too. Well, well. I shall look forward to meeting this paragon. Is he there now?'

'Yes, somewhere about.'

'Well, make sure he doesn't disappear before we get there.'

The phone rang as soon as Jade disconnected, and she'd only just finished a lengthy conversation with a woman who wanted a kitten for her daughter and sorted out a petfood delivery when the campervan drew into the yard and parked outside reception.

Callum and Sarah came in together and Jade looked at Callum's animated face and thought she'd never seen such a well-matched couple. She was surprised they hadn't decided to make their relationship more permanent. Maybe they had. Maybe they'd stopped by at Gretna Green on the way. No, she thought, stepping over sacks of dog biscuits that had just been delivered, and kissing them both on the cheek. Sarah would never have kept something like that to herself.

'The kettle's just boiled,' she told them. 'You can make a brew while I go and find Finn. He takes his white with two sugars.'

'Callum can make the tea, I'm coming with you. I want to see all these miraculous transformations you told me about.'

Jade laughed, knowing Sarah was far more interested in inter-rogating her than in Finn's handiwork, a fact that was confirmed as soon as they stepped outside.

'Now tell me the truth.' Sarah linked her arm through Jade's. 'You do like him, don't you? You can't keep something like this from me. I'm your best friend.'

'All right.' Jade knew she wouldn't get a minute's peace until she confessed. And she did want to talk about Finn. She'd spent an uncomfortable night torn between thinking she might be falling for him and wondering whether it was just because he'd been so kind when she was vulnerable.

'Yes, I do like him. And there is chemistry. I'm pretty sure he feels it too. But he is working for me. It's really early days, and I don't want to...'

'Rush into anything,' Sarah finished. 'Yes, I can see that. And I guess you don't need to, do you, seeing as you've got him exactly where you want him. I bet Aiden hates his guts, doesn't he?'

'He's not over fussed – how did you know that?'

'For someone who's so bright, you're amazingly dense where men are concerned,' Sarah said glibly. 'Aiden's had the hots for you for months.'

'I'm beginning to think you're right.' Jade told her about the date that never was at Da Vinci's. 'Don't you dare say anything to him, I'm not supposed to know. And if you say anything in front of Finn, I'm going to kill you.'

'About Aiden?'

'About anything. I don't want him frightened off. He's too useful.'

'Don't worry. I won't. I can see you're smitten. You're completely transparent, Jade. Well, you are to me. I'm really pleased for you, it's about time you fell for something with fewer than four legs. Hey, is that him?' She paused and shielded her eyes and Jade saw Finn up a ladder that was resting against the quarantine block.

'Yes. He said there were some tiles that needed replacing. I knew I should have bought new – it was a false economy getting second-hand.'

'You live and learn. He's pretty fit, isn't he? Very nice bum.'

'Sarah!'

'He can't hear us.'

They paused at the foot of the ladder and Finn acknowledged them with a nod and began to climb down.

'Sorry to interrupt,' Jade began as he reached the ground and turned, smiling, towards her, 'but I just wanted to introduce you to Ben's mum. Finn, this is my best friend, Sarah. Sarah, this is Finn.'

There was a pause, which got longer and longer, and Jade

stood in the winter sunlight, feeling a rising sense of bewilderment.

It was hard to tell what Finn was thinking, it always was, but Sarah looked as if she'd just seen a ghost, complete with severed head clutched under one arm and clanking chains.

Finn broke the awkward silence. 'We've already met,' he said, glancing at Jade. 'Although I don't think we were on first-name terms back then, were we?' He held out his hand, but Sarah didn't take it and after a few moments he nodded and let it drop back to his side. 'It was a long time ago,' he went on for Jade's benefit. 'It was a Christmas party, if my memory serves me right. And we'd both had way too much to drink.'

'I can't remember much about that party,' Sarah blurted, finding her voice at last. 'After about nine o'clock it's a complete blank.' She raked her fingers through her long hair and glanced at Jade. 'Must have been a good party. We went to lots of parties in those days, didn't we, Jade? You were probably there.'

'Yes,' Jade murmured, even though she was sure she hadn't been. She'd never been much of a partygoer. She'd always preferred quiet pubs and restaurants where you could hear yourself speak.

'I can't remember much either,' Finn said quietly, his eyes holding Sarah's, and she nodded and went scarlet and looked vastly relieved, all at the same time. Jade had the strangest feeling Finn was letting Sarah off the hook for something. But she had no idea what.

'Are you coming down for a cup of tea?' she asked him. 'Callum's just making it. Or shall I bring it down here?'

'I'm all right for now, thanks. I want to get these tiles done before it rains.'

'Right,' Jade said, glancing distractedly into a cloudless sky, and hurrying to catch up with Sarah, who was already marching back up the yard.

'What on earth's going on?' she hissed, falling into step beside her friend.

'Nothing. Nothing's going on.'

'Sarah, tell me. Oh my God.' Realisation hit her like a bucket of ice. 'It was *that* Christmas party. The Christmas party where you met the guy and... Oh, my God, Sarah, Finn's Ben's father, isn't he?'

20

Sarah folded her arms and shook her head. 'Don't be daft. Of course he isn't. It's nothing like that.' She tripped over a bit of uneven ground as she spoke and Jade caught her arm, feeling pain shoot through her own wrenched muscles in the process.

'Don't lie to me, Sarah, please. You have to tell me. It's important. Is Finn Ben's father or isn't he?'

'Keep your voice down,' Sarah pleaded, glancing over her shoulder. 'Look, I can't talk about this now. I've got to get Ben from Darren's.'

'I'll come with you.'

'No, you can't. What about this place? Someone might come in who wants an animal.'

'I'll lock up and I'll forward the landline to my mobile. Finn's here anyway. Please, Sarah, we can't just leave it like this. You have to tell me the truth. Best friends – remember?'

By the time they got back to reception, Sarah was almost in control of herself again. The colour was back in her face and her eyes were calm. They found Callum sitting reading a dog-homing brochure and there were four mugs of steaming tea on Jade's desk. He glanced up and smiled.

'Callum, I don't suppose you could do us an enormous favour and answer the phone for ten minutes while Jade comes with me to collect Ben?'

'Aye, sure I can,' he said peaceably, 'if that's what you want.'

'The parking can be tricky at Darren's. It'll be easier to park Jade's Land Rover than the campervan. And I'm sure Ben will want to say thanks to Jade for having him. We'll come straight back.'

He nodded and didn't question this change of plan and Jade found herself thinking that it must make it a lot easier to lie if no one asked you any awkward questions. And then she berated herself for prejudging her closest friend, because she had said that Finn wasn't Ben's father. And although Jade wasn't sure if she believed this, she was still clinging grimly on to the last shreds of hope that he wasn't. Because if he was, then it changed everything. She couldn't have a relationship with the man who was Ben's father. She couldn't even employ him any more. Not when a secret like that hung between them. Sarah might be prepared to lie to him forever, but she wasn't. It wasn't fair.

Worry and fear made her drive faster than usual and Sarah clung on to her seat belt as Jade hurtled around a corner.

'You'll get us pulled over if you're not careful,' she squealed. 'Oh, Jade, I'm so sorry. If I'd known he was working here, I'd have told you. I'd never have let you fall for him.'

'I haven't fallen for him. And you can't control how I feel.'

'No, I know, I didn't mean that. Oh my God, he's met Ben, hasn't he?'

'You know he has. I told you. They get on really well.'

'Well, he can't see him again. I don't want him in Ben's life. I don't want him to have anything to do with him.'

'Listen to yourself, Sarah. For God's sake, be reasonable.' Jade yanked the Land Rover into a vacant space close to Darren's house. 'So, I take it Finn is Ben's father, then, and you were lying just now when you said he wasn't?'

Sarah hesitated. 'I'm sorry. I was in shock. I never expected to see him again. Especially not here. Bloody hell, he mustn't find out, Jade, it'd ruin everything. You have to promise me you won't tell him.'

'I can't promise you that. You know how I feel about it – how I've always felt about it.' Jade stared out at the blue sky beyond the window in the suburban road and remembered the arguments they'd had. Dozens and dozens of arguments over the identity of Ben's father. She'd never won any of them and she had a feeling she wouldn't win this one, either.

'You're going to have to tell him, Sarah. It's not fair on either of them, not knowing. Not now they've met. They really like each other. Besides, even if you didn't tell Ben, how are you going to explain that he's not allowed to see Finn any more? He spends most of his free time at the rescue.'

'You could sack him. You don't even have to sack him, you could tell him you can't afford him any more. He's done masses of the work already and I told you Callum doesn't mind helping out. We'll spend every weekend there. You won't lose out.'

'No,' Jade said, meeting Sarah's blue eyes and seeing a mixture of fear and defiance in them. 'I'm not throwing him out just because you can't face up to the truth. That's even less fair. He's only been working for me for two weeks.'

They were still arguing when they got to Darren's front door. But they broke off as soon as it was answered.

'Mum,' yelled Ben, hurling himself through the doorway and into Sarah's arms. 'You're back. I didn't know you were picking me up.'

'I wanted to surprise you.'

Jade saw Sarah's face soften as she looked at him. And then Sarah was bending down to hug her son, who submitted to being kissed for a few moments, before pulling impatiently away.

'Hello, Auntie Jade. Where's Daddy Callum?'

'He's looking after the animals so Auntie Jade could come with me. That's nice, isn't it? Have you missed me?'

'A bit,' Ben said, rolling his eyes and checking over his shoulders to see if Darren was looking. His friend had come to the door more slowly. A woman who Jade presumed was Darren's mum was smiling from a few feet behind him.

'But I like staying at Auntie Jade's. I've been looking after the chickens. I've been a big help, haven't I, Auntie Jade?'

'A very big help,' she agreed.

'His bag's here.' Darren's mum came forward with the holdall.

'Thanks so much. Has he behaved?' Sarah asked as she took it.

'They've been very good.'

'Have you said thank you to Darren's mum, Ben?' Sarah took the holdall and Jade stepped back, feeling in the way of this mum-to-mum exchange.

'Thank you very much. I had a very nice time,' Ben said politely.

'Oh, and don't forget your picture, Ben. The boys were painting yesterday.' Darren's mum hurried off to get it and came back with a rolled-up tube of paper.

Another painting, Jade thought. Like father, like son. She remembered the night in the Red Lion, when they'd looked at her with identical expressions. It seemed so obvious now she knew.

* * *

Back in the Land Rover again, Ben was full of chatter about his week. 'I've been learning how to paint properly. Finn's been helping. He's a proper artist. I'm going to be a proper artist when I grow up.'

In the seat beside her, Jade saw Sarah flinch and she felt a wave of compassion. What must it be like to have the past suddenly turn up on your doorstep? The past that was going to threaten your entire future happiness. She might not approve of what Sarah had done, but she couldn't blame her for reacting like this.

'Do you want to see my picture of Candy's puppies?' Ben added. 'It's at Auntie Jade's. Finn said it's the best thing I've ever done. I want to show him my one I did last night. Can I show him when we get back?'

'I think he might be busy at the moment. He won't want to be interrupted.'

'He likes looking at my paintings,' Ben said, his lips tightening mutinously. 'He says he never gets too busy for that.'

Sarah blinked a few times and Jade swallowed a massive ache in her throat. How on earth had they got into this mess?

* * *

There was no sign of Finn when they got back to Duck Pond Rescue, much to Ben's obvious disappointment and Sarah's obvious relief.

'You'll have to leave your picture with Auntie Jade to show Finn, sweetheart,' Sarah told him as she began to carry Ben's luggage out to the camper van. She gestured through the reception window for Callum to come out. 'We need to get back. Anyway, don't you want to get home and see what we got you in Scotland?'

'Suppose so.'

Sarah met Jade's eyes over his head. 'Please don't say anything to him. Give me a couple of days. I need to think things through. Otherwise, the whole thing could be a nightmare. For both of them,' she added, glancing at Ben. 'You must know that.'

'All right,' Jade agreed, feeling the beginnings of a headache starting at her temples. 'I won't go blundering in – but you are going to deal with it, aren't you?'

'Of course.' Sarah dipped her head and Jade felt as though already there was a wall growing between them. An insurmountable wall. On the one side was her friendship with Sarah, and she would never betray Sarah; but in order to protect her, she was going to have to lie through her teeth to Finn.

* * *

Finn came in early that evening, which was unusual. Jade was washing up in the kitchen when she heard him taking his boots off in the hall and hanging his coat by the front door. She realised how used to his presence she had become, even after a fortnight. How much she liked him being around.

She thought he might go straight upstairs, but he came into the kitchen and asked her if she wanted coffee. She nodded, moving out of his way so he could fill the kettle, anxious that they didn't touch.

Finn spooned coffee into their mugs and Jade sensed his gaze on the back of her neck, but she didn't turn round. This was madness. He was going to guess something was wrong. How could he not?

'How's your back now?' His voice was mild. 'I bet you ache a bit today, don't you?'

'It's not too bad, thanks,' she said, still without turning.

'It'll be quiet without Ben around,' he remarked at the same moment as the kettle switched itself off.

'Oh, he'll soon be back,' Jade murmured, emptying the washing-up bowl and rinsing it out and wondering what else she could do to avoid meeting his eyes.

'Did his parents have a good time in Scotland? As good as they could, I mean, in the circumstances?'

'Yes, I think they did.' She found a teaspoon in the bottom of the sink and held it under the tap. At least that was one saving grace – Finn thought Callum was Ben's father, so he wouldn't be putting two and two together and coming up with the right answer.

'Your coffee's ready,' Finn said mildly. 'Jade, if that teaspoon's done, can you sit down a minute. I want to talk to you about something.'

She turned around and even though he was standing at the furthest point away from her in the kitchen, she still felt threatened. If he started asking her questions about Sarah, she was going to have to lie and he was going to see straight through her. She'd always been hopeless at lying.

'Is it to do with work?' she asked, glancing at the kitchen clock and racking her brains frantically for a cast-iron reason for rushing out. 'Because I've got to do a home check in Southampton in a minute, so I haven't got long. We've got a surplus of dogs at the moment, and I need the space.'

'It's not to do with work. No,' Finn replied, his voice casual. 'Actually, it's a bit more personal than work. Perhaps it would be better to discuss it another time. When you're not so rushed.'

'Much better,' Jade said, relief flooding through her as she hurried across the kitchen. 'Blimey, is that the time? I didn't realise it was so late.' She fled out of the door and then had to go back for the keys to the Land Rover, which she'd forgotten. She pulled back the main gates and locked them again behind her and wondered what had possessed her to say Southampton. What on earth was she going to do for the next couple of hours, so it would look like she'd been on a home check that was twenty-five miles away?

21
_____

Finn had gone to bed by the time Jade got home and she didn't
see him first thing in the morning either, which was a relief. But
she knew she couldn't avoid him forever.

Seeing Reg Arnold's van pull through the gates just before
lunch didn't improve her mood. He was another person she'd
have dearly liked to avoid. But it was too late to hide from her
most impatient supplier. He'd already seen her and was striding
up the yard.

'Jade.' His voice was ingratiating. 'Long time no speak. I was
just passing and as you never seem to return my phone calls, I
thought I'd pop in and see how things were.'

Chase me up for payment, you mean, Jade thought with a
surge of irritation. She couldn't be more than a couple of days
late. She paused from sweeping the yard and waited for him to
reach her. He was a stringy, wiry, grey-haired little man who
reminded Jade of a jockey.

He stopped in front of her, thrust his hands in his pockets and
said, 'This place is looking a bit more cared for than it used to. I
heard you had some help.'

'That's right.' She glanced at Finn, who was just going past with a hammer in his hand. 'I've got some temporary help.' She waited for Reg to make some comment about being able to afford to hire people, but not to pay him on time, but it wasn't forthcoming.

'Mind if I take a look around? I'm thinking of getting a dog myself, actually.'

'Help yourself.' She leaned on the broom and watched him heading up towards the kennels. He was probably just being nosy; he didn't strike her as the type who'd re-home from an animal rescue even if he did want a dog.

'I'll pop in and see you on my way out,' he called over his shoulder. 'You never know, I might see something I like.'

'Not that I'd let him have one of my dogs,' Jade told Finn in reception a few minutes later.

'Why not? I'd have thought being a pet food supplier would have made him quite a good proposition,' Finn said without looking up from the box of screws he was rummaging through. 'At least it would never go hungry.'

'He's mean-spirited and I don't like him,' Jade said, surprising herself. She hadn't realised she felt that strongly.

'That doesn't mean he won't be able to offer a dog a good home. Some people are better at communicating with animals than they are with their own species.' Now he did glance at her, raising his eyebrows and smiling slightly.

She flushed. 'You are talking about Reg Arnold, I take it? Or was that a cheap dig at me?'

'All I'm saying, Jade, is that for all you know he'd make a very good pet owner. Just because he's a bit short on the charm side, you shouldn't write him off. You were saying yesterday you could do with re-homing some dogs, so you ought to at least give him a chance.' He stood up then, having presumably found what he wanted, grinned at her, and went out into the sunshine.

Jade frowned. Irritatingly, he was probably right. But it was all pure speculation and not worth getting wound up about. Reg Arnold might not even find a dog he liked. She didn't want to admit that Finn's little dig about people who communicated better with animals than humans had irked her. Sarah had said the same thing plenty of times, but it was different coming from Sarah. She was her closest friend. She snapped her thoughts away from Sarah, not wanting to think about yesterday and what was going to happen to their friendship now.

She'd almost forgotten about Reg Arnold when he came into reception about half an hour later, rested his hands on the desk in front of her and said, 'I've found the perfect dog, Jade. Little lurcher bitch – got puppies with her.'

'Candy.' Jade looked at his lit-up face. She'd never seen him look so enthusiastic, with the possible exception of when he'd come in to collect a big payment. 'It'll be a while before she's ready to go to a home.'

'I can wait. I just had a chat with someone called Dawn. She said I could reserve her if I came and spoke to you.'

'We'd need to do a home check first,' Jade said, inwardly cursing Dawn.

'Home check? But you know me, Jade.'

'It's just a formality. I have to check your fencing, things like that. And Candy will need to be spayed, or at least have the arrangements made. Give me a ring in a couple of weeks if you're still keen. Then we can arrange a time for me to pop over and see you.'

'Yes. All right, I suppose, if that's what you have to do.' He looked disappointed. Straightening up, he ran a hand through his wispy hair and said, 'You know I really miss having a dog around the place. We had Jackdaw for nearly eighteen years.'

'Jackdaw?'

'He was a black Labrador. Had him from a scrap of a pup. Broke my heart when he went. Still, I suppose seventeen's not bad for a Lab.'

'No,' Jade agreed, thinking that perhaps she had misjudged him. 'Well, as I said, give me a ring when you've had a think.'

'You're the boss.' He hesitated. 'You're doing a great job here, Jade. I'm impressed. Maybe we could leave the payment...' He screwed up his face, as if he were having some internal battle with himself, and Jade held her breath. 'Until you come and do the home visit. That would help you out a bit, wouldn't it?'

'That's very thoughtful, Reg, thank you,' she said, trying not to laugh at the magnanimous expression on his face.

* * *

'Up until that moment I was starting to think he was a decent human being,' she told Dawn that afternoon as they walked dogs in the field. 'A few weeks' extra credit, whoopee do – he looked so pleased with himself.'

'I thought you were looking stressed,' Dawn remarked. 'Are you sure it's just Reg Arnold? Or is there anything else on your mind?'

They paused in the corner of the field to let a dog walker with a greyhound go by and Jade noticed a broken fence post by the road and made a mental note to tell Finn about it. There was a lot on her mind, but most of it was classified, she thought with a surge of weariness, aware that Dawn was waiting for her answer.

She shook her head. The older woman was kind and discreet

and could be relied on to keep quiet, but none of what was on her mind was hers to share.

They'd reached the end of the field and paused to let the dogs sniff a patch of grass, before turning to retrace their steps. Then, before either of them could say anything else, a rabbit shot past them with the greyhound, minus its walker, in hot pursuit. The terriers started to dance and bark on the ends of their leads and, despite the fact they were only small dogs, Jade felt the sudden wrench on her shoulders, which until then had been healing nicely.

The rabbit reached the fencing and shot through the gap by the broken post. The greyhound, unable to stop, crashed into the wire and yelped, then withdrew, limping and holding one dark paw in the air. The dog walker was running down the path towards them.

'Sorry,' she panted. 'Took me by surprise and I couldn't hold him.'

'Don't worry.' Jade knelt by the dog, trying not to wince at the re-awakened pain in her shoulder. 'He's probably just twisted it. No damage as far as I can see. Your rabbit-chasing days are over,' she said to the greyhound, who blinked his liquid brown eyes and licked her hand.

'He looked like he could still win a few races to me,' Dawn remarked.

'Yes.' Jade returned to the greyhound to his walker, glad the moment for confessions had passed.

* * *

She was about to shut the main gate that evening when Aiden's jeep drew up outside. He slid down the window and beckoned her across.

'You're late tonight. I was just locking up.'

'Sorry. I had an urgent call last thing.' He looked tired and there were lines of stress around his dark eyes.

'You don't have to come every night, you know,' she said gently. 'You should have left it. I can cope with Fang.'

He brushed a hand through his hair, a curious gesture of vulnerability that touched her. 'I'm all right. Long day, that's all. Have you eaten, Jade, only I was wondering if you'd like to come for a bit of dinner?' He reddened a little, his dark eyes even more intense than usual.

Jade hesitated. She was still aching like mad from her fall and all she really wanted to do was to lie in a bath and let the water soothe her wrenched muscles. Yet she didn't want to turn him down flat. Not after what Mike had told her.

'Not tonight, Aiden.' She kept her voice gentle. 'I need an early night. I'm really tired.'

He looked so defeated that she heard herself adding, 'I'd love to come another time, though.'

His face brightened and before she could qualify this by suggesting they go to Mike's one evening, he said, 'How about next Saturday? I could book somewhere. Do you like Italian?'

'Yes, why not.' She wondered if the same restaurant would let him book another table. 'But you'll be in before then to see Fang?'

'Of course. I could go up there now if you like?'

'I've just locked up. You'll disturb the others.' As she spoke, Finn came up the yard, heading towards the cottage, and she saw Aiden's cheekbones tense.

'I'll see you tomorrow, then.' He leaned out and touched her arm and Jade had the horrible feeling it wasn't for her benefit, but some signal of possession to Finn.

She stepped away. 'See you tomorrow.'

He gave her a quick smile and pulled out of the yard. She watched him go with mixed feelings.

Dusk was already creeping through the air, bringing a chill dampness with it that promised yet more rain.

'Going to stand there all night, or are you coming in?' Finn's voice interrupted her thoughts.

'I'm coming now.'

'Are you OK? You look shattered.'

Shattered just about summed it up – if she hadn't been so tired and distracted, she was sure she wouldn't have agreed to go out with Aiden. She glanced at Finn, longing for the easy rapport that had built up between them before Sarah had dropped her bombshell, but afraid to relax her guard. She wasn't like Sarah. She couldn't act as if nothing had happened. There was no way she could laugh and joke with Finn while she was also lying to him. She'd have been hard pushed to do it with a stranger, let alone someone she liked and trusted.

'I am tired,' she said, jolting away from him as they took their coats off in the hallway and their arms brushed accidentally.

'And jumpy,' he added quietly. 'What's on your mind, Jade?'

'Nothing.' She spoke too quickly, too sharply, and she saw his face tighten even in the dim light of the hall. 'What I mean is that...'

'You don't need to explain. I think I can guess,' he murmured.

God, she hoped not. Then it struck her he might think she was judging him for having a one-night stand with her closest friend. Every instinct she had urged her to tell him she wasn't.

But she didn't dare open that can of worms. She couldn't afford to let down her guard around him, not for a second. Not until Sarah had told him the truth.

22

There was no word from Sarah for the next few days and Jade was saddened, but not surprised.

Finn said no more about wanting to talk to her either, which was a relief. He too seemed to be keeping out of her way. The prospect of going out for dinner with Aiden loomed like a black cloud and she wished she could back out of it. But that would have been crueller than saying no in the first place. Why hadn't she said no? She berated herself for being a coward.

As she got ready on Saturday night, Jade realised she hadn't told Finn she was going out with Aiden. Not that she normally filled him in on her activities. But then she didn't normally go anywhere. She looked at herself in the mirror critically and wondered if she'd subconsciously chosen an outfit that covered every bit of flesh. Coffee-coloured skinny cords, a cream silk shirt she'd bought for interviews and boots with no heels because she was out of practice at walking in heels and there might be a walk between car park and restaurant.

She looked smart but casual. There was no way Aiden could get the impression they were off on a hot date. She checked there was no lippie on her teeth and opened the bedroom door to meet Finn coming out of the bathroom.

'You look nice.' There was a mixture of surprise and appreciation on his face and she didn't know whether to feel insulted or flattered. 'I take it you're going somewhere more interesting than the Red Lion?'

'Just for a pizza with Aiden.' She ignored the knowing look in his eyes. 'You up to anything?'

'I thought I might head down to the pub and see if Mike's sold any of my paintings yet.'

'I'll keep my fingers crossed for you.'

A few minutes later, the doorbell rang and Aiden strolled into the cottage. He made a big thing about giving her a bunch of flowers and whistling his appreciation of the effort she'd gone to. She knew he was being nice, but by the time she'd got him out of the door her face was flaming. This had been a crazy idea. She was never in a million years going to be able to let Aiden down gently after tonight.

* * *

Aiden was torn between worrying about whether Jade would like the restaurant he'd chosen and a tentative delight that their long-awaited date was finally happening. The Italian had been fully booked, so he'd picked an English restaurant that hadn't been open very long. She didn't seem overly excited about coming out with him, but this was new territory for them both. He'd decided to drive her himself and not have anything to drink. That way he could fully enjoy the evening. Unglazed by alcohol, he could also make sure he didn't commit any faux pas.

A waiter took their drinks orders and left them with leather-bound menus. Rather to his chagrin, Jade had asked for a Diet

Coke. But nothing really mattered, Aiden thought, as he watched her scanning the menu. The main thing was that she'd chosen to be here with him for the evening. He tried to suppress the tiny flicker of satisfaction that Finn would be sitting in the Red Lion on his own. It was petty and he could afford to be gracious now.

Knowing Jade was vegetarian, Aiden had decided to forfeit his usual rare steak and go for sea bass. But the sea bass was sold out, so he'd picked guinea fowl, which seemed the most innocuous of the remaining choices, with prawns to start.

'How's your soup?' he asked Jade, picking up a prawn and deftly snapping off the head.

'It's lovely, thank you, Aiden.' She dabbed her mouth with her napkin and Aiden looked around for a finger bowl and saw that there wasn't one. Unable to catch a waiter's eye, he had to resort to wiping his fingers on his own napkin. Preoccupied with this, he didn't notice until Jade was halfway through her soup that although they had butter on the table there was no bread.

'Would you like some bread with that?' he asked belatedly.

'No, I'm fine, Aiden, thanks.'

'Are you sure? I can get you some.' He stood up, knocking his fork on to the floor with the edge of his jacket.

Jade bent to pick it up. Fortunately, at that moment their main courses arrived. Or at least Aiden's did.

'Yours will be two minutes,' the waiter informed her.

Good manners prevented Aiden from starting without her and they talked shop while they waited. He asked her how the fund-raising was going and she told him about a woman who'd left a generous donation to them in her will.

'She took a cat from us when we first started up,' Jade told him. 'She was quite elderly and so we had an agreement that Felix would come back to us if he outlived her, which of course I was fine with. I had no idea she planned to leave us a legacy if this happened.'

'Wow.' Aiden shook his head. 'There are some lovely people around.'

'There are. Only last week a jogger brought in a mallard with an injured beak...' She broke off and glanced at his plate.

Aiden was distracted by the waiter arriving to apologise for the lateness of Jade's meal.

Saved by the bell, Jade thought, realising she'd opened her mouth before putting her brain into gear. Talking about the duck she was currently nursing back to health, when Aiden had a guinea fowl on his plate, suddenly seemed a bit crass.

She tore her gaze away from his plate, where a piece of bone, presumably the guinea fowl's leg, stuck out at an angle, the end of it trussed in white paper. Was the paper meant to be a disguise or decoration?

She felt a pang of sympathy for the bird, which had not only had to die, but had been made to look so undignified afterwards.

'Please start, Aiden, don't wait for me,' she urged, seeing that gravy was beginning to congeal on his plate.

He ate as slowly as he could, which was sweet of him, but he was still almost finished by the time her main course arrived.

'So sorry,' the waiter said, putting it on the table with a flourish.

Jade thanked him absently and he swept away, his nose in the air. She wondered what Sarah would have made of all this. She'd probably have laughed. And suddenly she felt overwhelmingly sad that Sarah felt she couldn't phone her for a chat, even if she wasn't ready to confess all to Finn.

Even when she'd been away in Bristol, they'd always kept in close contact, more like sisters than friends. It was impossible to believe this space had come between them so swiftly.

Jade turned down Aiden's offer of a dessert, and they drove back to the cottage in silence. A strained silence, Jade thought, or maybe it was just her. Aiden seemed OK.

She glanced at him and tried to work out the most diplomatic way of telling him that she'd had a lovely evening, but had no desire to repeat the experience. He'd refused to let her pay any of the bill, which made it all worse.

* * *

Aiden parked outside the main gates, switched off the ignition, and reached across to release her seat belt at the same moment as she pressed the button.

'It sticks a bit sometimes,' he said apologetically as their hands knocked against each other.

'It seems to be all right tonight,' she said, pulling her hand away.

Aiden leapt out of the car and came round to open the door for her.

'Thanks.'

'My pleasure.' He was wondering whether he should risk a goodnight kiss. The evening hadn't quite lived up to his expectations. Jade hadn't seemed as relaxed with him as she usually was.

She clutched her bag to her. 'That was a lovely evening, Aiden.'

They stood with a little gap between them below the sign for Duck Pond Rescue that Finn had made. It was a beautiful night, clear and crisp, the stars coldly bright above them. A perfect evening for romance, Aiden thought, taking a step closer to her.

She looked beautiful in the moonlight, her eyes wide and dark. He had an urge to put his arms around her, but he still wasn't sure. Eventually, cursing himself for his shyness, he bent and gave her a peck on the cheek. 'See you tomorrow, then.'

'OK. Goodnight and thanks again.' She made no move to invite him in and after a moment of awkwardness, he stepped back, still looking at her, and tripped over a tree stump. He put his hands out to save himself, then overbalanced completely and fell backwards into the hedge that ran alongside the cottage.

'Are you all right?' Her voice was all concern and she bent to help him up, which didn't help his ego one bit.

He scrambled to his feet, brushing dead leaves and bits of grass off his trousers and feeling like a complete idiot.

'I hope you're not driving in that condition.' They both glanced up to see Finn coming round the corner, presumably on his way back from the Red Lion.

'I'm not drunk.' Aiden flushed. Why was Finn always around when he made an idiot of himself?

'Hey – take it easy – I was joking.' Finn put up his hands in mock defence. 'You just didn't look too steady there for a minute.'

Jade, Aiden saw to his embarrassment, was pressing her fingers to her head and looking as if she'd rather be somewhere else, anywhere else. Some romantic finale that had been, he thought bitterly. 'I'll be off then,' he said, and, giving Finn a curt nod, he got into his jeep. When he looked in his rear-view mirror, Finn was saying something to Jade as he opened the gate for her. He felt a little twist of jealousy. He hated the thought of them going into the cottage and sharing coffee and perhaps a laugh at his expense.

Jade was too nice for that, he consoled himself, and she'd chosen to go out with him tonight, not Finn.

* * *

'Nice evening?' Finn asked, looking at Jade, eyebrows raised, as they got inside the cottage.

'Lovely, thanks.' It was a minor lie in the big scheme of things. 'You?'

'Not bad. You stopping up for coffee?'

'I'll just have a glass of water. I've got a bit of a headache.'

'Side effect from landing on it last week, probably.'

'Yeah, I expect you're right,' she said, although she knew her headache had nothing at all to do with last week, but more to do with the feeling she shouldn't have gone out with Aiden. At the very least she should have said something, but she hadn't been able to. Not after he'd landed in the bush in front of Finn. It would have been like kicking him when he was down.

Now it was going to be twice as difficult to persuade him she wasn't interested in him. Water splashed over her hands as she filled up her glass and she realised Finn was still standing in the kitchen.

'So, has Mike sold any of your paintings yet?'

'No, I think he's right. I'll have to do more local landscapes.'

'You could do more of Stonehenge. It's beautiful in spring.'

'Yes, maybe I will.' As she passed him, he handed her a foil-wrapped blister of tablets. 'Painkillers.'

'Thanks.'

Upstairs, Jade lay in bed, feeling curiously depressed. She and Aiden had a lot in common. It would have been nice if there was some chemistry, but there was no spark, none of the electricity that flared between her and Finn and left her disconcertingly breathless at the most inappropriate moments.

She blinked away the thought. Fantasising about Finn was both stupid and painful. In a few months' time, he'd be a distant memory because, despite what she'd told Sarah, she knew that when it came to it, her loyalty was to her best friend. If she had to choose between friendship and a crush on a man she barely knew, there was no contest.

23

Finn walked around Stonehenge, trying to find the best angle from which to paint it. But even when he'd found a spot and set up his easel, he still couldn't concentrate.

He'd got up early and, realising Jade hadn't surfaced, he'd gone and knocked on her door. When she hadn't responded, he'd been gripped by a sudden fear that she might not be all right. She never overslept and last night she'd complained of a headache. What if it was a delayed effect of the bang on the head when she'd slipped in the kennel? Deciding he couldn't take the risk she might be unconscious, he'd poked his head around her bedroom door.

She'd been lying on her front, one arm tucked beneath her head, her breasts crushed against the bottom sheet. The duvet had been at the foot of the bed and he hadn't been able to stop his gaze from travelling down her naked body. As well as the graze on her back, which looked as though it was healing nicely, there was a large bruise at the base of her spine, just above the gentle curve of her buttocks. There was another bruise at the top of one smooth thigh. Her face was peaceful, though, and she was breathing steadily. As he watched her, she stirred and murmured something. Finn closed the door, his heart beating too fast, feeling guilty that he'd intruded on her privacy.

Since he'd realised Jade's best friend was also his long-ago one-night stand, he'd been tearing himself apart over what to do for the best. Jade obviously knew about it. He knew enough about women to know they'd have discussed it in detail, and even if he hadn't, he'd have guessed by her attitude towards him. She'd begun to relax around him, but that had gone now. He was torn between telling her he wasn't in the habit of having one-night stands, and saying nothing at all. Least said, soonest mended, his father would have said, and perhaps he was right.

Not that Jade had given him much chance to discuss the subject. When he'd tried, she'd shut him down. He'd sensed it would be counterproductive to push her into a corner. The best thing he could do was to let some time pass, which meant that at the moment she was off-limits, but telling himself this did nothing to make the memory of her nakedness less evocative.

He'd been celibate since Shona and he was living in the same house as a gorgeous woman whom he'd wanted to take to bed from the moment he'd seen her. Sharing her routines, using the same bathroom, knowing she was sleeping in the room just below him. He'd have had to have been a eunuch not to be affected. He shook his head to clear it, knowing that way madness lay.

His thoughts drifted to Aiden. He'd been surprised when Jade had gone out for dinner with the bumbling vet, but perhaps he'd underestimated him. They were friends, after all. Perhaps she'd hoped to negotiate better discounts. Or perhaps it was some sort of signal to him that she wasn't available. He didn't think she was the type to play games, but then he still knew hardly anything about her.

Dismissing Aiden, he forced himself to concentrate on the ancient stones he was trying to sketch. Beyond them, the sky was a backdrop of blue with only the occasional cloud to break it, but despite the glorious spring weather there weren't many people about. Jade had told him that in another couple of weeks the place would be flooded with tourists. Today was a good day to come.

He worked for another couple of hours, the air soft on his face, the peace of the countryside slowly seeping into his mind. Then he got up and stretched and walked around a bit. Time to find himself a pub lunch.

It was after six when he got back to Duck Pond Cottage. Aiden's jeep wasn't around, he saw with relief. He had a feeling he'd seen quite a bit more of Jade this morning than Aiden ever had and he was not anxious to bump into him for a while. He wasn't keen on bumping into Jade either, come to that. What if some half-formed memory of him opening her door had been sharpening in her mind during the day? Perhaps she'd already packed his bags and was about to tell him he was sacked?

He parked the Toyota and opened the back to get his painting things out. When he straightened, he saw Jade coming down the yard. Seeing him, she frowned and came hurrying across.

'Hi, Finn, I'm glad you're back. Have you got a minute? I'd like a quick word.'

* * *

Finn looked guilty, Jade noticed as they went into the cottage. He'd jumped out of his skin when she'd spoken.

'Did you have a productive day?' she asked. 'Get much done?'

'Yeah, not bad, thanks. Very relaxing.'

He didn't look at all relaxed. She smiled at him. 'If you're rushing off somewhere it can wait. It's not important.'

'I'm not rushing off.' He leaned on the door frame of the lounge. 'Fire away.'

'There's a broken fence post in the dog-walking field and there's a little gap that leads out on to the road. I noticed it the other day, but I forgot to tell you. I'm worried a dog might get loose and go through there.'

'That's what you wanted to talk to me about?'

'Yes. Oh, and I also wanted to say that you really must have a day off in the week too. You must think I'm a slave driver.'

'Not at all. You're not exactly a slacker yourself, are you?'

She flushed. 'But I'm doing it for the love of it, Finn. You don't have to work such long hours. I probably don't tell you enough, but I really appreciate having you around.' She paused and flicked him an anxious glance. 'Wasn't there something you wanted to talk to me about?'

He hesitated. Would now be a good time? She looked on edge. He decided it would be better to wait. He wanted her to listen to him, to trust him, and she had to be relaxed for that.

'It'll keep.'

The relief on her face told him he'd said the right thing.

* * *

Jade waited until she was sure he'd gone to bed at the top of the house, then closed the lounge door and phoned Sarah, who rarely went to bed before midnight.

'Have you decided what you're going to do about Finn?' she said, launching straight in. 'Because he's been acting really strangely today and I think he might have guessed. I asked him what was on his mind just now, but he didn't want to discuss it.'

'He can't have guessed,' Sarah said stubbornly. 'Why on earth would he connect Ben with himself when he thinks Callum's his dad? Anyway, he said he couldn't remember what had happened.'

'I think he was lying, so as not to embarrass you. He's that type of bloke.'

'So as not to embarrass himself, more like,' Sarah snapped. 'It takes two, you know. I didn't drag him into that field.'

Jade flinched. She knew she was torturing herself, but she couldn't get the image of Sarah and Finn, backed up against a tree, or wherever it had happened, out of her head. She knew they'd been drunk and very young, but they'd still wanted each other, hadn't they? And they'd still produced Ben, so she couldn't even kid herself it had just been a desperate fumbling where not much had really happened.

'Jade, please give me a bit longer.' A note of fear had crept into Sarah's voice and Jade sighed.

'How much longer? A week, a few weeks, a few months? I hate this. I hate seeing him every day and knowing the truth. He's a nice bloke. He's going to be really hurt.'

'Yes, I know, but I've got to think of Ben. And there's Callum. I've got to find the right time to tell him, too. I love him, Jade. I'm scared of buggering things up between us.'

'But isn't sooner going to be better than later? And Callum loves you. It's not as though he thinks Ben's his.'

'No, but I told him Ben's father didn't want to know. I told him I'd had a relationship with this much older guy who left when I got pregnant. I know I should have told him the truth, but I wasn't expecting anyone to turn up and prove me a liar!'

Her voice was getting lower with each sentence, but Jade heard the message loud and clear. Of course Sarah wouldn't have told Callum about something of which she was deeply ashamed. She wanted him to think she was an independent single mother who'd been abandoned by the father of her child – just as she'd been abandoned by everyone else in her life. That she'd come through it all by her own strength of character. She didn't want the man she loved to see the flaws, the desperate insecurity that had been behind her decision not to contact a man whose name she hadn't even known.

In some ways, Jade couldn't blame her. Perhaps she'd have done the same in her place.

'And Jade, there's been a development I haven't told you about. Callum proposed yesterday. I've said yes. If I tell him the truth, the whole thing will be off. I can't risk it.'

'Congratulations,' Jade whispered, feeling a deep sadness welling up in her because once she wouldn't have had to call Sarah to find out this news. A few weeks ago, Sarah would have been straight on the phone.

'We're coming over at the weekend to tell you officially so pretend you don't know. And, Jade, please don't say anything to Finn. Let me do this my way.'

Blossom the colour of pink candyfloss was everywhere, and new grass had sprung up in the fields. Pink lilies appeared on the duck pond and the young female mallard Jade had nursed back to health had rejoined her emerald-headed partner. Every time Jade saw the duck couple, her heart warmed that she'd had a hand in their survival and when a string of yellow fluffballs appeared on the pond, she felt almost as proud as the new mallard mum.

There were hundreds of lambs, too. Aiden had been rushed off his feet with lambing and hadn't been such a frequent visitor. Jade felt relieved, even though she could never see lambs skipping after their mothers without feeling a pang of bittersweet poignancy, knowing they were destined for the table. Despite the fact Jade had been vegetarian since she was fifteen, she turned a blind eye to Finn cooking meat in her kitchen, although the subject had come up.

'I won't do it if it bothers you,' he said one morning when he saw her wrinkling up her nose as he fried bacon and sausages and Mickey watched him in anticipation, knowing he'd get a bit of sausage if he hung about.

'I'm not judging you, Finn. Do what you like. Just make sure you don't use my best non-stick pan, you'll wreck it.'

'Wouldn't dream of it. Doesn't the smell of frying bacon get your taste buds going even a bit?'

'Nope.' She shot him a glare, and he didn't push it.

Later that day, when they went to collect some new fence panels, a rabbit ran across the road in front of the car and he only just missed it.

'Why don't you try driving a bit slower?' she snapped.

On the return journey, Finn insisted she drive and when she'd slammed on the brakes to avoid something else in the road and a fence post had nearly skewered him in the back, he'd said crossly, 'For goodness' sake, Jade, was that really bloody necessary?'

'I didn't want to hit it. What was it anyway?'

He glanced out of the window. 'Can't tell, you've flattened it. Poor little thing.' Then, seeing her shocked expression, he'd winked. 'You just killed a defenceless plastic bag, Jade.'

For a moment he'd thought she was going to slap him, then she'd giggled and they'd both ended up in fits of laughter.

* * *

Apart from the lambs, spring was Jade's favourite season. Even the air smelt new, crisp and lemony with a hint of the summer that was to come. Rosanna was back from Puddleduck Pets. Finn had helped her collect the mare this time, as Aiden had been so busy, and again Jade had thought how lovely Maggie Crowther was.

In an effort to repay her kindness, she'd brought back a cat with eight kittens that had landed on Maggie's doorstep out of the blue. Maggie had been really grateful. Apparently she had a half-feral cat called Saddam who roamed around Puddleduck Farm and made things extra tricky. Jade had already got homes lined up for three of the kittens.

She had also decided to re-home Ashley, her frisky horse. Hopefully, this would happen before Rosanna came into season again. He was a handsome fellow and Jade had mentioned in her advert that the low price she was asking reflected some behavioural issues he had, which would be fully discussed with any potential owner.

Candy's pups had all gone to new homes, apart from Tiny. Jade told everyone that he needed a bit longer than the rest of the litter, being the weakest, but the truth was she didn't want to let him go. It was stupid, she knew. You couldn't afford to get sentimental about one perfectly rehomable puppy. Not when you had a whole kennel full of other dogs; but there was something special about Tiny. In her mind, Tiny's progress was tied up with the rescue centre's future and, in some strange way, her own.

It was superstitious nonsense, she knew, not far removed from the challenges she'd set herself when she was a child. If she could get down the whole street without treading on the cracks in the pavement then she'd have a good day at school. If she got top marks in maths, which she hated, then her mother would pick her up instead of sending the childminder. Life wasn't like that. You couldn't make bargains with some deity. But, however irrational it was, she couldn't shake off the feeling that Tiny's survival was tied up with the future of Duck Pond Rescue. If she kept him safe, the rescue would survive too. And the only way she could keep him safe was to keep him here with her.

Candy, though, would be going soon. Reg had called to arrange his home check, and Finn, who'd happened to take the call, had asked Jade if he could go with her to do it.

'Why?' she'd asked, curious. It was the first time he'd shown an interest in anything directly concerned with an animal.

'I just want to see what excuse you're going to find to say he can't have her,' he'd replied with a wry smile. 'Or are you going to be more professional than that and put Candy's welfare first?'

'I always put the animal's welfare first,' she'd said, 'not that it's got anything to do with you.'

'So can I come then? You can take me for a drink afterwards if you like.'

She'd been so taken aback she'd agreed, and they'd driven round to Reg Arnold's in her Land Rover. Despite what she'd told Finn, she *had* been thinking of saying Reg couldn't have Candy. Not because she didn't like the man, but because anyone as tight-fisted as Reg might skimp on looking after an animal. What would happen if Candy needed expensive veterinary treatment?

Jade parked outside the address that Reg had given her and they both got out and looked at the house.

'Bit posh,' Finn said, echoing her thoughts. He peered over the fence that surrounded an impressively large garden. 'Nice lot of space for a dog to run around. Candy would love it.'

She stood beside him. The garden was what an estate agent would have referred to as 'mature'. A long, sloping lawn flanked with bushes and trees led up to a big conservatory. The house itself was encircled by a gravel driveway, where Reg's delivery van and a five-year-old Jaguar were parked.

'Blimey, so that's what he does with his money. He could afford to wait weeks longer for his accounts.'

'Ah, but then he probably wouldn't be able to afford this lot.' Finn clicked his tongue. 'Made up your mind, then, have you, Jade?'

Ignoring him, she let them through the five-bar gate and they walked towards the house.

'Aiden's got a nice garden too,' Jade commented as they waited on the front doorstep. She glanced at Finn. 'How are you getting on with him, these days?'

'I don't think we're ever going to be best buddies,' he replied, but was saved from having to comment further when Reg opened the door.

'Come in, come in. Nice to see you both.' He ushered them into a country farmhouse kitchen, which wouldn't have looked out of place in a glossy magazine, and made them both coffee.

Supermarket own brand, Jade thought uncharitably, as he showed them the place next to the range oven where he planned to put Candy's basket.

'I just need to check your garden's secure,' she said, aware of Finn's eyes on her, but despite walking all the way round the quarter-acre plot, she couldn't find anywhere the little lurcher could possibly squeeze through.

'Can I have her, then?' Reg asked when they got back to the house again. 'Have I passed the test?'

'With flying colours,' she said, not looking at Finn. 'Just one question. Why do you want to take on a rescue dog? Why don't you just buy a Labrador puppy?'

'I like to do my bit.' Reg rubbed his hands together. 'As you know, Jade. Now, about your latest account. Maybe a little discount would help?'

'That's very generous, Reg. Thank you. There's an adoption fee payable when you come to collect Candy. Her inoculations are up to date, but she'll still need to be spayed. Either you can go through your own vet, or ours might be cheaper. If money was an issue, I mean?'

He cleared his throat. 'Of course. I'll – er – pop in next week and we'll discuss it.'

Afterwards, Jade drove Finn to the Red Lion and bought him a drink, as agreed.

'Satisfied yourself about my professional abilities?' she asked as she put the glass down in front of him.

'Perfectly. I was very impressed.' He winked. 'So you can't always judge people from what you see on the surface, can you?'

'And what's that supposed to mean?'

'Well, you thought Reg was an old skinflint who'd be a totally unsuitable dog owner, didn't you? But closer inspection proved that not to be the case. Am I right?'

She didn't answer and he sipped his pint of Guinness and went on idly, 'And I thought you were a crazy, idealistic animal lover, but there's a lot more to you than that, isn't there?'

'I should hope so.' She met his steady gaze. 'If I was just a crazy, idealistic animal lover I probably wouldn't have got this far. I'd have given up after the first three months when I found out that running a rescue is flaming hard work. Anyway, Finn McTaggart, enough about me, what about you?'

'What about me?' His voice was soft. 'What would you like to know, Jade?'

She wouldn't ask him about Sarah, she decided. Or about whether it was a regular thing for him to jump into bed with women he didn't know. Partly because she didn't want to spoil the easiness of the moment – she'd missed this easiness so much – and partly because she wasn't sure she'd like his answer. Besides, what business was it of hers what he'd done in the past? She thought about the photo of the little boy in his wallet. She couldn't ask about that either, since she wasn't supposed to know it was there.

She stared into her orange juice, aware he was waiting for her to respond, and kept her voice deliberately light.

'I don't know. Stuff. Like, have you got any brothers and sisters? What your dad does, that sort of thing.'

'OK. No brothers and sisters, and Dad's retired now, but he was a miner until the pit closed down. How's that?'

Jade would have liked to ask more about his mother, but she sensed that he'd clam up completely if she did, so she changed tack. 'Are you close to your dad? You could ask him down for a holiday some time, if you like? You said he likes dogs, didn't you?'

'Yes, he does like dogs. Thanks, I might do that.'

'I promise I won't interrogate him too much. What's his name?'

'Ray. And he'd probably enjoy being interrogated by you, Jade. Do you want another drink?'

She shook her head, and, before she could lose her nerve, went on softly, 'So why did you really move down from Nottingham, Finn? It must be quite a culture shock living here.'

He met her eyes steadily. 'I've always liked it here. I was down every summer when I was a kid. I was close to my grandparents. And there was nothing really to tie me to Nottingham when I lost my job. Apart from Dad, of course, but he's got a full social life. He belongs to a working men's club and he's got his old cronies from mining. Although there aren't as many as there used to be. They're all getting on a bit – and not many miners live to a great old age.'

Jade picked up a beer mat and twiddled it nervously. 'The girl you lived with in Nottingham – did she have any children? You don't have to tell me. If it's private... you know...'

'It's not private. Yes, Shona had a little boy.' He rummaged for his wallet and Jade felt her face burn as he slipped out the photo she'd seen and slid it across the table. 'This is Stewart. You've seen this photo already, though, haven't you?'

'It fell out of your wallet when you first started working for me.' She knew how unlikely that must sound. 'I wasn't prying, truly. But yes, I did see it.'

'Shona was married to my best friend, Andy,' Finn went on with a wry smile, so she wasn't sure whether he believed her or not. 'I was best man at their wedding. I was close to both of them, but then Andy started drinking heavily. It was soon after Stewart was born – I don't think he could handle the responsibility of being a parent.' His face clouded and Jade felt a tug of guilt because the one thing she was sure about was that Finn would make an excellent father.

'Andy started knocking her about,' Finn continued quietly. 'One evening he broke her arm because the carrots in his stew weren't cooked properly. She told me about it. She didn't want to tell me – she was desperately ashamed that it was somehow her fault – but she was terrified he might start on Stewart.'

'My God,' Jade whispered. 'That's awful. What happened?'

'She left him. She and Stewart came to live with me for a while because she didn't have anywhere else to go. I cared about them both.'

He hesitated. 'Andy found out where they were, turned up one night and gave me a good hiding. I pressed charges and he ended up in prison. Which was actually the best thing that could have happened in some ways, because he got treatment for his drink problem.'

'And you ended up with Shona?' Jade asked, fascinated.

'We were never a proper couple,' Finn told her, raising his eyebrows, and Jade wondered whether he meant they didn't sleep together, but his next words shattered this. 'Basically, she needed someone and I was there. We sort of drifted together, but I was a lot more involved with Shona than she was with me. She still loved Andy, you see. When he came out of prison, she went back to him. I think I always knew she would.'

He sipped his pint, his eyes serious. 'I shouldn't have got

involved – in any sense of the word, I guess. But it's difficult not to in a situation like that.'

'And are they OK now?' Jade asked, wanting more than anything to take his hand, but not sure if he'd let her. He certainly didn't want her sympathy; she could see that in his face.

'Yes, I think so. Dad keeps a discreet eye on them both. He lives nearby. Dad would let me know if they needed me. He adores Stewart; he takes the lad fishing. He's the grandson he never had.'

His eyes held hers and eventually she had to drop her gaze. Finn had a son and Ray had a grandson and they should be sharing his life, but they didn't even know he existed. Jade ached with the deceit of it all.

'It's OK,' he murmured, catching her stricken look. 'I'm over Shona. I got more involved than I should have done. I knew deep down she was always going to go back to Andy and I'm glad that they're happy. Even if I did lose a mate. Are you sure you don't want another drink?'

She couldn't sit here any more, listening to him opening his heart when she couldn't do the same. She forced lightness into her voice. 'No, I guess we should get back. Getting out for a while feels like playing truant from school.'

His eyes warmed. 'I've never met anyone who works as hard as you do.'

'Is that supposed to be a compliment?'

'Yeah, I guess it is.' He leaned across and picked up their glasses and for a second he was very close to her. She could smell the faint citrus smell of something he wore and she felt a little shiver of excitement run through her. She glanced at him and their eyes held and Jade knew he was as conscious of her as she was of him. Supercharged with awareness, she couldn't breathe.

He dropped his gaze and got up to take their empty glasses across to the bar. Jade hugged her arms around herself and tried to get the bittersweet ache of longing out of her throat. By the time he came back, loping in that casual, easy way he had, she was in charge of her breathing again.

They drove back in companionable silence and Jade thought once again about Sarah. Since she and Callum had come over to announce their engagement, they'd been rushing around organising things and hadn't been over to the rescue much. And although Jade knew the real reason why Sarah kept away, she'd tried to put it to the back of her mind. Fortunately, Finn hadn't asked about Sarah. Neither had he mentioned the painting lessons he'd offered Ben. Maybe he felt embarrassed about their past encounter. Whatever the reason he kept quiet, Jade was relieved.

Let Sarah have her happiness. Until this conversation with Finn, she'd even begun to think Sarah might be right. What Finn didn't know couldn't hurt him. But now the doubts that had nagged at the corners of her mind came crowding back. Finn wasn't just some faceless stranger any more. He was the sort of person who cared – he'd put himself in danger to protect someone else's wife and child. Jade was very aware that he must have known exactly what he was risking when he'd taken in Shona and Stewart, but he'd done it anyway.

She sighed as Finn pulled up outside Duck Pond Rescue and he looked at her quizzically.

'Penny for them.'

'I was just thinking about what you said in the pub.'

'Ah – my murky past,' he said dryly. 'You must tell me about yours some time, Jade.'

'Yes,' she gulped, leaping out of the car and hurrying towards the house. Fleetingly she hated Sarah for putting her in this position, but she hated herself more. What would Finn do when he found out the truth and the part she'd played in keeping it from him?

25

Prompted by the chat she'd had with Maggie Crowther about animal sponsorship, Jade had decided to set up her own scheme. Dawn said she'd take photographs of their most photogenic animals, while Jade wrote a piece about each one. The idea was that prospective sponsors paid an annual fee and received an adoption pack, which included a photograph and information about their chosen animal.

When Finn saw their photographs, he offered to do some sketches.

'It would be a bit different, don't you think? Might help to drum up business.'

'All right, but you must let me pay you for doing them. You work enough hours already.'

'Don't be daft, Jade, I enjoy it. It's a pity Ben doesn't come over so much these days. He could help. How's he getting on with his painting?'

'Great,' Jade muttered, aware of his curious gaze and feeling heat in her face. 'But they've got masses on at the moment, what with organising their wedding.'

'I'm sure they have.' Finn's voice was ultra-casual and, anxious to get off the subject of Ben, Jade said, 'How's your dad now? Is he over his flu bug yet? Did he say when he wants to come down?'

'He's still coughing. But he sounds a lot better than he was. I spoke to him last night. If it's still OK with you, he'll probably come for a week in May.'

'Yes, that'll be great.' Jade's mobile rang and she made her escape. The caller turned out to be Sarah, wanting to know if she fancied a drink at the Red Lion that night to discuss wedding plans.

'Of course, I'd love to come. Will it just be the two of us?'

'Yes, Callum's babysitting, and we haven't had a girlie night for ages, have we?'

'No,' Jade said pointedly, but if Sarah heard the irony in her voice she didn't comment.

* * *

As she got ready to go out that night, she decided to make a supreme effort to keep the talk on weddings.

Sarah was already there when she arrived, sitting at a table with two large glasses of wine and a pile of glossy wedding magazines in front of her.

She waved as Jade came in and Jade flew across to hug her and then sat opposite.

'So how's it all going? I haven't seen much of you lately.' She glanced at the pretty diamond ring on Sarah's finger – Sarah had at least popped in briefly to show her that – and tried to keep her voice neutral. It was like treading on eggshells talking to Sarah these days.

'We're getting there. We've booked the registry office for next April, third weekend. I know it's ages away but put it in your diary. After, we'll go down to the Red Lion for pie and mash. There'll just be a few friends, Callum's family, and my parents, we don't want a big fuss.' She paused. 'Although that's one of the good things that's happened lately. I'm on speaking terms with my parents again. I took Ben to see them this week. He's thrilled at the idea of Callum being his dad. He's thrilled at the idea he's got some new grandparents too.' Her eyes willed Jade not to say he might have another set, so she didn't.

'That's brilliant news.'

'Isn't it?' Sarah flushed and changed the subject. 'Dawn said she'll do the photographs for us. I was wondering if you fancied coming to help me choose a dress some time? There's no rush – I'll probably get it a bit closer to the date.'

She looked so happy that Jade felt herself softening; how could she not be happy for her?

'I'd love to. You know I would.' She caught Sarah's hand across the table. 'I'm so pleased for you. Callum's lovely, isn't he?'

'I know.' Sarah's smile was radiant, and there was a little pause and Jade let go of Sarah's fingers and wished things were different. Wished that Ben's father were some unknown stranger, far away from here, and not someone she cared about so much. And she did care. It was rapidly becoming pointless to try to deny it – even to herself. She dropped her gaze, but Sarah didn't miss the look.

'Please don't be angry with me, Jade. I am going to tell Finn. But just not yet.'

'I'm not angry, just worried. I don't want all this to backfire on you.'

'How can it?' Sarah pursed her lips. 'You're the only other person in the world who knows the truth about Ben's father.'

'Yes,' Jade murmured, wondering whether she should tell Sarah how she felt about Finn. Not that she was 100 per cent sure herself. She seemed to go through the whole range of emotions when he was around. Lust, fear, warmth, tenderness, guilt. Guilt had been the main one lately. But then she'd always been plagued with that. It was part of her genetic make-up, she sometimes thought.

She sipped her wine and changed the subject to safer territory. 'Aiden asked me out again last week.'

'What did you say?'

'No, of course. He didn't take it very well. I felt really guilty.' She paused, deciding it would probably be better not to tell Sarah what else Aiden had said.

'It's him, isn't it? Finn.' He'd spat out the word as if he didn't want it in his mouth. 'I knew this would happen.'

She'd drawn back from him, alarmed by the pain on his face.

'It's got nothing to do with anyone else. Honestly, Aiden. I just don't want a relationship. Not with you. Not with anyone.'

And though finally he'd seemed to accept it, she still felt uneasy. He was back to coming daily to socialise Fang. Fortunately, so far, Finn had kept out of his way.

'Aiden will get over you sooner or later,' Sarah murmured, taking a gulp of wine and not meeting Jade's eyes. 'It's a shame you don't fancy him, because...'

'Then you'd be off the hook,' Jade finished, regretting the words as soon as she'd said them.

'No, I didn't mean that. I just meant you deserve someone nice, and he is nice, isn't he? I want you to be happy, Jade. I want you to feel what I'm feeling.'

There was an awkward little silence, which was broken by Mike striding over to their table, rubbing his hands together. 'Evening, ladies. Is Finn coming in tonight by any chance? Only I've got some good news for him. I've just sold one of his paintings.'

They glanced up at his happy, bearded face.

'Er, I'm not sure.' Jade smiled back at him. 'Which one? Stonehenge?'

'No. It was the one of the little girl on the beach. To the woman in the twin set and pearls over there. Said it reminds her of her granddaughter.'

The woman, who was sitting on a bar stool, raised her glass to them.

'She said she'd like to meet the artist. Could you give him a ring on his mobile, Jade?'

'Of course.' Jade glanced at Sarah.

'My cue to go, I think.' She stood up. 'Don't worry, I've got to get back anyway. I can't drink any more, I'm driving. Thanks for tonight.'

'Something I said?' Mike asked, raising his eyebrows as Sarah hurried towards the door.

'She's got a lot to do, wedding things,' Jade told him, glancing at her watch and deciding she'd have to wait for Finn. She couldn't just phone him and disappear. He'd be hurt.

* * *

He arrived surprisingly promptly. He was wearing his smartest jeans and was freshly shaven. He looked nervous, she saw with a little tug of tenderness. When he saw her, he headed across and pulled out a chair.

'So is she still here then, this woman? Or are you going to tell me this is a wind-up?'

'Of course it's not a wind-up. You should have more faith in yourself. You're really good.'

He reddened and Jade touched his arm. 'I'm serious, Finn. She's sitting at the bar. Go over and Mike will introduce you.'

'I'll get you a drink.'

'I'm up to my limit already.'

'Oh, go on. You're not driving and you can't celebrate with me unless you've got a drink.'

* * *

'She wanted me to write on the back of it for her,' Finn said when he finally came back with their drinks. 'I didn't like to just rush off.'

'Don't worry. It gave me the chance to sober up. Congratulations. Is that your first sale?'

'To a stranger, yes.' His grey eyes were warm. 'A few people back home have bought them, but I was never sure if they were just being nice.'

'Here's to many more,' Jade said, and they clinked glasses. Then they chatted for a while longer about art until eventually Jade stood up. 'I'd better get back. Are you staying?'

'No, I'll walk with you.'

It was relaxing walking back with the darkness settling around them and the odd nocturnal rustle in the hedgerows reminding them they weren't the only living creatures out in the still night. The blackthorn was in flower, its sweetness scenting the air, and there was a new lemon sliver of a moon. Above their heads, thousands of stars speckled the clear sky.

'Have you ever tried to count them?' Finn asked, tilting back his head and standing still for a moment in the middle of the country road.

'No.' Jade looked at him, surprised.

'Sometimes, if I can't sleep, I count the ones I can see out of my skylight. Twenty-three's the record so far. Might just beat it tonight.'

'Do you often have problems sleeping?'

'Not really. But I'll definitely have problems tonight. You must think I'm mad, getting all excited over a painting.'

'I don't think that at all. But then maybe I'm not a very good person to judge the sanity of others – being a bit mad and idealistic myself.'

'Ouch. And there was me thinking you'd forgotten that conversation.'

'I don't forget much, Mr McTaggart.' She went across and stood next to him in the middle of the road. It must be the wine. Maybe she wasn't as sober as she'd thought. Or maybe it was because tonight his face was unguarded and happy and his enthusiasm was infectious.

'Your dad's going to be pleased too, isn't he?'

'He'll be surprised I've sold something. He's always insisted there's no money in painting. But yes, I think he'll be pleased.'

Impulsively, she caught hold of his hands. 'You've got artists' fingers,' she said, lifting them up and studying them. 'Do you get those from your dad?'

'I'm not sure. I'll have to check.' There was a moment's silence, as if each of them had suddenly become aware they were holding hands. And in the silence Jade realised her heart was thumping very quickly. She dared not look at him for fear he'd read her expression and guess she could have stood here all night, just holding hands with him, it felt so right.

Shocked at the strength of her feelings, and still without looking at him, she said, 'So what's the plan, then – with your dad, I mean?' Because suddenly words were ambiguous.

'He's a lot better. I said I'd phone him tomorrow to firm up dates. He'll come down by coach. We'd better get going; we'll get run over, standing in the middle of the road.'

He withdrew his fingers gently from hers.

26

They walked back with a little space between them, although Jade wasn't sure who was creating it.

When they reached the cottage, he went ahead of her into the kitchen and leaned back on the worktop beside the kettle. 'I think I'll skip coffee; I could do without the caffeine.'

'There's half a bottle of wine in the fridge.' Jade liberated it and when he nodded, she poured them both a glass. 'Shall we drink these in the other room?'

They went through and sat where they usually sat: Jade on the sofa and Finn on the armchair opposite. Mickey, who'd come to greet them, got back in his basket and went back to sleep.

'It's very peaceful here,' Finn said after a few moments' silence. 'Perhaps that's why I couldn't sleep when I first came here. I was so used to the noise of the traffic. My flat in Nottingham was close to a main road and there was always traffic. Even in the early hours of the morning.'

'Yes, I found the same thing when I first came back from Bristol. Although to be honest I don't think I'd have slept wherever I was. I felt too guilty about Mum. If I'd have taken over Arleston

Court like she wanted me to, she wouldn't have been so stressed. But I couldn't do it. I loathed that place and Mum and I always had such a difficult relationship.' She stared at her hands.

'With hindsight, I wonder if I was just being selfish. Maybe she wouldn't have had that final stroke if I'd done what she wanted me to do.' Where had all that come from? She definitely shouldn't have had that last glass of wine. She shifted uncomfortably, aware of Finn's eyes on her.

'You came back when she needed you. You gave up your dreams of being a vet.' His eyes were soft. 'I don't call that selfish.'

'That wasn't the only reason I gave up being a vet. I realised I couldn't do it anyway.' She told him about the slaughterhouse, expecting him to make light of it – say it was a hard fact of life she needed to get used to – like her mother had said, and since then one or two other people had echoed.

But Finn didn't make any trite remark. He just nodded and listened and so she went on.

'It was too little, too late,' she whispered, feeling the familiar ache of grief inside her and for once putting how she felt into words because it was easy to talk to Finn in the peace of this little room. 'She might not have died if I'd have been a better daughter – if I'd done what she wanted.'

Now he leaned forward in his chair, chin on hands, his eyes serious. 'Don't torture yourself, Jade. Everything's easy with the benefit of hindsight. You did what you thought was right at the time.' He paused. 'So why this place? Why an animal rescue?'

'Because by then I'd realised that a vet is a silly place to work anyway if you really love animals.' She gave him a bittersweet smile. 'People used to bring them in and ask us to put them down. For all sorts of reasons. They were moving house, having babies, changing jobs. It used to break my heart.' She sipped her wine and looked at him. 'Am I being boring?'

'Not at all, I'm interested.'

So she carried on – telling him how the vets almost always became philosophical across the years. It was better for a dog to be humanely destroyed than dumped on a motorway.

'I knew that they were right – well, the logical part of me did, but I wanted to do something concrete. When I was at the practice where I did day release, I felt so helpless about all those unwanted animals. I set up a mini-rescue scheme, but I used to dream about having a place like this. Then, when I lost Mum, well, I thought it was a good time. I had the money from the sale of the hotels. They were bought by a big chain, and I wanted to do something with it. Something all-consuming. Something that would help me get over her death.'

She glanced at him. 'I got dumped by my boyfriend, too. He was a couple of years older than me – he was a vet at the practice in Bristol. We used to work together – but what I didn't realise was that he didn't restrict himself to one woman at a time. He had three of us on the go.'

'Tosser,' Finn said, and she glanced at him.

'You don't approve, then? Some men would.'

'I'd say that one woman at a time was more than enough trouble.' His eyes were warm. 'It's gone midnight, Jade.'

'I know. I suppose we'd better go up. Although I can't say I feel particularly tired.' She took their glasses back out into the kitchen. When she came back, he was waiting for her at the foot of the stairs.

'Would you like to come and count stars?'

For a moment, she just stared at him. 'I'm not propositioning you, Jade. I'm serious. I bet you've never looked out of that skylight at night, have you?'

'I don't think I've looked out of it in the daytime, either.'

He started up the stairs and she followed him. On the landing by her bedroom door he glanced at her, the hint of a challenge on his face, and she amazed herself by going straight past her room and following him up the rickety staircase to his. He opened the door and gestured her ahead of him, but he didn't put on the light, and she had to stand for a few seconds to let her eyes adjust.

His room smelled faintly of citrus and that indefinable scent of man that was so hard to put into words. Jade felt relaxed and also emboldened by the wine. She glanced at the outline of his face. She could scarcely breathe.

'There's a perfect view if you lie on the bed,' he said, 'but to prove my intentions are honourable, you can probably see just as well if you sit on the end of it.'

She giggled and sat down and he came and sat beside her, the bed dipping under his weight. Their legs were touching. It was impossible not to touch, sitting side by side on the end of his single bed. Did he feel like she did? If he did, he must have had amazing self-control. If he made the tiniest move towards her, she knew she'd have no defence. She so badly wanted him to make the first move.

He didn't. Instead, he tilted his head back. 'We should have more or less the same angle like this. Let's see if we can beat twenty-three.'

They sat in silence and Jade began to count. At first, she could only see six, but then she realised he was right, there were a lot more. Much fainter, but just discernible. She still couldn't get past sixteen, though. Disappointed, she told him, 'I'm sure I could see more if I cleaned the skylight. It's got bird droppings all over it.'

'I can see twenty-seven,' he said with obvious satisfaction. 'Try looking harder.'

They sat a bit longer. It was odd how comfortable she felt sitting on Finn's bed in the dark. She sneaked a glance at him. His head was still tilted back, his strong face in profile, but he had his eyes closed.

'You're asleep,' she accused.

'No, I'm not.' He opened his eyes and gave her a sideways glance. 'I was just thinking how peaceful it was.' He held her gaze for a few seconds, his eyes soft in the half-light. She stared back at him. It was like being on the edge of a precipice. One more step and she'd be lost. The moment stretched out and she knew he was aware of it too.

'Still not tired?' he murmured.

'No, but we've got to get up early in the morning.' She felt so short of breath she could hardly speak. Dragging her gaze away from his, she said, 'I'm sorry, I'm keeping you up.'

'I'd be happy if you kept me up all night, Jade.' He touched her face with his fingers, the most fleeting, the most gentle of touches. 'But we'd probably regret that tomorrow.'

'Yes.' She ached for him to touch her again, but she made herself stand up, wondering exactly what they might regret. Then he stood up too, slightly taller than her. They were still facing each other, but they weren't as close as they'd been on the bed. It was easier to get things in perspective standing up. Easier to control her breathing and the frantic thumping of her heart.

'Night, Finn.' She forced herself to move across the room. When she reached the door, she looked back at him. He was still standing beneath the skylight, his face in shadow so it was impossible to tell what he was thinking.

'Night, Jade. Sweet dreams.'

It was only as she closed her own bedroom door that she realised how much tension was tightening her muscles. Tension because she'd ached for him to touch her, or because she was terrified he would? It was impossible to tell; she felt so weak and giddy. She undressed and got into bed, shivering slightly as the duvet touched her over-sensitised skin.

'Get a grip, Jade,' she told herself. But when she closed her eyes, all she could see was his face. And she knew she'd been kidding herself thinking that it didn't matter that a huge lie stood between them. She wanted nothing between them. She wanted him totally and utterly and she thought of Sarah's words: 'I want you to be as happy as I am, Jade.' And she thought how ironic it was that the one man she knew she could be happy with was as out of her reach as the stars.

27

'I hear Finn's sold a painting,' Aiden said. 'Clever bloke, isn't he?' He'd just arrived to take Fang out and caught Jade in reception.

'News travels fast.' She paused from the list she was making on her 'Things to Do' pad and glanced up at him. There were tight lines of stress around his eyes and his mouth was drawn into a thin line.

'I went into Mike's for a drink last night and he said you'd all been in together on Saturday.'

'It was just me and Sarah, actually,' she said, wondering why she felt the need to explain herself. 'Mike asked us to call Finn because the woman who was buying his painting wanted to meet him.'

'So what's she like then, this woman?' His voice was conversational, but there was a hint of something else in his eyes. Something she couldn't quite put her finger on.

'In her fifties, fairly posh. Why do you ask?'

'Mike said she was quite taken with "The Artist". I thought she might want to whisk him off to do some special commissions for her.'

'I doubt it. She's just an ordinary tourist, Aiden. She's staying in the village in an Airbnb with her family. I think the painting only caught her eye because it reminded her of her grand-daughter.'

Aiden came across to the desk, sat heavily in the swivel chair opposite her and twisted it from side to side so it squeaked. 'Pity.'

'He's not a bad guy. I don't know why you dislike him so much.'

'I don't dislike him, but I thought this was only going to be a temporary arrangement. I thought he was just working here while he looked for another job. One more suited to his many talents.'

There was that edge to his voice again. It was beginning to annoy her. 'Maybe he just hasn't found one yet. There's not a lot going round here.'

'There was the perfect job for him in the *Farming Times*. Maintenance Engineer at Jacob's pig farm. That's what he does, isn't it – maintenance?' Aiden produced a slip of paper from his pocket and pushed it across the desk towards her. 'I cut it out for him. Just in case he'd missed it.'

'That's nice of you, Aiden,' she said evenly, folding up the paper without looking at it. 'I'll make sure he gets it.'

His dark eyes flashed and he stood up. 'It's curry night at the Crown and Anchor on Friday. Do you fancy coming with me?'

'I can't, Aiden, no. Finn's dad is coming on Friday. They've asked me to go to Mike's with them in the evening for something to eat.'

He didn't reply, just gave her a curt nod, and the momentary pang she felt at not inviting him along passed. Besides, she was sure he knew Finn's dad was coming on Friday. Mike would no doubt have passed that on, too.

She watched him stalk out of reception, stiff-backed. Then the phone rang again and she found herself speaking to a nurse who'd seen Jade's advert and was interested in re-homing the horse with behavioural issues, depending on what they were. In her excitement, Jade forgot all about Aiden.

* * *

'Are you staying there all night?' Finn came into reception just as dusk was beginning to creep across the yard. 'Only I was just going to lock up.'

She yawned. 'I've been immersed in paperwork. Time flies when you're enjoying yourself, doesn't it! Anyway, isn't Aiden still here?' She glanced out of the window and answered her own question. 'That's strange, he didn't say goodbye.'

'I don't think he was in a very good mood,' Finn said. Actually, that was the understatement of the year, but he didn't intend to tell Jade about the little exchange they'd had earlier.

'He brought this in for you.' She handed him a slip of paper and he scanned it.

'Pig farm assistant, eh?'

'Is that what it says?' She looked startled. 'He told me it was a maintenance engineer job.'

'His idea of a joke, I expect.' Finn crunched the paper into a ball and tossed it into the wastepaper basket by the desk. 'He doesn't like me very much, does he?'

'He can be a bit spiky at times. He'll get over it.'

Finn doubted that. Aiden was besotted with Jade. It didn't take a genius to work out that he thought Finn stood between him and the object of his affections. Some hope, he thought wryly, when she was still keeping her distance from him. It had to be because of Sarah. He was sure she had feelings for him and he could think of no other reason for her reticence. Perhaps she was waiting for him to bring up the subject, but it was a hard subject to raise. He could hardly just say, 'Oh, about that one-night stand with your friend. It didn't mean anything, we were both too drunk to know what we were doing.' Well, he supposed he could, but it wouldn't be very tactful. Jade and Sarah were close. He didn't want to say anything that would put Sarah in a bad light. And the only other way to do it was to say he'd taken advantage of her – which would be worse. It was a catch-22 situation.

'So are you looking for another job, then?' She was watching him, her dark eyes serious.

'Why? Had enough of me?'

'No, of course not.' She smiled and his stomach twisted. Why was it so difficult to just walk across the room and tell her he really cared about her? He'd never been so hesitant with a woman before. But then he'd never cared so much before about the possibility of being rejected.

'I keep an eye on the papers, but there isn't a lot around. You'll say, though, won't you, if it gets tricky to pay me?'

'I think I can afford you for another couple of months,' she said lightly.

They went into the cottage and Finn found himself checking over his shoulder, just in case Aiden had decided to make a re-appearance. Crazy, he knew, but then there'd been craziness in the guy's eyes earlier when he'd cornered him up at the kennels.

'Think you've got your feet right under the table now, don't you, mate?' had been his opening sentence.

'I'm not with you,' Finn said, playing for time.

'Jade's not interested in you, you know. So don't start getting any ideas.'

Finn had met Aiden's furious eyes with a calmness he didn't feel. 'Look, whatever problem you've got, it's in your own head. I work for her. That's it. Not that it's got anything to do with you.'

'You think you've got a right cushy number, don't you?' Aiden had been almost dancing around in his anger. 'You might share the same house, but you'll never get any further than that with her. Not while I'm around. Got it?'

If it had come to a fight, Finn had no doubt he could handle Aiden, but he knew that flattening him in the middle of the yard, however tempting, wasn't the answer. Jade was not going to be impressed if she had to scrape her vet off the concrete, and he didn't fancy getting sacked over Aiden. With a huge effort of will, he'd turned away from the almost palpable anger in the other man's face.

'I'm not interested. So just leave it, will you.' Eventually his words had registered and Aiden had stalked away towards the kennels. It could have been nasty, though, he thought now. And he couldn't see the situation improving. Not while Aiden was still pursuing Jade.

'You look miles away.' Jade's voice interrupted his thoughts. 'Did you have anything to eat earlier, or would you like some tea? I've got some quiche if you fancy it.'

'No, I'm all right, thanks. I grabbed a sandwich earlier. Think I might just finish that painting I started.'

'The one of the magpies?'

'Yeah. All right if I shower first?'

'Feel free.' She was frowning now. 'Did Aiden say anything to you earlier?'

'Not much. See you in the morning.'

* * *

Jade spent the days prior to Ray's visit cleaning the cottage from top to bottom, helped by an interested Mickey, who followed her around because she quite often discovered forgotten dog toys down the sides of cupboards or interesting out-of-date food.

'There's really no need,' Finn told her when he caught her on her knees, scrubbing out the kitchen cupboards at 11.30 p.m. one night. 'He'll take us as he finds us.'

'I don't want him to think you're living with a complete slob,' she said, smiling at him. 'Anyway, you're just as bad as me. I've hardly seen you this week, there can't be anything else that needs doing outside.'

'I've been painting. The light's perfect in the evenings at the moment and Mike wants me to fill the space on his wall.'

'What about all those little signs you've been putting up everywhere? I notice you've renamed the quarantine block New Arrivals.'

'It's so Dad can find his way around. He hasn't got a very good sense of direction.'

Jade looked puzzled, but Finn didn't tell her the real reason he'd been carving and painting the wooden signs was because it kept him outside for longer hours. If he were out of Jade's way, he wouldn't be tempted to proposition her. As soon as Ray's visit was over, he decided he would sit her down and talk to her about Sarah. Then he would tell her how he felt about her and if she threw it back in his face, well, he'd have to deal with it. It had to be better than carrying on like this. Being so close to her and yet so far away – it was agonising.

28

The day before Ray's visit, the nurse who was interested in re-homing Ashley came to see him. Jade didn't know what she'd expected, but it wasn't the stunningly attractive girl who came rather uncertainly into reception and introduced herself as Kate Turner. She had long, coppery gold hair and intense dark eyes and she was younger than she'd sounded on the phone. She looked as though she'd be more at home on a catwalk than a hospital ward, Jade decided, feeling dowdy in comparison. She found herself hoping, somewhat irrationally, that Finn wouldn't materialise while they were talking.

Kate was wearing jodhpurs and carrying a riding hat and obviously expected to ride Ashley, which threw Jade a bit because the horse was still in his field. She'd groomed him, first thing, but she hadn't thought to bring him in.

'How come Ashley ended up here?' Kate asked as they walked up to see him.

Jade hesitated. Kate was a nurse, for goodness' sake, so why did she suddenly feel embarrassed at bringing up the subject of Ashley's overdeveloped sex drive?

She was saved from having to answer straight away by Kate's exclamation of delight. 'Oh, wow, is that him?'

They'd reached the paddock and Ashley, spotting the bearer of polo mints, pricked his ears and came trotting across to greet them. His summer coat was coming through and it gleamed chestnut in the morning sunshine. He looked the picture of health, his head and tail high, as he wheeled to a halt by the gate. Compared to the other horses in the paddock, he looked a prince, Jade thought with a little rush of pride.

'Yes, this is Ashley.' She stroked the horse's nose and fed him a polo.

Kate patted his neck, her face animated. 'He's very handsome. I never expected him to look like this. How high is he? He's obviously easy to catch.'

'About fifteen two, I think. And yes, he's never been a problem that way.'

'But he is a problem in other ways?' Kate's voice was doubtful as she picked up on Jade's tension. 'Does he buck or something? I don't want to take on a dangerous horse.'

'He's not dangerous,' Jade rushed on, annoyed with herself. She was going to blow this if she didn't get her act together. 'He's just...' Why on earth couldn't she bring herself to say the words? She could see Finn heading towards them. God, she was going to have to say something before he reached them.

'He's rather fonder of the ladies than he should be. Actually, well, to put it bluntly, he's a bit of a sex maniac.'

'He's a sex maniac!' Kate repeated loudly, and Jade realised, with intense embarrassment, that she'd followed her gaze and was looking at Finn as she spoke. 'Haven't you had him gelded, then?'

'Sounds like an interesting conversation,' Finn said, shooting a sideways look at Jade. 'She'd have everything neutered round here if she had the chance.' He grinned at Kate and added, 'But I haven't let her catch me yet.'

Jade glared at him. 'Did you want anything in particular, Finn?'

'I was just going into town for bits and pieces. Need anything picking up? I hear they've got some DIY gelding kits on special offer. I could get probably get a discount on a bulk buy.'

'No, we don't need anything. Thank you.'

Finn, completely unfazed by the sharpness of her voice, just nodded. Then, with another grin at Kate, he loped off down the yard.

Jade turned back to Kate, who was looking puzzled at this exchange. 'He's got a strange sense of humour. Anyway, as I was saying, Ashley's here because he embarrassed his previous owner by – er – mounting a mare in the show ring. Unfortunately, the mare already had a little girl on her back.'

Kate clapped a hand over her mouth, her eyes widening.

That's it, Jade thought. She won't want him now. But, to her surprise, Kate seemed more amused than anything else.

'Is it all right for me to have a ride on him? Or perhaps I should rephrase that?' She giggled and Jade found herself warming to her.

'I'll nip and get his tack for you. It's in the house.'

Finn was getting into his car as she passed. He winked at her and drove off before she could say anything.

Twenty minutes later, Jade leaned on the fence and watched Kate trot Ashley round the field. He tossed his head and high stepped and generally looked very full of himself, which wasn't surprising, Jade thought, as no one had ridden him since he'd been here. She'd meant to take him out herself, but she never had time to do much that wasn't essential, and she'd also worried about falling off. She couldn't afford to be injured.

Kate could ride, though, she observed, pleased. She looked good on him, her auburn hair streaming in the sunshine, her back very straight.

Rosanna, who was grazing with Conker and Sparky on the other side of the field, lifted her head to watch and Jade started to feel optimistic. It would be such a relief if Kate took Ashley on. She wondered if she should mention his escapist tendencies. Perhaps not. It wasn't as if he'd jumped out of the field lately, or undone any bolts, but then he hadn't had any reason to.

Kate trotted the horse over to the fence where Jade stood. 'He's lovely,' she said when she'd got her breath back. 'Just what I'm looking for. I've always wanted a horse, but I never thought I'd be able to afford one.'

'They're not cheap to keep,' Jade cautioned.

'I know, but I'm lucky there. My Uncle Arthur owns Willett's stud farm on the other side of Salisbury. It's where I'm planning to keep Ashley. That shouldn't be a problem, should it? It's not as though he's going to be able to get in with any mares.'

Jade looked up into her enthusiastic face and her conscience got the better of her. 'Ah. I'm afraid that might be more of a problem than you think. He's a good escape artist too.'

Aiden arrived just as Kate and Jade were carrying Ashley's tack back towards the cottage. Jade felt herself tensing as he parked up, but all he did was give her a cursory nod and go into reception.

He was sitting in a chair when she went back in with Kate.

'I've just brought in a couple of invoices. Is there any particular reason why your post box is taped up?'

'There's a pair of great tits nesting in it, I didn't like to turf them out.'

Aiden shook his head in mock exasperation, but he didn't

smile and Jade had a horrible feeling he was going to have another go at her about Finn.

'Kate's thinking of having Ashley,' she said, deciding that at least he'd be pleased about that. 'We've just been chatting about his problems.'

'Yes, it's a shame because I really like him. But I'm going to have to rethink my stabling arrangements. I was going to keep him at Willett's stud farm, you see, but in view of his, er – tendencies, Jade thinks that wouldn't be a good idea.'

'It'd be torture for the poor sod.' Aiden gave Jade a pointed look. 'I'd go so far as to say cruel.'

Jade flushed and wondered if Kate was aware of the atmosphere, but she didn't seem to be. She turned back to Jade, her eyes warm. 'I'll have to try and find some cheap alternative stabling. I'll be in touch – it's good that you've ruled out a hormonal problem. A behavioural problem might be easier to sort out. I'll have a word with my uncle and see what he thinks.'

'Of course.' They shook hands and Kate nodded at Aiden and went out into the yard. Jade watched her through the window.

'Pity about that,' she said to Aiden. 'She'd have been ideal.'

'You'd better keep your fingers crossed that something can be done about his urges, then,' he remarked, giving her another black look. 'Is it all right if I nip up and see Fang?'

Jade nodded. It was on the tip of her tongue to say something, but Finn would be back any minute. There was no way she could start a 'clearing the air' conversation if there was a risk of him walking in on them. She took the invoices. Their talk would have to wait. With a bit of luck, in another week or two it might not even be necessary. Aiden might get over his crush on her. One thing was certain. If he didn't get over it soon, then she was going to have to seriously think about getting another vet.

* * *

She told Finn about Kate's stabling problem later that night as she washed up the plates from their tea. 'It's such a shame. It was going so well. Although I could have done without your smart remarks about DIY gelding kits.'

He picked up a tea towel and grinned at her. 'Touch a nerve, did I?'

'No, you did not touch a nerve.'

'You mean you don't want to neuter all the males in the vicinity? How about Aiden?' His grey eyes challenged hers.

Was he insinuating she'd led Aiden on? She was already regretting she'd ever gone out for that meal.

'Why don't you mind your own business?' she said, more abruptly than she'd meant to.

He put the tea towel down and raised his hands in self-defence. 'Oooh, I have touched a nerve, haven't I?'

'Don't be ridiculous.' Forcing indifference into her voice, she met his eyes and hoped he wouldn't be able to read her expression and see how close he was to the mark. Though it wasn't Aiden she was wary of. She was sorry he'd read more into their friendship than there was. But time would sort things out between them.

Finn, however, was a different matter. He unnerved her. Made her feel as though she could break apart under his gaze. Especially the way he was looking at her now. Half quizzical, half knowing. Sarah had a lot to answer for, she thought, blinking and turning away from him to study a damp patch on the wall just above the kettle.

It was a huge effort to keep her voice casual. 'I'm just disappointed that Kate's not taking Ashley. They'd have been good for each other. I feel as though I've failed him.'

'You haven't failed him.' Finn's tone changed completely, and he came across the kitchen. 'No one could work harder than you do, Jade. You go well beyond the call of duty for this lot. At the risk of you telling me to mind my own business again, I'd like to recommend that now and again, you spare a thought for yourself. There's a world out there, you know.'

She looked at him. All traces of mockery had gone from his face now and she felt choked.

'I'll bear that in mind,' she said and fled before he could take advantage of her shattered defences.

29

The following morning, escorted by Mickey, Jade walked round Duck Pond Rescue checking all was as it should be. Finn had left half an hour ago to pick up his father from the coach drop-off point. They'd be back soon. At least the sun was out, she thought with relief. Everything looked better when it was sunny. Diesel was lying on top of the chicken run, eyes closed, the tip of his black tail flicking.

'Monster,' she said as she passed, and he blinked sleepy golden eyes at her.

Satisfied that all was as it should be, Jade headed back towards reception. She planned to close up as soon as Finn's dad arrived. Anyone with a dire emergency could park outside the cottage and ring the bell.

She was just writing a note to put on the front gate when Finn's car drew into the yard. Iron-grey hair and a tweedy jacket were Jade's first impressions of his father. She waited while Finn switched off the engine and went round to open the passenger door, and then she went out to greet them.

'So this is that slave driver boss of yours. Ray McTaggart at your service,' the old man said as Finn introduced them.

Jade added a gravelly voice, a firm handshake and a direct gaze to her first impressions. 'Slave driver, hey? Is that what he's told you?'

His eyebrows arched above grey eyes that were very similar to Finn's, and to Ben's, and Jade was struck, once more, by the painful realisation that it wasn't just Finn she was deceiving.

Ray pumped her hand. Deep lines etched his face and he looked older than she'd expected.

For a moment he looked quite stern and then his face cracked into a smile. 'It's grand to meet you at last, my dear. Hope he's not been causing you too much trouble.'

'None I can't handle.' She glanced at Finn as she spoke, aware of his amusement. 'Well, would you like coffee before you start your grand tour?'

'I'd like a rollie,' Ray said. 'But I don't suppose that's allowed with all the straw an' stuff round here, is it?'

'Just make sure you put it out, and don't leave the butts on the ground.'

'I wouldn't dream of it.' Ray produced a portable ashtray from his pocket. It was stainless steel with a lid. 'I came prepared.'

'Great.'

'Don't encourage him,' Finn said. 'I've told him this is a strictly smoke-free zone.'

The phone rang and Jade apologised. 'Excuse me a minute. I'll put the answer machine on and catch up with you.'

* * *

By the time she'd dealt with the phone, locked up the main gate and got into the cottage, they were installed in her lounge, talking animatedly.

'So, did you have a good journey?' She sat next to Finn on the sofa and addressed his dad, who was in the armchair opposite. 'How long did it take?'

'Not bad and too long.' Ray winked at her. 'But that's coaches for you. At least they've got conveniences on them these days.'

'And coffee, Dad. You said that was quite good.'

'Aye, I suppose it wasn't bad. Not as good as yours, though. Or maybe it's the company.' He shot a glance at his son and Jade was struck by the pride on his face. Struck too by the warmth in Finn's eyes. Neither of them was the type for big declarations of emotion, she thought, but there was a lot of love there.

It was heart-warming to see. 'So, what are your plans for today?'

'First of all, I'm going to pick out the dog I'd most like to take home,' Ray said. 'Not that they're allowed on coaches, I shouldn't think. And then...' He was overtaken by a fit of coughing that seemed to rack his whole body. It was painful to listen to and when he finally stopped, Finn said, 'That's why he shouldn't be smoking.' There was a mixture of crossness and sadness in his voice.

'Stop fussing, lad.' He winked at Jade. 'I think it's a picnic lunch, isn't it? And then tonight I'm going to check out Finn's local – see if they've got any decent paintings on the walls.'

'You are still joining us later, I take it?' Finn added.

'I'm looking forward to it. Now, how about I show you around?'

As they went past the locked reception, Jade heard Finn say, 'That flu took a while to get over. What did Dr Jenkins say about it?'

'Not much. Seeing as I didn't tell him I had it. What's the point? Can't do 'owt, can they?'

Jade was following a couple of steps behind them, feeling a little surplus to requirements, when Ray suddenly turned. 'Now then, young lady, when does the grand tour begin?' He raised his eyebrows. 'I want to know all the ins and outs of the place.'

He wasn't joking either, she realised as they went round. At the hospital block he wanted to know all the details of the animals that had recently been treated there. Jade told him about the red kite with the injured wing that now regularly flew over the land, and about the mallard with the injured beak who was now back with her mate on the duck pond he'd passed on the way in. She told him about how Mickey had ended up becoming a permanent resident, and about Candy's pups and how even Candy herself had been re-homed with their pet food supplier. Reg had kept his promise and given Jade a proper discount on her pet food too.

She glossed over the fact she still had Tiny. He was the last of the pups and at twelve weeks old had just had his second vaccination, but Jade hadn't found a good enough home for him yet.

Then Ray wanted to know all about the current residents of the cattery and how come that black beggar had escaped and was sitting on the chicken run, looking like he owned the place.

'Diesel,' Finn explained, repeating the story of how the big black cat had had much of his fur burnt off when he'd been trapped under the bonnet of a diesel truck.

And why did they have chickens anyway? What did they need rescuing from?

'They're ex-battery hens,' Jade said. 'They don't have very long lives in battery farms. It's too intensive and as soon as egg production goes down, they're for the chop. But once they get back to something resembling a normal life, they start laying again. We sell the eggs to raise funds.'

Eventually, they went up towards the kennels, stopping short of the gate that led to the first two kennel blocks.

'Once we go in, we won't be able to hear ourselves think,' Jade told Ray. 'So I'll tell you about the dogs out here, then you can have a wander round. I'll sit in the sun and wait for you.'

They weren't gone long, five minutes or so, and Jade sat at the wooden picnic bench, with her face turned up to the sun, and felt very relaxed. Two magpies had just flown into the tree in the field next door. Two for joy, she thought, remembering the old rhyme. A good omen for today.

Then the gate clanged, and Finn called, 'Is it all right if I take Dad up to New Arrivals? He wants to see Fang.'

'You carry on. You can take her out if you like. She doesn't normally get a walk at this time of day.'

Ray and Finn reappeared with Fang on a lead. The small dog was wagging her stubby tail and looking very pleased with herself. She and Mickey sniffed noses and did some more wagging.

'Aiden's done wonders with that dog,' Jade called out to them. 'A couple of months ago and she'd have had your hand off. Mind you, I still wouldn't trust her with a child.'

'Would you trust her with an old man?' Ray asked. 'She's my type of dog, she is.' He bent to fondle the Jack Russell's head and she pricked her ears.

Finn came across to where she sat and put his hand on Jade's arm. A casual little gesture, but as she glanced at his fingers, she was reminded of the night she'd held them and asked him if he'd inherited them from his father.

'Dad could have a dog, you know. He's got a lovely little

garden. And no cats for her to terrorise. She'd have a nice life with him.'

Jade smiled up at him. He'd had his hair cut for his father's visit and his face was tanned from being outside and she was very aware of his touch.

'Well, she's up for re-homing like all the rest of them. Why doesn't he take her for a walk round the field? See how he gets on.'

* * *

Aiden frowned as he parked outside the cottage, read Jade's note and unbolted the side gate. He was sure Jade had said they were going out this evening, not out to lunch. She never closed the place up in the day. What if there was an emergency?

Then something else struck him. She'd been offish with him all week. Perhaps she'd just said they were going out this evening so she didn't have to go out with him. He wandered up the yard, opened the little gate that led to the upper part of the sanctuary, and froze.

Ahead of him by the picnic table, an old guy, presumably Finn's father, was bending down and petting Fang. The little Jack Russell, far from snapping and growling, had rolled over on to her back and appeared to be enjoying the attention. For weeks, Aiden had been the only one allowed near her, yet, as soon as his back was turned, Jade had let some unqualified bystander take her out without so much as a by-your-leave.

Jade was sitting at the table and Finn stood just beside her, one hand on her arm. She was looking up into his eyes and smiling that beautiful smile. Jealousy so sharp it was a physical pain cramped Aiden's abdomen and he could feel a pulse beating in his head. He clenched his fists into balls. Finn had been sniffing around Jade ever since he'd arrived and, not content with stealing her, he was after the little dog too. Something snapped inside Aiden's head and he stormed up the yard towards the group. It was high time Finn got what was coming to him.

30

Jade was the first to notice Aiden heading towards them. Even before he reached them, she could tell from his body language that he was furious, although she didn't have a clue why. She stood up uneasily, aware that at the same moment Finn had taken a step back from the table. 'Hi, Aiden. How's it going?'

But if Aiden heard her he didn't react. He just marched straight up to Finn and threw a punch at him.

Finn, who'd sensed what was about to happen just before it did, dodged. He didn't get the full fury of Aiden's fist, which was just as well or it would probably have broken his nose, but the blow still knocked him off balance.

'Good God.' Ray, reacting more quickly than any of them, dashed to his son's side, elbowing Aiden to one side in the process. 'Are you all right, lad?'

'What the hell do you think you're doing?' Jade yelled at Aiden at more or less the same moment. 'Have you gone completely mad?'

Aiden stood blinking in the sunlight, as if he wasn't fully

aware of what he'd just done. On his right, Finn held a hand to his bloody nose and straightened up slowly.

'Well, let's hope that's finally got it out of your system,' he said, his voice icy.

Jade could feel herself trembling. 'I think you'd better leave, Aiden. Before Finn takes it into his head to press charges for assault. Or I do.'

Aiden looked at her, confusion in his eyes. 'But what about Fang?'

'You've scared the life out of her.' Jade crouched down and held out her hand to the little dog, who was hiding beneath the picnic table, close to the security of Mickey, her whole body trembling violently. 'Get out of my sanctuary, Aiden. Before I call the police and have you thrown out.'

He turned, his shoulders round with defeat, and retraced his steps slowly down the yard.

For a few seconds, no one spoke, and then Finn said quietly, 'I think that if he's definitely gone, I'll just go and clean this up before I bleed all over my clean tee-shirt.'

'I'll come with you and make sure.' Jade glanced apologetically at Ray. 'I'm so sorry about that. He's normally such a mild-tempered chap. I'll be back in two minutes.' She went with Finn. 'Are you OK?'

'I'll survive. It's just a pity he had to pick today to stake his claim.'

'What claim? What are you talking about?' Jade went across to the main gate and saw to her relief that the jeep was gone. Finn didn't say anything else until they were standing inside the front door of the cottage.

'What all that was about,' he said looking at her, 'is that Aiden is in love with you. And he thinks I'm the reason you don't return his affections.'

She stared at him, confused. 'But you're not... I mean, we've never even – well...'

'It's not about us.' Finn's voice was unusually sharp. 'It's what's inside Aiden's head that counts.' He frowned and touched his face. 'Can I borrow your first-aid box? I think I'll sort this out in the bathroom. Come up a minute.'

'What about your dad?'

'He'll be fine. I expect he's having a sneaky rollie to calm his nerves.'

Upstairs, she sat on the edge of the bath while Finn sponged the blood off his nose. There was a small cut just above his lip.

'Does that hurt?'

'Yes, it does a bit.' He met her eyes in the mirror. 'But not half as much as it would have done if I hadn't ducked at the last minute.'

'I'm really sorry. I mean, I know he had a bit of a crush, but I'd no idea he was going to get violent about it. Or take it out on you.'

'It's not your fault. He's been getting crosser and crosser for a while. He had a go at me the other day when he brought the advert for that pig-farming job in. Perhaps I should have mentioned it, but I honestly didn't think it would come to this.'

'What did he say?'

'He warned me off you. That was about it. I certainly didn't wind him up. At least I don't think I did.' He dabbed at the cut. 'Mind you, having Fang out probably didn't help. His dog and his woman. He just exploded, didn't he?'

She nodded, clenching her hands in her lap. 'I'm not his woman. I'm not anyone's woman. What do you think I should do? About him hitting you, I mean. I can't let him think he's got away with it.'

'I don't think you should do anything. I think he shocked himself as much as he shocked us. I bet he's already regretting it.'

He sat beside her on the edge of the bath. 'Don't upset yourself over Aiden. I'm not. I just wish he hadn't done it in front of Dad.'

She reached out and touched his face just above the cut. 'That won't do much for your love life, will it?'

'You don't think so?' There was a softness in his eyes that belied the facetiousness of his voice. Then he caught her hand and kissed the tips of her fingers very gently. She looked at him, trembling slightly.

'Are you cold? Or just shocked?' Letting go of her fingers, he cupped her face in his hands and kissed her mouth and she found she was trembling again, not for either of the reasons he'd suggested, but because she was filled with a sudden desperate longing for him. She kissed him back, scared of hurting his mouth, but never wanting it to stop. At some point, as if by tacit agreement, they stood up, but even when they finally drew apart they were still holding hands.

'Seems to have done wonders for my love life,' Finn remarked. 'Maybe I should get myself thumped more often.'

'We're steaming up the mirror,' Jade whispered, looking up into his grey eyes, half enjoying the frantic flutterings in her tummy and half afraid of them.

'You're such a romantic.'

'Do you think we'd better go downstairs?'

'I can think of lots of things I'd much rather be doing, but yes, I think we'd better.' He searched her face. 'I wanted to do that the other night. You did too, didn't you?'

She hesitated, battling with the urge to tell him he was right and inwardly cursing Sarah because she couldn't let this go further. If she told him how she felt then she'd have no excuse to keep the distance between them. Finn could crash through her barriers and she wouldn't be able to stop him.

'Are you two all right up there?' Ray's voice came up the stairs.

'Only I reckon we should have a stiff drink with our lunch. Good for shock. I brought a bottle of nice malt down with me for Finn. Should I get the top off?'

Finn smiled, a little uncertainly. 'He never misses a trick.'

'So I see.' She pulled her hand from his, rubbed a patch in the mirror and glanced at her flushed face. 'Can we talk about this later?'

'Sure. You go down.' He indicated the first-aid box still open on the loo seat. 'I'll just clear up and I'll be with you.'

* * *

Half an hour later, once Jade had resettled Fang in her kennel and Mickey was mooching around the yard, they were sitting around the picnic table. Finn had brought out the sandwiches and crisps he'd got ready earlier, and Ray had sloshed a generous helping of malt whisky into his and Finn's glasses. Jade had said she'd stick to orange juice.

'Are you sure you don't mind me gate-crashing your lunch as well as gate-crashing your evening meal?' she asked Ray again. Joining their picnic hadn't been a part of the day's plan, but then the whole day was beginning to take on an unreal quality.

'Course not, lassie.' He chucked back his Scotch. 'I figured you might want some company in case that maniac turned up again. Are you sure I can't tempt you into a whisky? What'll you do, Finn?'

'Nothing. I'm sure it was a one-off. Aiden's not normally prone to violent mood swings. He must have had a bad morning. He's Jade's vet, Dad.'

'Is he now?' Ray swallowed thoughtfully. 'Not a very James Herriot thing to do, is it? Going around punching your customers. He could probably get struck off for that, couldn't he?'

'I'm not sure if vets do get struck off, as such,' Jade said, frowning.

'Well, I certainly won't be complaining,' Finn told him. 'Least said, soonest mended, I'd say.'

'Yeah, you're probably right. And there was me thinking the countryside was a nice, peaceful place where nothing ever happened. Still, there's nothing like a bit of excitement to work up an appetite. These sarnies look all right, lad. Shall we tuck in?'

Jade glanced at Finn. He was smiling, but he looked awfully tense. She wondered if he was regretting kissing her. And what had he meant about wanting to do it the other night? She'd wanted to do a lot more than kiss him on the night they'd counted stars. She'd wanted to take him to bed. She'd ached to feel his body pressed against hers. She still did. But the image of him with Sarah haunted her. And what if they did go to bed? Wouldn't that just make things worse? While she kept the distance between them, the fact that she was keeping Sarah's secret didn't seem so traitorous. She wasn't sure if she could sleep with him and still lie to him. She sighed, and then aware that neither she nor Finn had answered Ray's question, she fixed her attention on their guest.

31

Aiden drove away from Duck Pond Rescue with his head throbbing. There was no way he could go back to the practice. They'd have to cancel the rest of the afternoon's calls. He dialled the practice on his mobile, his hands shaking so much it took four attempts. Then he headed towards home. He pulled up in his driveway, switched off the engine and put his head in his hands. What the hell had he done? He wasn't aware of the tapping on the driver's window until it became a frantic knocking.

'Mr Southerland. Excuse me. Are you all right there?'

It was Emily, his next-door neighbour, he realised with a start. He lowered the window.

'I took a parcel in for you, this morning,' she said, her face wrinkling up into a frown. 'It was too big to go through your letterbox. Are you all right? You don't look very well.'

Aiden got out. He was about to say he was fine, but somehow the concern in her face made him feel even worse. He stood swaying in his driveway.

Emily put a hand on his arm. 'You're not all right, are you? Come and sit in my kitchen and I'll make you a nice cup of tea and you can tell me what's happened. Was it a bad case you've been to?'

He didn't have the energy to argue so he followed her through her yellow-painted front door into a hallway that smelt of lavender furniture polish. Despite being well past seventy, she trotted ahead of him and pushed open the kitchen door.

'Now, sit yourself down,' she bossed, indicating a stool along-side a modern breakfast bar.

Her kitchen wasn't what he expected. It wasn't an old lady's kitchen at all, but a modern affair, with yellow sunflower wallpaper, wooden cupboard doors and a top-of-the-range dishwasher and microwave. On the breakfast bar was a flat white parcel with his name on it.

'There you are.' She put a mug of tea beside him and nudged the sugar bowl across. 'Your colour's coming back now. You looked right poorly out there for a minute.'

Aiden smiled, despite himself. Emily reminded him of his own gran. She had the same inquisitive chocolate-button eyes and thought tea was the answer to everything. Unlike his gran, though, who'd had short cropped white hair, which she'd said was befitting when you got to a certain age, Emily had a long grey plait, which was coiled on top of her head in a sort of bun. It must take her ages to do that, he thought as she perched on a stool opposite him.

'What do you think of the kitchen, then? Kate, my youngest granddaughter, designed it for me.'

'It's very nice.'

'Yes, she's got good taste. Takes after me, see. Only I wanted something modern and I wouldn't have known where to start. Are you going to open that?' She glanced at the parcel, which had a label in one corner with the name Perfect Pooches emblazoned in gold across it.

'I already know what it is. It's a designer dog collar.'

'I didn't know you were getting a dog.'

'I'm not. It's for one of the dogs at Duck Pond Rescue.' Aiden closed his eyes and thought what lousy timing. The dog collar was for Fang. But she'd never see it now. He'd probably never see her again. Never see any of Jade's animals, come to that. She was hardly going to let a half-crazed vet back onto her premises. He'd be lucky if she didn't put in an official complaint. How could he have been so bloody stupid?

'Anyway...' Emily regarded him over her mug, her head on one side like a bird. 'Tell me what's been happening to you this morning. Cruelty case, was it?'

He sighed. She knew what he did because once, when he'd come back from a particularly bad case, he'd confided how much he hated that part of the job.

Since then, she'd taken a keen interest in what he was up to and often timed her outings to coincide with him getting into his jeep so she could interrogate him. To Aiden's shame, he'd taken to avoiding her. Not because she wasn't a sweet old dear, but he was normally running late and didn't have time for the long conversations she was fond of.

'I've done something really stupid.' He sipped his tea and met her eyes. 'I'm not sure if I can even bring myself to tell you.'

'I've done plenty of stupid things in my time. Nine times out of ten, we think they're a lot more stupid than anyone else does.'

'Not this time.' He fiddled with the sugar spoon and lowered his eyes. 'I've screwed up big time. I'm in love with this woman and I've just blown any chance I ever had with her.'

'It can't be all that bad. If she loves you too, you'll soon sort it out.'

'That's the trouble,' Aiden said bleakly, putting the sugar spoon down with a small clink on the breakfast bar. 'I don't think

222 DELLA GALTON

she's ever seen me as anything other than her vet. And after this morning, I'll be lucky if she ever speaks to me again.'

* * *

'The best thing you can do is to go round there and tell her you're desperately sorry,' Emily said after Aiden had told her the whole story. 'Explain you'd had a bad day, a moment of temporary insanity – whatever. If she's half the woman you say she is, I think she'll forgive you. Maybe not straight away, but in time.'

'Should I take flowers?'

'No, I don't think you should, love. Just take yourself and convince her you mean it. And don't forget to apologise to the lodger too. However much you dislike him. The sooner the better.'

Aiden thought about this conversation all afternoon. Emily was right. It wasn't just his professional reputation on the line, although that was reason enough to go back as soon as possible, it was his friendship with Jade. In every quiet moment, he could hear her shouting, 'Have you gone completely mad?' Every time he closed his eyes, he could see her shocked dark eyes. And then the coldness in her face when she'd told him to get out before she called the police.

Finn had looked pretty shocked too. In that moment, just after his fist had connected, he'd been sure Finn would hit him back. Sure he'd see his own furious anger reflected. Yet, there had been no anger in the bloke's eyes, just a kind of resigned acceptance. It was that expression, as well as Jade's horror, that was tormenting him.

It was the first time Aiden had ever punched anyone. Violence sickened him. It had done ever since school when he'd been bullied by Terry Bradshaw and his gang – held face down in the mud one sunny winter afternoon because he'd come top in English, biology and maths.

'Filthy little swot,' Terry had snarled, tipping his books into the puddle, too, and then stamping on them for good measure.

When his mum had asked him what had happened, he'd told her and she'd gone straight to the headmaster, demanding action. All the boys had been disciplined and after that he'd been beaten up regularly. Except that the gang were then careful where they put the bruises. Nowhere that showed. His groin or his lower back.

'Snitch again and you're dead,' Terry had told him one terrifying night. 'And don't think we don't know how.'

Aiden had believed them. He'd done his best to keep his head down after that. He still worked hard, but he was careful not to come top in anything again. Academic subjects were a doddle to him. It was easy enough to put in the odd wrong answer, which would keep Terry off his back. When it came to the real thing, he could just fill in the papers properly, secure in the knowledge that none of his classmates would ever know his final exam grades.

In some strange way, though, it was Terry's bullying that shaped his future career. Aiden had left school with twelve GCSEs and four A Levels and a burning passion to do something that would enable him to protect the vulnerable. He wasn't sure exactly what. Something in the social services possibly. He knew social workers got a bad press, but he'd be different. Idealistic and desperately shy, he'd got as far as doing the first year of the course. The academic side was a breeze, but he'd found it difficult to form relationships with the other students. He was too insular, too inward-looking, his tutors said. He should lighten up a bit. In the end, Aiden decided that working with people wasn't for him and left. Then his Uncle Seth had suggested that with his academic background he ought to try and get into veterinary college.

It made sense. Aiden didn't know why he hadn't thought of it before. Within a month of beginning, he knew he had found his vocation.

But today he'd been the perpetrator of exactly the sort of violence he'd always sworn to oppose. He sat at his kitchen table, which was a lot scruffier and less modern than Emily's breakfast bar, buried his head in his hands and felt sick. It was just after 8 p.m. and he hadn't eaten all day. Maybe that was the cause of the hollow dizziness in his stomach. Or maybe it was as Emily had said. He wouldn't feel better until he'd put things right. He couldn't go up there now because Jade had said they were all going to the Red Lion. On the other hand, he couldn't wait until tomorrow because if he did, he'd never get any sleep. He decided he'd have to go tonight when they were back from the pub. They wouldn't be that late. They had an early start the next day. Saturday was one of the rescue's busiest days.

* * *

'I don't know about you youngsters, but I think it's time I headed for bed,' Ray said, draining the last of his Guinness and clunking the glass back on the table. 'Quite an eventful day, one way or another.'

Finn glanced at Jade. 'Are you ready?'

She nodded. She looked strained, but then she had all evening. Earlier, when he'd kissed her, she'd been soft, almost vulnerably open. Now she seemed to be deliberately blocking him out again. Was she regretting it? Or was he being over-sensitive?

He took their empty glasses to the bar and walked back to the table, rubbing his eyes. He was tired and his face was sore where Aiden had hit him. Jade stood up as he reached them. She looked a bit lost and he had an urge to put his arm around her, tell her that everything was going to be fine. Maybe when Ray had gone to bed, they'd get the chance to talk. Really talk this time. He'd put off this conversation for long enough.

They walked in silence for the first part of the journey back. There was none of the easiness they'd shared the last time they'd walked home. There were no stars tonight either; clouds covered the sky and the air felt hot and oppressive.

'How's your face?' Jade asked him.

'Fine now.'

'I still think you should report that maniac to the police,' Ray muttered gruffly.

* * *

The lights of the cottage came into view as they reached the final stretch of the lane. What had gone wrong? Jade thought. How could Finn be so gentle and warm one moment and so distant the next? Maybe it was because Ray was with them. Maybe this was some sort of macho pretence that he was OK for his father's benefit.

She wondered what would happen when they got back. Would they just go in this awful, stiff silence to their respective rooms? Maybe it was best if they did. It was obvious Finn was finding the prospect of talking to her a huge ordeal, which, she decided, meant he was regretting kissing her earlier. Tonight, she'd touched his arm and he'd jumped away as though he'd been stung. She didn't need him to spell things out.

As they reached the hedge that surrounded the cottage, a shadow detached itself and materialised into a figure and Jade, already edgy, jumped out of her skin.

'Aiden!'

She heard Ray's sharp intake of breath and she could feel Finn's sudden tension beside her. 'What are you doing here?'

Aiden raised both hands, palms facing them. 'It's OK. I'm not here to cause trouble. I've come to apologise.' He hesitated, his face shadowy in the moonless night. 'To all of you. I'm so very sorry about earlier. I just wanted you to know.'

Jade didn't reply. She glanced at Finn, who'd gone very still as soon as Aiden had stepped out in front of them. Now, he cleared his throat, but he didn't say anything. There was tension in his shoulders, though, and she noticed he was keeping his distance from Aiden, as if he was worried the vet might suddenly change his tune.

'That's all I came to say,' Aiden went on quietly. 'I won't hold you up. I just wanted you to know how sorry I am. I couldn't have slept otherwise. Of course I appreciate that you'll be employing another vet. If you still want to use the practice, I'll make sure someone else responds to your calls.'

He looked diminished and Jade stepped forward so she was facing him. 'It's all right,' she said, looking into his dark, troubled eyes. 'We know it was out of character. I'm glad you came. We both are.' Half turning, she included Finn in the conversation and he gave the slightest of nods.

'Perhaps it would be best if you didn't come to the rescue for a while, though,' she said, hating to kick him when he was down, but knowing she owed that much at least to Finn.

'Of course. Good night.' He took a few steps away, and then, as if suddenly remembering something, he hesitated. 'I hope you don't mind, but I got this for Fang.'

He thrust a package into her hands and then turned and went to his jeep, which was parked out of sight, just beyond the entrance to the rescue. Only when she'd watched his taillights disappear around the bend in the road did Jade feel herself relax.

'You OK?' Finn was standing behind her.

'Yes. You?' She turned to look at him, but once again his eyes were unreadable.

'I'm glad I don't have to keep looking over my shoulder any more. Come on, let's go in.'

'Did you still want to have that talk later?' Finn asked once Ray had headed, yawning, for bed.

'No, I'm too tired. Like you said earlier, least said, soonest mended.'

'I said that about Aiden.'

'Goodnight, Finn,' she said, without looking at him. 'And thanks for the meal, I enjoyed tonight.'

He looked defeated, but he left the room, and once again Jade cursed Sarah for putting her in this position. It took every bit of self-control she had not to race after him.

32

Finn came into reception one morning, a couple of weeks after Ray's visit, looking worried. Jade steeled herself. Finn hardly ever looked worried, but there had been a slight awkwardness between them lately.

She hoped Ray was OK. He hadn't taken Fang in the end. He'd confessed that his health hadn't been so good lately and he wasn't sure he was up to the challenge of taking on such a young fit dog.

Finn cleared his throat and Jade saw he had a piece of paper in his hand. Maybe he was going to hand in his notice, show her the details of some new exciting job.

'Yes?' she said, a lot more tersely than she'd intended.

'I've just been talking to Dad.'

'Ah. Is he OK?' she asked anxiously.

'He's fine, Jade. Thanks for asking.' There was surprise in his voice and she felt a little stab. Had they got so far apart that he thought she didn't care?

He smoothed out the paper, which was creased, as though it had previously been screwed up. It looked innocuous enough.

There was a phone number scrawled on it with a code she didn't recognise. Finn retrieved another piece of paper from the pocket of his jeans and unfolded it so she could see. 'I wasn't going to show you, but the interfering old bugger said if I didn't mention it he'd phone you himself.'

It was a news item about a donkey that had been abandoned on Skegness Beach. It was being looked after by a local woman, who was appealing for someone to re-home it urgently because she only had a small back garden. The newspaper was asking for information that might lead to tracing the donkey's former owner, but so far no one had come forward.

'I'm not surprised,' Jade said, looking at the photo. 'He's not exactly in tip-top condition, is he? The RSPCA would probably prosecute.'

'Dad saw it in a free newspaper when he went to visit a mate at Skeggy. He's got it into his head that you might want to bring it here.' Finn sounded apologetic. 'Like you haven't got enough to do without trekking up there and getting yourself another load of trouble.'

'Donkeys aren't much trouble.' Jade read the feature and felt her insides turning over. 'Poor love's had a hard time of it.'

'Going up to get him would be a fair bit of trouble,' Finn said, quietly reasonable.

'It's not that far.'

'There's a time limit,' Finn pointed out. 'And who's going to look after the sanctuary if you go gallivanting off on a donkey rescue at the other end of the country?'

'Sarah and Callum would probably do it if I asked them. And Dawn would help out, I'm sure.'

'It's going to take you longer than a couple of hours to drive up to Skegness.'

Jade sighed. His quiet logic was gradually overriding the

impulse she had to go up there now, this minute, but he was right. It would take some organising. Thinking quickly, she said, 'I'll phone Sarah. I'm sure she'd say yes. If I went up in the evening, I'd only be away for a day and a half.'

Finn sighed and Jade felt touched, knowing he was only trying to protect her. So perhaps he did still care a bit. 'It's what we're here for, Finn,' she murmured.

'It's a flaming long trek there and back in a day.'

'I won't do it in one day.' She was determined not to be deflected now she'd made up her mind. 'I'll book into a Travelodge the night before. That'll be cheap enough. Then I can pick up the donkey in the morning and drive him back here.'

'A B&B would be cheaper and probably nicer. There are loads in that neck of the woods. I'll come with you. I can drive. It's the least I can do, seeing as it's my fault you've got to go in the first place. Don't worry, I'll pay for my room.'

In the end, Jade agreed because sharing the driving was sensible. And the prospect of spending some time away with Finn was appealing. Maybe, once they were away, she could get a different perspective on the situation. Maybe she'd even realise she didn't like him so much, after all.

* * *

A week later it was arranged. Jade had talked to the woman who was looking after the donkey. 'She's keeping him in her back garden,' she told Sarah, shaking her head. 'Are you sure you don't mind looking after this place?'

'Of course we don't.' Sarah had agreed instantly once she'd known Finn wasn't going to be around. 'It's the least I can do and Ben's in his element. He said he can't wait to have Mickey on his bed for a bedtime story.'

* * *

They left mid-afternoon on Wednesday, having given Sarah a long list of instructions.

'Just get going or you'll hit the rush hour at Newbury. I'll phone you if there's the slightest problem.'

It was strange driving away from the rescue. Jade hadn't left it for more than a few hours since the day she'd opened it. This is how it must feel if you were a new mother leaving your baby with someone else for the very first time, she thought idly. It was strange being alone with Finn, too. She sneaked a glance at him. He looked very at home driving the horsebox and she found herself wondering if there was any situation he wouldn't look at home in.

'What?' he said.

'Pity we haven't got time to pop in and see your dad.'

'If he'd have kept quiet you wouldn't be having to drive two hundred miles to pick up another load of expense and hassle,' Finn grumbled.

'I'm not driving, you are. And anyway, I don't look upon the donkey as a load of expense and hassle. Poor love.'

He shot her a look of exasperation and shook his head.

'And don't think I'm falling for that hard man, I wouldn't care if he ended up in French stew, act, either. You're as worried as I am.'

'I'm not worried in the slightest. He'll be living the life of Riley once you get him back. Why should I worry about him?'

He raised his eyebrows and shot her a speculative glance. She and Finn were good like this. Light-hearted banter. She could cope with this.

They reached Newbury just ahead of the rush hour and hit Oxford and Milton Keynes without any hold-ups either. They didn't talk much, but it was an easy silence. She felt safe and cocooned by the darkness and the rumbling rhythm of the engine. The road snaked ahead of them, the headlights and tail-lights of the rest of the traffic like bright strings of rubies and diamonds. All the same, she didn't realise she'd fallen asleep until she woke up with a start, aware they were no longer moving.

'Are we in a traffic jam?' she asked, sitting up and feeling groggy.

'No, we're here.' Finn yawned. 'I'm just going to see if this place has got any rooms. The car park's a bit full. I guess we should have booked, after all.'

'I'll come with you. Blimey, I must have been asleep for ages. What time is it?'

'Just gone nine. We ought to think about getting something to eat. There's a nice-looking Italian around the corner.'

They went into reception and were greeted by a harassed-looking woman, who shook her head when Finn asked for two rooms.

'Normally you'd be fine mid-week, but we've got a writers' conference here at the moment. Romantic novelists. Sorry, I think we're fully booked.'

'Completely fully booked?' Jade asked, dismayed.

She frowned and opened an iPad. 'Hang on a sec. I don't think they have room seventeen. I'll just go and check.'

She came back smiling. 'You're in luck. I'm afraid it's only a twin, but I could do you a discount. Is it just for one night?'

Jade glanced at Finn and he said, 'Your call. We can try some-where else if you like.'

She looked at his tired face and knew she couldn't ask him to drive any further. 'No, it's all right. A twin will be fine.'

The receptionist directed them up two staircases and Finn

opened the door on to a sloping-ceiling attic room with a skylight.

'Home from home,' he said, bending his head as he put their bags on to one of the single beds.

'Actually, it's not bad,' Jade said, looking around. There was a pine wardrobe and dressing table and the beds had crisp white linen. On one wall was a print of a girl with a straw hat.

Finn sat next to the bags on the bed. 'Shall I see if we can get a table in the Italian, or don't you want to bother?'

'Yes, let's go out. I've never been to Skegness. Anyway, you haven't eaten all day. You ought to eat something after all that driving.'

Half an hour later they were sitting in La Mamma's, which had a friendly, busy atmosphere, smelt delicious, and was surprisingly full for nearly ten o'clock on a Wednesday. There was a Courvoisier bottle candle on their table, the wax of countless evenings forming a waterfall of colour down the glass.

'If I fall asleep halfway through my pizza, can you give me a prod?' Jade said, putting down her menu and yawning.

'Am I that boring?'

She shot him a look and saw humour in his grey eyes. 'Stop fishing for compliments.'

'Fancy some wine to go with your pizza?'

'I don't know if the budget can stretch to that.'

'Well, we've saved on the room.' He raised his eyebrows. It was the first time either of them had mentioned it, but before she could respond, he added, 'Besides, this is my treat. What would you like, red or white?'

'I don't mind. You choose.'

'There's one here called Bugger,' Finn said, looking down the menu. 'Made of classic Bordeaux grapes, apparently.' He pointed it out to her. 'Perfect with pasta and pizza according to this.'

'It says Boeger, pronounced with a soft J,' Jade said, trying not to sound smug. 'But yes, let's give it a go. Are you having pizza, then?'

'The biggest they do with as many extras as they can cram on to it.'

'I think I'll join you.'

'Ah, you like one bottle of the Bugger,' the waiter said when he came to take their order a few minutes later. 'Good choice.' As he swept away, his order pad in hand, Finn glanced at Jade and she laughed.

'OK, Mr McTaggart, you win.'

'I don't suppose that's really how you pronounce it. I think it's more likely that the waiter shares my warped sense of humour,' he said, and she thought how different this evening was from the one she'd spent with Aiden.

The waiter came back with their wine and uncorked it at the table.

'You like to try?'

'I'm sure it will be fine,' Finn said, indicating he should pour for them both.

When he'd gone again, Finn picked up his glass. 'Perhaps we should have a toast. What do you think?'

'How about to a successful donkey rescue mission tomorrow?'

They clinked glasses and Jade reflected that the last time she'd felt this easy around him was the night they'd counted stars in his room. It seemed like an eternity ago, a night imbued with magic, and as the evening wore on and they ate and laughed and drank the wine, which was smooth and velvety, it was as though some of that magic had found its way here to this little restaurant in Skegness.

33

'Are you too tired to walk back?' Finn asked when they finally rolled out of the door at half eleven. 'I could get an Uber.'

'No, let's walk. I'm just getting my second wind. What's the nightlife like here?'

'You never stop surprising me.' He shook his head. 'I haven't a clue. But if you're not tired, I could give you the grand tour. Dad brought me here quite a bit when I was a kid. It was the closest beach.'

'Then lead on, McTaggart.'

They went past a theme park and he pointed out the big wheel and the roller coaster, which were shadowed and silent, like great, hulking monsters, asleep until daylight.

'We used to come for the day quite often,' Finn said. 'And a day was a whole day. No messing about. We'd catch the train, get here about eight and then walk around shivering in our shorts and tee-shirts until the sun warmed us up. Dad always insisted we wore our shorts because we were at the beach and it was bound to be sunny.'

'I thought Skegness had a reputation for bracing winds.'

'It does, but whatever the weather we had a strict routine. Breakfast in a beach café, slot machines until lunchtime and then the theme park. That was always Dad's favourite.'

'He liked going on rides?'

'Oh, he didn't go on anything. He liked watching me clinging on for dear life. He used to stand on the ground slapping his leg and roaring with laughter every time my carriage came past. I bet he didn't strike you as sadistic, did he? I was terrified most of the time.'

'You weren't, were you? I can't imagine you being terrified of anything.'

'You'd be surprised.' His face darkened and then he grinned. 'I'm winding you up, Jade. It was a good sort of terror. The sort that gets your heart thumping, even though you know you're quite safe, really.'

She nodded, aware that her own heart was thumping a bit. She couldn't decide whether it was his proximity, or simply because they were in an unfamiliar town at night.

They went past a closed-up ice cream kiosk with red and white striped shutters, a shop that sold buckets and spades and inflatable animals in garish colours, and then finally he led her along a dark street that went past a golf course.

'Where are we going?'

'Wait and see.'

At the end of the street, the tarmac gave way to a track and then to sand and there was a new, salt freshness in the air. Finn gestured her down some steps ahead of him and she realised they were on the beach. The tide was out, leaving a great expanse of sand stretching towards the dark sea. A moon path lay across the water, a strip of silver glitter on a piece of black paper. Like a child's drawing, Jade thought, reminded of Ben and his pictures, as she followed Finn towards the hard sand at the water's edge.

She was amazed how easy she felt in his company. Or maybe it was the alcohol relaxing her. They'd followed up their pizzas with espressos and Amaretto on ice, which Finn said was the only way to finish a meal, but rather to Jade's surprise, she didn't feel tired or particularly drunk. She just felt warm and happy.

'Your turn,' Finn said as they listened to the soft swish of the waves. 'Tell me about your childhood.'

'It was great. I had a pony and a dog and a cat. I was really lucky.'

'No brothers or sisters?'

'No. Mum was a businesswoman. She didn't really want any children. Neither did my dad. I was a mistake. She told me once that's why he left.'

'I'm sure that wasn't true,' Finn murmured, his eyes narrowing. 'Parents say a lot of stupid things.'

'Mum didn't have time for children anyway. She was too busy building up her business empire.'

'And your dad didn't stay in touch with you?'

'No.' She glanced at his face. 'The same thing happened to you, didn't it? Only it was your mum.'

'We're talking about you, not me.' His voice was light, but his eyes darkened. If she wasn't mistaken, Finn was still hurting over that. So he wasn't as indifferent as he liked people to think.

'So, come on, what else?' he went on.

'I spent most of my time living a life of luxury,' she said flippantly. 'I was utterly spoilt.'

She gazed into the frill of the tide, remembering, and Finn reached for her hand and said, 'Then why do you look so sad? What are you thinking?' And she wished for the hundredth time that he couldn't read her so easily.

'I'm not sad,' she said, leaving her hand where it was, but not looking at him. 'This is a lovely beach, isn't it? Did you have animals when you were little?'

'We had the odd dog, but not till I was older. Dad worked long hours at the pit and I was at school and he didn't think it was fair to leave a dog on its own all day.'

'I spent more time with animals than with people,' Jade said dreamily. 'It was easier for us because we lived in the country. Right out in the sticks with no other houses within walking distance. I suppose Mum thought it would give me something to do. She wasn't around very much.' She paused, aware he was looking at her, his face soft in the light of the moon.

'What have I said?'

'Nothing that surprises me. Is that really why you didn't go into the family business, Jade? Because you resented the hotels for keeping your mum from you?'

His eyes were gentle and she shook her head and then decided it was pointless denying what he'd already worked out and added, 'Partly, I suppose. I did feel that the business came before me. Well, with hindsight, I guess it had to. It was what supported us.'

'Is that why you sold the hotels?'

'Yes. I needed to draw a line under the past.' She met his gaze and said, 'I thought it would make me feel better. But it just made me feel guilty.'

'And so now you bury yourself in work. Just like your mother did.'

'But I don't have children,' she said sharply. 'So it's hardly the same thing. Come on. Let's walk.'

For a while, he didn't say anything else. They were still holding hands and she was glad they were. It felt so natural walking along the beach with him, listening to the lap of the waves and being fanned by the faint sea breeze. Every so often they climbed over groynes that were barnacled and frilled with seaweed. At one of them, she'd just put her feet on the ground when she spotted something on the sand ahead of them, a dark shape. As they got closer, she realised it was a crab on its back, its legs paddling the air, but slowly, as if it had been there a long time and had given up hope of ever righting itself.

'Let's take it back to the sea,' she said.

'Never off duty, are you?' His voice was teasing, but it was he who picked up the crab and he who got his feet wet when he misjudged the waves to put it back.

'You're a big softie at heart, aren't you, Finn?'

'No way. I just know better than to argue with my boss. Anyway, I seem to remember you're scared of spiders. I thought you might not want to pick it up. All those legs wriggling about. Not so different, are they?'

'I'm not that scared of spiders,' Jade protested.

'You could have fooled me. I've heard of rain dances, but never a spider dance.' He sounded amused and she felt a prickle of embarrassment.

As though sensing her discomfort, he changed the subject and said, 'How long have you known Sarah, Jade?'

'Since we were small,' she murmured, deciding she wanted to talk about Sarah even less than she wanted to talk about the spider dance.

But for once Finn was oblivious to her thoughts.

'Have you always been close?'

She hesitated, knowing where this was leading, but not knowing how to stop it, and then she realised they'd come to a halt on the shoreline and that Finn was holding her hand once more, so there was no escape.

'She was the sister I never had. Actually, I think we were probably closer than sisters. We were soulmates. When she got pregnant with Ben, she asked me to be his godmother because...' She came to an abrupt halt, realising she'd almost given herself away.

'Because what?'

'Because we were close, I guess.'

'Ben's a great kid. It's a pity we haven't seen so much of him, lately.'

'Yes.' She didn't meet his eyes, suddenly terribly afraid that he'd already guessed. And he'd brought her here to ask her for the truth. She was going to have to lie and he'd know she was lying.

'Jade. Do you trust me?'

'Of course I do. What sort of a question's that?' She could hear the bleakness in her voice. Here it came.

'Then why do you keep me at arm's length? Is it because of Sarah? Because of what happened at that party?'

'No.' She met his eyes, glad of the darkness. It was easier somehow to lie in the darkness.

'Then why?'

'I don't know. I'm...'

'Scared?' he asked quietly. 'I'm not going to hurt you. I'm not in the habit of having one-night stands. That time with Sarah was a one-off. A mistake I've regretted ever since, not because she wasn't a lovely girl, but just because it wasn't something I did. Not even then, and certainly not now.' He paused. 'Do you believe me?'

She nodded, not trusting herself to speak, and he stroked her hair. It was agonising, being so close to him. She felt dizzy with wanting him. All she had to do to stop this was to tell him the truth. Then he wouldn't look at her like that, as if he wanted her, too, and was waiting for her to reciprocate. But she couldn't find the words. And he was still looking.

'I wanted you to know that, Jade. In case it made a difference.'

'It doesn't.' She forced brightness into her voice. 'It was a long time ago.'

'Then I assume there's some other reason you don't want things to go any further between us,' he said lightly. 'Or have I misinterpreted the situation completely? Have I just made a complete fool of myself?'

34

All she had to do was nod and she'd be off the hook, but she couldn't bring herself to do it. Not even for Sarah.

In a voice that didn't sound like hers at all, she said, 'No, you haven't done that, Finn.'

He let go of her hand. 'Good. I'm glad we've got that sorted out.'

She felt so weak with disappointment and relief she thought she might collapse at his feet. Then it struck her that perhaps he meant they could spend the night together now. This night. She'd have to think of some way of stopping it. She shivered. The effects of the alcohol were beginning to wear off, and it was starting to get cold. A stiff breeze had come up since they'd been walking, turning the breakers milky white and whisking up the top layer of sand.

He glanced at her. 'It's nearly one o'clock, Jade. We ought to get back soon, or we'll never get up in the morning.'

* * *

The B&B's lounge was still full of people when they got back and as they hesitated outside the door, they could hear a lot of rather slurred talk about plots and agents and six-figure advances.

'Different world,' Finn remarked as he followed her up the stairs to their room. He wished fervently they weren't sharing. The barriers between them had crashed down again tonight, but he wasn't going to push her. She had to come to him. He didn't know how much longer he could stand it if she didn't.

She went to get undressed and clean her teeth in the en suite and Finn sat on his bed. He felt ragged. When he'd suggested bringing her up here, his motives hadn't been entirely altruistic. He'd thought if he got her away from home for a couple of days, it would be easier to tell her about Sarah. Easier to find out how she felt, and now he had a clue that she did feel the same as he did, he wasn't sure what to do about it. He'd shot himself in the foot telling her about Sarah tonight. If he made the first move now, she might think he'd just been saying that to get her into bed.

He frowned. She'd opened up to him for the first time, let him see a little of what was behind the wall, and in doing so she'd been enormously vulnerable. He'd have been taking advantage of the situation if he'd done what he really wanted to do and made love to her right there on the beach.

Jade came back into the room, her robe belted loosely around her. There was a sprinkling of talc on her toes, he saw. He tore his eyes away, the intimacy of the moment catching in his throat.

'Forgot my slippers,' she said, following his gaze. 'Bathroom's free.'

'Thanks.'

As he cleaned his teeth, he wondered if perhaps he should sleep in the bath. It would be a damn sight easier than sleeping in the same room as Jade. He shook his head. That was a crazy idea.

He had to get a grip. He'd waited all this time, he could hold on a bit longer.

When he went back into their room, she'd turned the bedside light off and was curled away from him, the duvet moulding around her slender figure. He could hear her quiet breathing and realised with a little stab of irony that she was oblivious to the effect the evening had had on him. She was already asleep. He got into his own bed, swallowing an unfamiliar tenderness that was somehow metamorphosing into pain in his throat.

* * *

Jade kept her breathing as even as she could. She wasn't asleep. But pretending to be was the only way she could guarantee she wouldn't give herself away to Finn. One wrong move, one wrong look, and she had no doubt they'd have spent the night wide awake. They'd have pushed the two singles together and then... She halted her traitorous thoughts. It couldn't happen. Pretending she was asleep might be the coward's way out. But it was for the best.

* * *

The next morning, they had breakfast in a pink and white room, amidst dozens of romantic novelists who didn't look in the least hungover.

'Hardened drinkers, obviously,' Finn said, pouring Jade's tea. 'How are you feeling?'

'I'm all right.'

The truth was that she felt edgy as hell. She should have told him she wasn't interested in him. She should have made some excuse about not mixing business with pleasure and, now she hadn't, it was only a matter of time. So close and yet so far, she thought, hating herself for her weakness.

'You look tired, Finn. Wasn't the bed comfy?'

'It was fine. What time did you say we were seeing this woman?'

'Ten.' He seemed tense too and he was having trouble meeting her eyes. Perhaps he was as embarrassed as she was. Perhaps she'd read more into what he'd said last night than had been there. Maybe he just wanted her to know that he wasn't a one-night stand kind of man. Wanted the slur on his character gone.

'I'll just go and settle up,' she said, getting up. 'I don't think I can manage a full breakfast this early. I'm still full from last night.'

'I've already done it.'

'But you can't pay for the room, that's not fair.'

'I was going to pay for mine so it makes no difference.' He frowned at her and she got up anyway.

'I'll go and get the bags, then.'

'Whatever.' He made no move to follow her. 'If it's all the same to you, I think I'll have breakfast. I doubt we'll have time to stop for lunch.'

* * *

They found the address of the woman with the donkey easily. She lived in the middle of a housing estate.

'No wonder she can't keep him here,' Jade said, looking over the wall into what looked like a back garden, but was obviously the right place because a grey donkey was tethered to the fence. He was painfully thin, his head lowered in resignation as if nothing much surprised him any more.

'I shouldn't think the neighbours are too impressed,' Finn remarked, opening the gate to let them in. 'Do donkeys kick?'

'He might. Best keep away from his rear end.' They walked cautiously past, but they needn't have worried about kicking. The donkey cowered away from them, particularly from Finn.

'Poor little sod,' he muttered. 'Doesn't look like he's been a much-loved pet.'

'I thought you didn't care.'

'I didn't say I didn't care.' He glared at her and Jade felt almost as cowed as the donkey.

'Blimey, you did get out of bed the wrong side, didn't you?'

Finn didn't reply and she decided he was the most contrary man she'd ever met. Last night on the beach he'd been so warm, tender almost. And now he couldn't be more different. Was it any wonder she preferred animals? She stormed ahead of him and rapped on the back door. At least animals were consistent. You knew where you were with them.

* * *

Aiden was thinking exactly the same thing. He'd just been treating a goat for mastitis and her owner, Jimmy Stanton, had been issuing dire warnings from the moment he'd got there.

'Molly's a mean-tempered bugger,' he'd said, as he'd introduced Aiden to his patient. 'Mind you stay out of the way of her back legs and her teeth, or she'll 'ave you.'

Molly had flicked her ears nonchalantly, as if attacking vets was the last thing on her mind and she'd submitted patiently to Aiden's examination so that he'd wondered what on earth the man was talking about.

'Watch yerself,' Jimmy yelled excitedly as Aiden had moved around the goat, with apparent disregard for his warnings.

'I'm pretty nifty on my feet,' Aiden reassured him.

'Not as nifty as Molly. She had my boy the other day. Sunk her teeth right into his hand. Little bitch.'

Aiden wondered what exactly the boy had been doing. Molly was one of the quietest patients he'd ever come across. But he'd decided it was best not to say anything. Animals were always fine with him. Like little Fang at the rescue, he thought with a pang of regret. She was supposed to be a raving lunatic, but she'd never so much as lifted her lip at him. It was all about how you treated them. Animals weren't like humans. They didn't make unprovoked attacks. He frowned, remembering Finn. How stupid that had been. He wondered how much longer he would need to leave it before he did as Emily suggested and called by Duck Pond Cottage – just to see how things were going. He finished his examination of Molly and she glanced at him, a benign look on her whiskery face.

'You can put her back in her field,' he told Jimmy as he packed away his vet bag and opened up the back of his jeep to put it away.

He was just about to close the back doors when he heard a shout of warning and, almost at the same time, felt a stabbing pain in the back of his thigh.

'What the hell?' Jerking away from the pain, he half turned and saw Molly, head down, lining herself up for another attack. Without stopping to think, he hurled himself into the back of his vehicle, bashing his head on the open door in the process, and landed in a heap amid a couple of cat baskets and some old blankets that smelt of dogs. Molly skidded to a halt in a cloud of dust.

'You little bitch. You cow!' Through the series of lights shooting in front of his eyes, Aiden was vaguely aware of Jimmy Stanton, dancing around in a fury outside the jeep. Then he passed out. He couldn't have been out for more than a few seconds because when he came to, very much the same scene was going on outside, only now someone else had joined in. A younger version of Jimmy, presumably his boy, was also dancing around with what looked like a rope lasso in his hands. Molly had turned from the picture of docility to a raving nutter and was charging about the yard like a beast possessed. They'd never catch her like that, Aiden thought groggily. He put a hand up to his head and felt stickiness. Blood, he saw, lowering his hand and gazing at it. Or at least he thought it was blood. Everything kept going in and out of focus. Deciding he was no longer interested in Molly's welfare, he lay back down again. His right buttock was on fire and a hot pain was spreading down the back of his leg. He shifted gingerly, turned his head to look, and saw there was a hole in his trousers and, more worryingly, a gash in his leg. Groaning, he stayed where he was, partly because it didn't sound as if they'd caught Molly yet and partly because he felt too sick to move.

* * *

'Are you sure you don't want me to drive?' Jade asked Finn again. They'd just stopped at a service station to give him a break and refuel and he looked worn out, his grey eyes shadowed and a little sad. Where was the sadness coming from? 'I shouldn't have kept you up so late,' she added, biting her lip. 'It was all right for me, I slept in the horsebox yesterday, but you've been on the go the whole time.'

'I'm all right, Jade, really.' Finn leaned into the driver's section of the box and opened a little hatch so they could check on Richard.

The woman who'd rescued him had called him Richard – after her late husband apparently – and Jade had promised her they'd keep the name. His real one being unknown.

Richard hadn't minded going into the horse box at all and he looked peaceful enough now. He was standing with his head down but he flicked his ears, clearly aware of their presence.

'I wish I knew what had happened to him,' Jade said. 'I don't think it's just cruelty. His teeth aren't good. Which means he probably can't eat properly.'

'Poor beggar.' Finn's voice softened. 'He'll be fine. It's the future that counts, not the past. And his future is looking rosy.'

'Yes.' Before they'd left Skegness, Jade had phoned Maggie Crowther for some advice and Maggie had told her donkeys were quite social animals and much better when they weren't alone.

'He'll perk up when he's around his own kind,' she'd added and then continued brightly, 'Jade, I'm more than happy for you to bring him straight here. I've got three neddies already. One more won't make any difference.'

'Are you really sure?' Jade's heart had lifted. 'That would be amazing. I'll pay for his keep.'

'No, you won't. I'm happy to help. I owe you one for taking those kittens.'

'Which have all been re-homed,' Jade had told her happily.

So they were now taking Richard straight to Puddleduck Farm, which meant they'd be back at Duck Pond Cottage slightly later than planned.

* * *

As it turned out, they were home by six and were met by an anxious Sarah as they drove through the gates.

'What's happened?' Jade asked, leaning through the window. 'Is Ben OK?'

'Everything's fine. How's the donkey? Did you drop him off OK?'

'We did.' Jade felt a thread of unease run through her because Sarah's smile looked forced. Perhaps she suspected that away from the sanctuary Jade had caved in and told Finn the truth.

'It's OK, I haven't said anything,' she murmured so only Sarah could hear. 'If that's what you're worried about.'

'What? Oh, no, it's not that. Actually, it's Aiden. That new vet, Paul, came by earlier to drop off some antibiotics and he said Aiden had just been taken to hospital. He was attacked by one of his patients this morning. I know you've fallen out with him, but I thought you'd want to know.'

'Is it serious? What happened? Not a dog, surely?'

'No, it was a goat. It – er – charged him from behind, apparently, and took a chunk out of his rear end and he knocked himself out trying to get away from it.'

Finn, overhearing this bit, snorted and Jade glared at him. 'It's not funny, Finn.'

'Paul seemed to think it was quite funny too. Poor Aiden does seem to get himself into trouble, doesn't he?'

'It couldn't happen to a nicer chap,' Finn said, ignoring Jade's chastising look. 'Are you dashing up to the hospital to play Florence Nightingale, Jade?'

'No. I'm not.' She was about to say something else, but he was already striding away.

'What did happen in Skegness?' Sarah asked when he was out of earshot.

'Nothing,' Jade said shortly. 'Nothing at all.'

Sarah coloured up. 'Sorry. That was insensitive. You still like him, don't you?'

'It doesn't matter how I feel about him, does it? Tell me about Aiden. It must have been pretty nasty if he had to go to hospital. Did Paul say which hospital?'

'It's Salisbury. Why? You're not going to visit him, are you? I thought you wanted to keep out of his way.'

'Yes, you're right. I suppose it would be best not to go.'

But a bit later when Sarah had left and Finn had disappeared somewhere, in that way he often did, she decided she would go and see Aiden. He'd be feeling pretty sorry for himself and she'd never intended to bar him forever, just for long enough to make him realise she wouldn't tolerate any more of his antagonism towards Finn.

35

At Salisbury hospital, Jade asked to be directed to Men's Surgical.

'Bay four, bed three, love,' said a sweet-faced nurse on the nursing station when Jade arrived at the right ward.

She found Aiden sitting up in bed, reading a veterinary journal, which he put down as soon as he saw her.

'Jade! Hi!' He sounded so pleased to see her that she felt terrible.

'Hello, Aiden. How are you feeling?'

'All the better for seeing you.' His whole face lit up. Then he shifted in the bed and winced, and the journal slipped off his lap on to the floor.

'Are you very sore?' she asked, reaching to pick it up.

'No, not really. It was my own stupid fault for thinking I knew best. Molly – she's the goat who put me in here – gave me the impression that butter wouldn't melt in her mouth, although her owner did try to warn me.'

'What happened?'

'Basically, she head butted me with her very sharp horns. And while I was trying to get out of her way, I knocked myself senseless on the door of the jeep. Didn't take a lot of doing. I was halfway there already.'

She wondered if he was referring to hitting Finn. Not sure how to respond, she glanced around the room. There was a card on the bedside table. She gave him the box of chocolates she'd bought in the hospital shop.

'Thanks. How are things at Duck Pond Rescue? How's Fang? Is she still there?'

Jade nodded, relieved Ray had decided against having Fang in the end. It would have been horrible having to tell Aiden he wouldn't see the little dog again. 'She's fine. She misses you. We all do,' she added impulsively. 'You'll have to pop in and see us some time. If you want to, I mean.'

'I'd like that very much.' He turned towards her, and Jade saw the bruise and a small cut on the side of his head.

'That looks nasty. Is that why they're keeping you in?'

'Yes. Just for the night, with a bit of luck. I can hobble about all right, but they don't like to take any risks when you've knocked yourself out. How did you know I was here?'

'Paul popped in this morning.'

'I bet he was laughing his socks off.'

'No, I don't think so. I wasn't there, as it happens. I was in Skegness rescuing a donkey.'

'That's a long way to drive – did Finn go with you?'

'Yes, he did.'

'Things are working out all right with Finn, then?' There was a hint of resignation in his voice and Jade nodded, reminded suddenly of the same look of resignation in Richard's eyes.

Compassion rose in her, and she said, 'I shouldn't think he'll stay around much past the end of the summer. He'll want to get something better.'

'I'm glad. That things are working out, I mean.' Aiden's eyes warmed. 'I guess I ought to prepare myself for being the butt of a few jokes when I get out of here. Literally, in my case.'

They both laughed and the tension left the room.

They talked for a bit longer about the animals she'd taken in and re-homed and then Jade said, 'I'd better get off. It's later than I thought.'

'I really appreciate you coming, and I'd love to see Fang some time. That's if you're really sure?' He lifted his hand but at the last minute seemed to think better of it and dropped it back on to the bed.

'Of course I'm sure. Give me a call first and I'll make sure I'm there.'

And she'd make sure Finn wasn't, she decided as she drove home. Perhaps asking Aiden back hadn't been such a good idea. It had seemed the right thing to do, but Finn might not be quite so enamoured with the news.

* * *

'It's up to you, Jade,' Finn said, not looking up from the Wordle he was doing when Jade got back to the cottage. 'As long as the bloke doesn't have another pop at me. I might hit him back next time.'

'I'm sure he won't. It'll be a while before he can even work again.'

Finn didn't answer and she sat on the sofa. He might say he didn't mind her inviting Aiden back, but the temperature in the room had definitely dropped since she'd told him.

'Thanks for coming to Skegness,' she added, anxious to get things back on an even footing.

'Like I said, it was my fault you had to go there in the first place. It was the least I could do.' His voice was cold and suddenly she was angry.

'What is the matter with you?' she demanded, getting up from the sofa and storming across to him.

He looked startled. Then he stood up so they were facing each other.

'I just can't work you out.' She knew her voice was rising. 'One minute you act like a normal human being. Quite a decent person, in fact. And the next you're a bloody iceberg.'

For a moment he didn't say anything, just looked at her with an expression she couldn't fathom. Then he grabbed hold of her arms, pulled her roughly against him and kissed her. It was such a shock she felt her legs melting beneath her. Or maybe it was the passion in his kiss. Iceberg-like, it was not. There was no tenderness there, either. Not like the last time they'd kissed, at all. Ribbons of fire flicked through her at his touch.

When she'd recovered the use of her legs, she tried to pull away from him, or at least that had been her intention, but somehow she found herself kissing him back. It was impossible not to – every defence she had was gone and she never wanted him to stop. When he did, she felt too weak even to slap him.

'Was that bloody normal enough for you?' he growled, and she saw that his grey eyes were blazing. And then he spun around and slammed out of the room.

Jade sank on to the sofa, so shocked she could hardly believe it had happened. Perhaps she should go after him. She dismissed the idea immediately. She'd provoked him quite enough for one evening. Best to let the dust settle.

She touched her lips, which still tingled from the roughness of his kiss. She wanted to cry and laugh at the same time. She took a few deep breaths until the hysteria subsided. Well, it had certainly proved one thing. Indifferent to her he was not. Her mind leapt ahead to work and the normality she'd been trying to recapture. Oh my God. What on earth were they going to say to each other tomorrow?

* * *

Fortunately, they didn't have to say anything because when she got up the next day he was already out working. Deciding there was a better chance of them resuming a professional relationship if as much time as possible passed before they saw each other again, she threw herself into the routines of the morning.

Finn kept out of her way for most of the day. Around teatime he called across the yard that he was going to wood stain some fences and that he'd probably be a while.

Jade locked up and took her paperwork into the cottage. He'd have to come in sooner or later.

It was dusk and she was sitting in the lounge, showered and changed and having extreme difficulty concentrating on a batch of invoices, when the front door banged.

'Is that you, Finn?'

'No, it's a burglar.' His footsteps slowed outside the lounge door, but he didn't come in.

Jade leapt up and went into the hall. 'I want to talk to you.'

'I'll get changed first. I'm covered in wood stain. Is there any hot water left?'

When he came down, his hair was still damp. 'I'm all yours,' he said, stepping into the room, his face guarded.

She'd been going to hedge round the issue, but now she was facing him, she couldn't, so she just launched straight in. 'Why did you kiss me last night? And I want a straight answer. I've had enough of your games.'

'I'm not playing games.' He gave her a direct look. 'I thought we'd got that clear in Skegness.'

'Just tell me why you kissed me.'

He looked uncomfortable. His gaze flicked around the room and he took a step away from her. Then he brushed a hand through his hair, leaving a spike of it sticking up so that Jade had a strong urge to go across and smooth it down for him. 'I guess because I couldn't help myself. I'm sorry. It shouldn't have happened. Do you want me to go?'

'No, of course I don't want you to go.' She watched his face. He rarely looked unsure of himself, he hardly ever looked vulnerable, but she could see he was both, now. She wanted to make him feel better and she'd had enough of keeping this forced distance between them. She was tired of pretending and she was worn out with lying – not just to him, but to herself.

'I enjoyed it,' she murmured. 'Didn't you?' She'd surprised him, she saw, but then she'd surprised herself, too. In for a penny, in for a pound. She took a step towards him. 'Am I embarrassing you?'

'No.' He stayed where he was.

Just two more steps to the point of no return, Jade thought, wondering who would be the one to take them. Or were they going to turn away from each other again? Keep pretending there was nothing between them? She could feel the electricity sparking, but she also had a feeling that if they stopped now they'd never reach this point again. Then, making a decision she knew she would live to regret, she took another step. But it was he who took the final one. He put his arms around her and gave a small moan.

'Bloody hell, Jade.' His arms tightened and he buried his face in her hair and then his lips found hers and she knew he wanted her as much as she wanted him, and that this time they weren't going to stop.

She forced herself to break the kiss and he looked at her, his eyes quizzical, but before he could speak, she grabbed his hand and led him out of the room.

Her bedroom door was open and they went inside wordlessly.

She sat on the bed and he knelt on the carpet in front of her. 'Are you sure this is what you want?' His voice was little more than a whisper, his eyes smoky with desire, and in answer she kissed him again and drew him up onto the double bed beside her.

* * *

In the morning, when Jade woke up, there was an empty space beside her and she thought for a moment it had all been a wonderful dream. But she could still feel the effects of his body on hers, a delicious awareness that was replaced by a quiver of lust when she thought about what they'd spent the night doing. So the love gene hadn't been missing in her, as she'd always suspected; just buried, she reflected, rolling over and burying her face in his pillow. What a pity she hadn't discovered it before. She'd been missing out.

Last night when they'd made love, she had never felt so on fire, so much at one with another person. She had gazed up at the outline of his face. His eyes, dark with passion, were totally unguarded. It was like looking into his soul. In that moment none of the past had mattered. She had felt as though she was exactly where she was meant to be. As if her whole life had been leading up to this point and if there was no more time left to her afterwards, it wouldn't matter.

So where was he now?

36

Concerned, she sat up, and then the door opened and Finn stood there with two mugs of tea. He hadn't bothered dressing to make it, she saw, but suddenly shy of her own nakedness she hugged the duvet around her breasts. He smiled, and to cover her confusion she said flippantly, 'You'll frighten the post lady walking around like that.'

'So, I'm frightening now, am I? Don't worry, it's too early for the post lady. It's only just gone six.'

'Is it? It feels much later.'

He put the mugs on her bedside table. 'Am I allowed back in, then? I'm feeling at something of a disadvantage.'

She turned back the corner of the duvet and he climbed in beside her. Then he propped his head on his elbow and looked at her. 'I was going to make some toast as well, but I wasn't sure how hungry you'd be.'

'Not hungry in the slightest.'

'Maybe you need to work up an appetite.' He pulled the duvet away from her and without taking his eyes from her face, he traced the curve of her breast with his fingers.

'You're a tease, Finn McTaggart.'

'Shall I stop?'

'Don't you dare.'

By the time they'd worked up enough of an appetite for their toast, the tea Finn had made was too cold to drink.

* * *

Jade spent the morning in a haze of happiness, which was only slightly marred by the fact that nothing had really changed. One night of passion, amazing as it had been, did not alter the fact that Finn was Ben's father and that she and Sarah had been lying to him for the past four months. Bathed, as she was, in the afterglow, she managed to put this out of her mind, more or less.

Sarah had promised she'd tell Finn – and Callum – the truth about Ben before the wedding, but that wasn't until next spring. Aeons in the future. Maybe when the time came, Jade and Finn could somehow work things out. Maybe he'd be involved enough with her to forgive her for not telling him a secret that wasn't hers to tell.

She was midway through cleaning out the chickens when this thought struck her. Crouched there, amidst the smell and the soft flutter of the birds, she knew for sure that she was kidding herself. What did she think he'd do? Forget he had a son? Walk away? Finn wasn't the type of man to do either. All she'd done by sleeping with him had been to complicate things further.

But she'd known that, deep down, hadn't she? She stretched out her fingers to stroke Masie, who was the tamest of the ex-batteries and had strutted across to see what she was doing.

'You wouldn't be so silly, would you?' she murmured, the bird's feathers downy soft beneath her fingers. 'Life isn't so complicated in Little Red Hen land, is it?'

Masie blinked and leaned into her touch.

'Having fun?' Finn's voice made her jump and she banged her head on a jutting-out bit of wood.

'Ouch.'

'Sorry, didn't mean to take you by surprise. Are you OK?' His voice was solicitous.

She rubbed her head. 'It wasn't your fault. I was miles away.'

'Somewhere nice, I hope.'

She glanced at him and reflected that they couldn't be in more unromantic surroundings, yet all she wanted to do was go to bed with him again. One night hadn't been nearly enough. She wanted to spend every night in bed with him.

'I was thinking about what to get Sarah and Callum for their wedding present,' she improvised hastily. 'I managed to prise the list off her the other day.'

'Maybe we could get them something together,' Finn suggested. 'Or am I being too forward here?'

'No, of course you're not. Great idea. We'll catch up later.'

Halfway through the morning, Aiden phoned to say he'd been let out of hospital, but was off work for a while and would call in and see Fang when he felt more up to it.

'I'll look forward to it,' she said, meaning it. Hopefully, he'd come on Sunday when Finn wasn't around. She didn't think Aiden would be in any hurry to bump into Finn.

By 6 p.m., Jade felt as if she'd spent the whole day with the phone pressed to her ear. She was just about to lock up reception when the phone rang again.

'Could I speak to Finn McTaggart?' said a woman's voice.

'He's not about at the moment. Can I take a message and get him to call you back?'

There was the faintest of pauses on the other end and the woman said, 'To be honest, it's quite urgent. Is that Jade?'

'Yes.' Jade was suddenly apprehensive.

'I'm Shona Brewer. I'm a friend of his from Nottingham. I hope you don't mind me calling, but I can't seem to get Finn on his mobile.'

'We're not in a very good signal area,' Jade murmured, feeling a small flicker of jealousy, which she knew was irrational. Why shouldn't Shona call Finn – they'd obviously been close once. 'I can take a message if you like,' she offered.

'Thanks. I wanted to speak to Finn about Ray, actually. He was supposed to take Stewart, my son, fishing last night, but he didn't turn up. He's not answering his door and I've checked at the pub and he hasn't been in. I just wondered if he was all right. He's had this awful cough, but he won't go to the doctors, stubborn old bugger. I don't like to think of him holed up in that house on his own.'

'No,' Jade said, concern instantly replacing the jealousy. 'Thanks very much for phoning, I'll get Finn to call you.'

'Oh, no, don't worry, I just thought I'd better pass it on. It might be that Ray's gone away for a few days, but he didn't mention it.'

Jade hung up, worried, and switched on the answer machine. She was about to go and find Finn when she saw him coming down the yard.

He wiped his hands on his jeans and came across smiling. 'God, it's still hot, isn't it?'

'Finn, I just had a phone call for you, from Shona – in Nottingham.'

His smile vanished and concern leapt into his eyes. Jade had to swallow more jealousy.

'Shona? What on earth did she want?'

Jade told him and his face grew even more serious.

'Well, he's certainly stupid enough not to go to the doctor.

And, thinking about it, he didn't answer his phone earlier, when I tried to ring. I'll try him again on his mobile. I should speak to Shona, too. Is it all right if I use the reception phone?'

'Of course it is. I'll just lock up the other end.' She rushed away, not wanting to hear Finn on the phone to his ex. When she came back down the yard, Finn was shaking his head. 'I can't get any answer from his mobile or his landline, and Shona seems really worried. I know it's short notice, but would it cause you a problem if I took a couple of days off and drove up there?'

'No, of course not. Will you go in the morning?'

'Actually, I think I might go now. If I put my foot down, I'll be there before ten.' He hesitated. 'I'm sorry, this is really bad timing, but I am a bit worried.'

'Don't be silly. Of course you must go. You will phone and let me know how he is, won't you?'

'Sure.' His eyes were distant, as if he'd already left. Jade felt chilled despite the balmy air. She'd liked Ray, too, and she hated the thought of him being ill and alone. Though she wasn't keen on Finn driving up to Nottingham, not when he was worried sick. Her feelings had nothing to do with the fact she wasn't keen on the idea of him spending time with Shona, she told herself. But as she waved him off, she found herself regretting, for the first time, her decision to run a business that you couldn't leave.

* * *

Despite putting his foot down wherever he could, Finn didn't get to Nottingham until gone eleven. The whole country was obviously heading in the same direction. He'd tried ringing his father a couple more times on the way, but still got no answer and he grew more and more worried. Even if Dad had nipped out, which didn't seem very likely from what Shona had said, he'd surely be back by now.

He couldn't find a parking space anywhere near the little end-terrace house, so eventually he had to park in the next street and walk. Dad's house, like the one next to it, was in darkness. He banged on the door and wondered what he'd do if he couldn't get in. After about five minutes with no response from either knocking or carefully aimed stones at his father's bedroom window, he climbed over the side gate, which was locked, and went round the back.

The back door was locked, too. He supposed he could smash the glass and let himself in that way, but if Ray had just unplugged the phone and gone to bed for an early night, he'd scare the life out of him. Somewhere under one of the numerous flowerpots in the garden, there was probably a spare key.

He decided to work his way methodically through all the likely hiding places and struck gold in the sixth flowerpot, when his hand closed over an old baccy tin that rattled when he shook it. When he managed to prise the lid off, he found a key on a bit of frayed string which fell apart in his fingers, so that the key tinged onto the path. Cursing, Finn fumbled around for it.

Twenty minutes after he'd arrived, he let himself into his father's tiny kitchen and switched on the light. Tidy, as always, but there was something missing. He frowned. Tobacco smoke. Conspicuous by its absence. He couldn't remember ever walking into this kitchen without noticing its pungent smell.

Alarmed now, he went through to the back room, which was where his father ate his tea, watched TV, had his after-dinner Scotch, did practically everything, in fact. The room was empty. Finn closed the door quietly and stood at the bottom of the stairs. 'Dad!' he shouted up. 'Dad, can you hear me?'

No answering cry greeted him. Suddenly Finn didn't want to

go up there. Didn't want to walk into a room and find his father collapsed unconscious on the floor. Or worse, still and unmoving in bed. How long did it take for the smell of tobacco to vanish so completely from a house? Surely, by now, it would have seeped into the very walls themselves. He put his foot on the first brown-carpeted stair and it creaked beneath his weight. 'Dad?' he called again. It was no good. He would have to go up.

On the landing, he hesitated. His father's bedroom door was ajar. He pushed it open and stuck his head around the door. Even in the dim light he could see the bed was neatly made and his father wasn't in it. He didn't realise he'd been holding his breath until he started to breathe again.

Without much hope, he checked the rest of the house. This was all very strange. According to Shona, his father had been at death's door the last time she'd seen him. Certainly too ill to go out. It didn't make sense. Not only was he obviously not here now, but Finn would have laid bets he hadn't been here for days.

He phoned Jade and updated her, then he texted Shona and told her he didn't think there was anything to worry about, but he was on the case. Then, because he wasn't sure what else he could do, he got comfy on the sofa with the aid of a brown throw he found in the hall cupboard and settled down to wait for his father's return.

* * *

Finn was rudely awoken from one of the deepest and most exhaustion-fuelled sleeps he could remember. Someone was prodding him with a stick, the wrong end of a broom, he saw, as he opened his eyes and tried to remember whose sofa he was lying on.

He'd been covered by the throw, but his assailant, a fair-haired, sixty-something old lady with cross blue eyes, had removed it, presumably with the broom, which she was still jabbing around. The throw was now lying in a crumpled heap on the floor and Finn, wearing only his boxer shorts, felt rather vulnerable.

'And who exactly might you be?' she demanded. 'Come on – get up and explain yourself.'

Finn sat up and glared at her. 'I could ask you the same thing. This is my father's house. What are you doing here?'

'Oh, so you're Ray's son, are you?' Her face broke into a smile. 'Why didn't you say so?'

He resisted the urge to point out she'd attacked him before he'd had the chance and said coolly, 'So, where is my father? I thought he was ill.'

'Ill...? Ray...?' She sounded so incredulous that, for a minute, Finn wondered if he'd tumbled into some alternative reality.

'Well, isn't he ill, then?' he said irritably.

'No, dear.' She gave him a look he'd have described as coquettish in someone a few decades younger. 'He's a little tired, but that's probably because he's not used to all the exercise.'

'I'll just get dressed, and you can explain what you're talking about.'

'Now tell me what you'd like to know?' she said a few minutes later as they sat at opposite ends of the sofa he'd just vacated, sipping the coffee she'd made them. 'I'm Dorinda, by the way.'

Finn shook his head, not entirely sure he wasn't still dreaming. 'Where Dad is now would be a good start.'

'That's easy. He's at my place. Three doors down,' she added, as if this explained everything.

'And he's definitely not ill?'

'No, dear.'

'He's never mentioned you.'

'No, well, we haven't known each other long.' She fluttered her eyelashes, which looked too long and black to be her own. 'He's mentioned you a lot. Said you were a fine-looking young man, but you can't always tell. Sometimes it's parental pride. Not in your case, though.' She giggled and Finn felt heartily relieved he hadn't been sleeping in the nude as he usually did.

'Do you want to tell him I'm here? Or shall I come to your house and see him?'

Dorinda glanced at her watch. 'He'll be along in a minute, he was having a shave when I left. Then he was popping up to get a paper and a pint of milk. We haven't been here for a while and he didn't think he had any in. I said I'd come and put the coffee pot on. Open a few windows and such like.'

'You're living together?' Finn felt his eyebrows rising in amazement.

'Don't look so shocked. You youngsters don't have the monopoly on living in sin, you know. Us oldies could show you a thing or two, I can tell you.'

Finn had no doubt whatsoever about that. It was just that his father hadn't lived with anyone since his disastrous relationship with Finn's mother. He'd always been dead set against the idea, so why change his mind now when he was in his mid-sixties?

To his huge relief, the door banged at that moment and he heard his father's voice.

'I'm back, Dorrie, love. Where are you?'

'In here, Pumpkin. You've got a visitor.'

Finn had never in his life imagined he'd hear his father be called Pumpkin. He stood up wearily as Ray came into the room. 'Hi, Dad. Sorry to barge in on you like this, but I came up last night and when you weren't here I crashed on your sofa. Hope you don't mind.'

'No, lad. Course I don't mind. I see you've – er – met Dorrie, then.'

'Yes, we're well acquainted,' Dorrie interrupted. 'I'll leave you two boys to catch up. Will you be stopping to dinner tonight, Finn? Because if you are I'll book another seat at the Cock and Bottle.'

She rose gracefully without waiting for an answer and left the room. Finn and his father stared at each other.

'You could have warned me you were coming,' said his father, looking sheepish.

'I didn't know I was until the last minute. Shona phoned and said you were ill. And when you didn't answer your phone, well, I didn't know what else to do.'

'Shona said I was ill?'

'Yes. She said you were supposed to take Stewart fishing and you didn't turn up.'

Ray clapped his hand over his mouth. 'Bugger – I'd forgotten all about that. I'll have to phone the little lad and say I'm sorry.'

'And you haven't been in the pub either, have you? Shona said your cough was so bad she was worried it was bronchitis again. She told me that's what you had last time, not flu at all.'

'Ah – yes... well, same difference.'

'It's not the same thing at all,' Finn said, exasperated. 'So why haven't you been in the pub? It's usually your second home.'

'If you must know, I've given up the dreaded weed and Dorrie's not keen on my usual local.'

'You've given up smoking!'

'Aye. Dorrie made me.'

'Well, good for you. But, Dad, how long's this been going on? Dorrie, I mean. You never said anything about her when you came down. Or when you phoned up about the donkey, which is no longer – you'll be pleased to hear – slumming it in someone's back garden.'

'No – no, I didn't, did I?'

'Why not, for God's sake? I nearly had a heart attack when I woke up and saw a strange woman standing over me.'

'If I'd known you'd be on the sofa, I would have mentioned it, lad. But I didn't. Strikes me we've both not been mentioning things.'

This argument was so devoid of logic that for a few seconds Finn was speechless.

'Besides – I wasn't sure you'd approve,' Ray added. 'It was a bit of a whirlwind romance, Dorrie and me.'

He narrowed his eyes. 'So how's the gorgeous Jade? Have you asked her out yet?'

37

Aiden woke up late on his first morning home. He hadn't set the alarm and the painkillers he'd taken the previous evening must have knocked him out. He got out of bed and limped across to the window to see what sort of day it was. Bloody hell, he felt sore. He drew back the curtains and saw bright sunlight. Beyond his garden he could see mist curling off the fields that led down to the river. So far, July was as blazing as June had been.

He thought about Jade's visit. It had been good to see her. He was no longer kidding himself that Jade would ever feel the same about him as he felt about her, but he longed for them to be friends again. Also, she'd mentioned that Finn would be gone by the end of the summer. That was good news too. He knew he'd never feel comfortable around Finn.

When he went to collect his recycling bins, Emily was just getting hers.

'Aiden, how are you, love?'

'I'm getting there. Thanks for the card. How did you know I was in hospital?'

'That nice young vet told me when he brought your jeep back.

Now, you are going to take it easy for a few days, aren't you? No dashing about.'

'I don't think I'll be dashing anywhere for a while.'

'Poor lamb. It'll do you good to slow down. You work far too hard.' She put her head on one side so that he could see the coil of her grey plait and added casually, 'You could pop by the animal sanctuary, couldn't you, dear? See how young Jade is.'

He grinned. 'Young Jade came to see me in hospital.'

'That sounds promising.'

'Don't get too excited. I don't think there'll be any more candlelit meals, somehow.'

'Maybe there wouldn't have been even if you hadn't thumped her lodger,' Emily mused. 'My Kate's coming over to see me later. She likes animals. Talking about getting a horse, she is. Maybe you could take her along to the sanctuary with you.'

'Maybe,' Aiden said, although he knew it was the last thing he'd do. Women were not top of his agenda right now. 'I might see if I can bring Fang home for a while,' he went on. 'Seeing as I'm going to be here a few days. It would do her good.'

'Kate likes dogs, too.'

'Does she?' Aiden gave her a quick smile and closed the door. He made himself breakfast and dressed with difficulty. The doctor at the hospital had advised him to take at least a week off work, not least because it would be difficult to drive. Getting to Duck Pond Rescue was going to be tricky, but Aiden was firmly of the opinion that anything was possible if you wanted it enough, and Jade had invited him. If he waited, she might have second thoughts and tell him not to come.

He got there just after eleven and found a very harassed Jade trying to do several things at once.

'Where is everyone?' he asked as she fielded phone calls and advised various walkers which dogs could be walked together without a fight.

'Dawn's looking after her grandchildren today and Finn's gone to Nottingham to see his dad. He's worried about him. He has health problems.'

'I'm sorry to hear that,' Aiden said, although he certainly wasn't sorry that Finn wasn't around. 'Let me answer the phone for you. I can't do much else at the moment, but I can sit in here, no problem.'

'Are you sure, Aiden?'

'Course I'm sure. Go on, you get up the yard and do whatever needs doing. I'll be fine.' He eased himself into the chair and, with a grateful glance at him, Jade disappeared out of the door.

He watched her go, deciding that fate moved in mysterious ways. When she'd banned him from the sanctuary, he'd hit rock bottom and when that blasted goat had attacked him, he'd thought things couldn't get any worse. But now it all seemed rather fortuitous. It was a shame about Finn's dad, but apart from that, he thought with a sigh of contentment, the timing was absolutely perfect.

* * *

Jade was shattered. It had been one of the busiest Saturdays she could remember. They'd had an influx of dogs, which often happened in the holiday season. It amazed her how many people would rather re-home their dogs than pay out for kennel fees.

Aiden grinned at her as she went into reception. 'You look worn out, Jade. Do you fancy coming for a pint and a pie up the road? Save cooking?'

What she really wanted was to collapse in exhaustion, but she couldn't because she had a home check in Salisbury. She looked at Aiden doubtfully.

Misreading her expression, he said, 'I mean as friends, Jade. No strings attached. I admit I used to hope it could be more, but those days are gone. Truly.'

'I could meet you there later, if you like. I must owe you several drinks after today. How about eight o'clock?'

'Great. See you there.'

As she drove to Salisbury, Jade wondered if she should have agreed, but Aiden had seemed genuine and she was tired of looking for ulterior motives where probably none existed. They'd have their own vehicles and she wouldn't stop long. Besides, going out had to be better than being alone in the cottage and jumping out of her skin every time the mobile rang in case it was Finn.

The home check took longer than she expected. The woman, a sweet old lady who Dawn had recommended, wanted to chat, and Jade didn't want to rush her, but she finally got away. At this rate, she was going to be at least half an hour behind Aiden. She hoped he wouldn't think he'd stood her up.

* * *

It wasn't until Aiden was home and trying to shower without getting any water on his stitches that he remembered he hadn't asked Jade about Fang. He'd mention it later, he decided, wincing as he moved too quickly. Rather to his consternation, the prospect of meeting Jade at the Red Lion, with no Finn around to muck things up, did not give him the pleasure he'd anticipated. True, he'd told her there were no strings attached, but he hadn't realised he'd meant it quite so unequivocally.

It had been great to see her again, but some of the bittersweet pain he always felt when he was around her, that 'so near, so far' feeling, had been missing. It was as if somehow the time they'd spent apart had dulled his feelings, taken the edge off his passion, and it hadn't really sunk in until today. A self-defence mechanism, maybe, now that he knew they were never going to be more than friends. He wiped the mirror clean of steam and shaved.

Perhaps Emily was right and he was finally acknowledging the truth. Jade wouldn't have ended up declaring undying love to him, even if he hadn't thumped Finn.

He was rinsing out his mouth with Listerine when the doorbell rang. Deciding to ignore it, he spat into the sink and dabbed his mouth dry, but the caller was persistent. Frowning in irritation, he pulled his bathrobe from the back of the door and, twisting the cord around his waist, limped along the landing and went carefully downstairs.

Pulling open the front door, words of irritation half formed on his lips, he stopped dead in his tracks. A gorgeous redhead was standing on his doorstep. She looked familiar and he frowned, trying to remember where he'd seen her before.

'Sorry, have I called at a bad time? I'm Kate, Emily's granddaughter. She said you wouldn't mind if I called round and saw your new dog. I know you from somewhere, don't I?'

'Kate.' Aiden's mind was spinning. It was something to do with horses, something to do with Jade. 'Come in,' he said, deciding now was not the time to confess that Fang wasn't actually in residence. If he didn't let her in now, he might never see her again. 'Go through to the lounge and make yourself at home. I'll just get dressed. Won't be two minutes.'

Upstairs again, he dressed as quickly as he could, splashed liberal amounts of Tom Ford over himself and went out on to the landing. Deep breaths. No need to get flustered, she was just Emily's granddaughter. Why hadn't Emily told him how gorgeous she was? Come to think of it, Emily had probably been pretty gorgeous herself in her younger days. She had the high cheekbones of timeless beauty and she still had long hair, albeit grey and plaited and coiled up on top of her head. He should have guessed Kate would be lovely too. He wished he could remember where he'd seen her.

Outside the lounge door, which Kate had closed behind her, he took more deep breaths and then went casually into the room. She was standing by the French windows, her back to him, her long hair cascading like a mane of gold in the evening sunlight.

'What a beautiful garden you have.' She turned and smiled at him. 'You must spend hours on it.'

'It's a hobby,' he murmured, moving to stand beside her.

'And now you're going to have a little dog racing about digging up the flower beds. Won't that be an awful pain?'

'I love dogs and she'll soon learn where she's not supposed to go.'

'I love dogs too. Where is she, then?'

The jigsaw pieces came together in his head. 'That's where I've seen you before. At Duck Pond Rescue.' He'd clearly noticed her, even though she hadn't had the same impact then as she was having now.

'Wow, you've got a good memory.' She was looking at him with those amazing eyes. They were the colour of Bournville, flecked with gold. 'That's right. I'm having a horse from her.'

'It's where my dog's coming from, but I'm not picking her up until tomorrow.' He shook himself. 'Can I get you a drink of anything? Coffee? Or perhaps a glass of wine?'

'Wine would be lovely,' she said, showing no signs of wanting to dash off. 'Is it all right if I go outside and have a look? I love gardens.'

Enchanted, Aiden unlocked the French windows for her.

'I'm always telling Gran she should get someone to do her garden,' Kate said, stepping out on to the immaculate lawn. 'Is it all right to walk on this? I don't want to leave heel marks. How do you get it to look so perfect?'

'It is hard work,' Aiden admitted, forgetting about the wine and following her outside. 'Maybe I could give your gran a hand. I didn't realise she needed someone.'

'I'm sure she'd like that.' Kate bent and slipped off her strappy sandals. She had slender brown feet with some sort of sparkly pink varnish on her toenails. 'Oh, it feels just like walking on luxurious carpet, only cooler.'

'Does it?'

She glanced at him. 'Gran likes you, you know. She often mentions you when I visit. Strange we've never bumped into each other here before.'

'I'm out working a lot.' He followed her across the lawn to a rose bush where she dipped her head to the pink blooms. 'These smell gorgeous. Most of the roses in florists don't smell these days. I think it's a dreadful shame.'

'Me too. I'll – er – just get the wine.'

When he came back with wine for her and coffee for him, she was sitting on the little wooden bench he'd found on Gumtree and restored to its former glory.

'Shall we have it out here? It's such a beautiful evening.'

'Why not?' He sat beside her awkwardly and saw concern spring into her eyes.

'Gran said you'd had a problem with an ungrateful patient.'

'I got savaged by a goat. Not my finest moment, I'm afraid. It's a bit uncomfortable but I'm on some heavy-duty painkillers. Hence the coffee.' He was suddenly aware his soreness was not the reason he no longer fancied Jade. Not if his reaction to this girl was anything to go by.

For a few moments, neither of them spoke. Then, putting his mug down for a moment, he got up, crossed to the rose bush and snipped off the most perfect yellow bloom with the secateurs he'd brought with him from the kitchen. He handed it to Kate.

'Thank you, Aiden.' She dipped her head and breathed in the scent of the rose, her eyes half closed. She had freckles on her nose, he saw wonderingly. And long eyelashes and full lips the colour of palest pink that turned up at the corners, even when her mouth was in repose. Why hadn't he noticed how gorgeous she was when he'd seen her at Duck Pond Rescue?

He realised it was because he'd been too tied up with Jade.

When she looked back at him, she was smiling again, her eyes soft. Aiden felt his heart flip.

* * *

Jade got to the Red Lion at twenty to nine. She'd been stuck behind a tractor most of the way back. She hoped Aiden hadn't got fed up with waiting. Parking the Land Rover, she tore into the Red Lion, glanced around the crowded bar and felt her heart sink. There was no sign of him. Waving over the head of a man in a deerstalker hat at the bar, she tried to get Mike's attention. 'Has Aiden been in at all?'

'Haven't seen him, Jade. Hey, didn't the silly bugger have some run-in with a goat and end up having stitches in his behind? Are you sure he's not still in hospital?'

'Positive, he's been at the rescue today.' She felt annoyance rising at the amusement on Mike's face. Why couldn't he ever take anything seriously?

'You're looking a bit stressed yourself, love.' He studied her and his expression changed to concern. 'Want your usual?'

She nodded. 'Finn's away. And I've had a nightmare of a day.' She took the glass he gave her and carried it to a table by the window that a giggling couple had just vacated. It was the table where she'd seen Finn on the night she'd asked him if he wanted a job. He'd been staring out of the window, a pensive expression on his face.

She hoped he was OK – he'd texted earlier to say his father was fine and he'd call later, but he hadn't yet. She knew it was stupid, but she couldn't shake off the feeling that he might regret their night together once he saw Shona again. And even though she knew it shouldn't have happened because it made everything a hundred times more complicated, she didn't think she could bear it if he regretted it.

She glanced at her mobile. There were no missed calls or further messages. It was almost ten to nine and it was beginning to look as though Aiden wasn't coming. She finished her drink, waited another ten minutes, then got up to go.

'Tell Aiden I was here, if you see him,' she called to Mike, who was collecting glasses. 'But I've got to go. I've got a bit of a headache.'

He abandoned the glasses and came over and patted her arm and the gesture of kindness brought tears to her eyes. She must be more tired than she'd realised, she thought, turning away so he couldn't see.

'Take it easy, Jade. And I hope Aiden's OK. He's a decent bloke.'

'Yes, he is. Thanks, Mike.' She left the pub before she gave herself away, shivering as the coolness of the evening hit her. It was another clear night. Thousands of stars studded the velvet sky. The night when she and Finn had sat and counted them seemed a long time ago. As distant and as untouchable as the pale moon that hung in the sky above her.

The cottage seemed curiously empty because she knew Finn

wasn't in it. Even Mickey didn't bother getting up from his basket, just gave her a cursory wag and went back to chewing what looked like one of Finn's boots.

'Bad dog,' Jade chided half-heartedly, prising it out of his mouth. When she straightened, she saw, with a little jolt, that the answer machine light on the landline was flashing.

The first message was from a farmer wanting to know if she'd take a litter of puppies. His best working bitch had escaped during her season for a romp with the local stray and the resulting brood was no use to him at all. His voice was so accusing he sounded as if he held Jade personally responsible for the dalliance.

The second message was from Finn. He was somewhere noisy; it sounded like a busy restaurant. Jade could hear laughter and the clatter of cutlery on plates in the background. 'Sorry I missed you, Jade, but just to let you know Dad's fine. A case of crossed wires. See you in a couple of days. Bye.'

She replayed the message over and over. His voice was curt. Finn's pet hate was leaving messages on answer-machines. Or maybe he just hadn't wanted to phone her. Maybe he was out with Shona, comforting her because her husband had left her again.

Cursing herself for her overactive imagination, she rubbed her eyes, which felt gritty with tiredness, and picked up her mobile to call Sarah. But before the call could connect, she cancelled it because she had no idea what she would say. She didn't want to tell Sarah her relationship with Finn had moved up a gear – that they'd slept together now and that it had felt so right, so gloriously, painfully right.

She phoned the farmer instead to tell him she'd take the puppies as soon as they could leave their mother.

'They can leave their mother now, as far as I'm concerned. They're all weaned.'

'I'll call you tomorrow to make some arrangements about when you can drop them off,' she said crisply, not wanting him to think she was too much of a pushover.

He grunted a thanks and disconnected.

Jade's thoughts returned to Finn. Maybe he wasn't as keen as she was. Surely if he was, he'd have come back tonight and not just left her a message telling her he'd decided to stop in Nottingham for a couple of days. And, as she stood there, staring into space, all the old, old insecurities came flooding back. She wasn't a nice enough person to interest anyone for long. She would always come second, never first in anyone's life. Except for the animals, who depended on her.

She took Finn's boot back out to the front door and then in a sudden burst of frustration hurled it at the wall. Feeling sadder and more alone than she had for years, she went upstairs.

38

Aiden woke up on Sunday morning feeling deliriously happy. For a few moments in the hazy gap between sleep and wakefulness he couldn't remember why. And then it all came flooding back. Sitting in the garden with Kate until they'd been forced indoors by the midges.

They'd talked and talked. She'd told him all about her job as a nurse at Odstock Hospital, and she'd listened, enthralled, by his version of 'it shouldn't happen to a vet'. Her warmth and enthusiasm had melted away his usual shyness. As the evening stretched on, they'd gone further back into each other's pasts. He'd even told her about being bullied at school, he remembered with a hint of embarrassment, but she hadn't laughed, she'd put her slim hand over his, empathy shining out of her beautiful eyes.

'So that's why you're so passionate about animals. They're so vulnerable, aren't they?'

He'd looked at her wonderingly. He'd never felt so at ease with anyone in his life.

At the end of the evening, when she'd said reluctantly she should get back or Emily would worry, they'd stood at his front door, Kate holding the yellow rose he'd given her. Then, having extracted a promise that she'd come and collect Fang with him the next day, he'd climbed upstairs, the pain and stiffness forgotten, and collapsed on his bed, ecstatic with happiness. It was only as he was dropping off to sleep that he remembered with horror he'd been supposed to meet Jade at the Red Lion.

Now, as he went downstairs to get coffee, he hoped she hadn't been too put out. Perhaps she'd been relieved when he hadn't turned up. She hadn't exactly looked thrilled at the prospect of meeting him in the first place. But no, that was unfair. Jade had just been tired – she'd probably been cursing him for dragging her out for nothing. Maybe he ought to pick her some flowers to take to the sanctuary as a peace offering. No, not flowers. He'd decided last night that from now on, the only woman he was ever going to give flowers to was Kate.

He'd arranged to give her a knock just before ten so they could head over to Duck Pond Rescue together.

He went into the lounge. An empty wine glass and a mug sat on the coffee table where he'd left them. So it hadn't just been a beautiful fantasy. As he crossed the room to get them, he noticed something yellow on the floor. A rose petal, he saw, bending with difficulty to pick it up. He held it to his face and breathed in its delicate scent.

Last night had been the start of something wonderful, he was sure of it.

* * *

When Aiden's yellow jeep drew into the yard just after ten thirty, Jade was on the phone to the farmer with the collie-cross pups. She glanced up and saw Aiden go round to open the passenger door to let out an attractive, vaguely familiar girl. His movements were almost reverent, she noticed with a mixture of affection and amusement. She wasn't the betting type, but she'd have put money on it that the flame-haired beauty had something to do with him standing her up last night.

Aiden came into reception and put a tub of Quality Street on the desk in front of her. 'I'm really, really sorry, Jade. I – er – completely forgot we said we'd meet.'

'And that's a peace offering, is it?'

He nodded. The girl, who was standing behind him and a little to his left, stepped forward.

'Kate,' Jade gasped, recognising her. 'I didn't know you two knew each other.'

'My gran lives next door to Aiden. Small world, isn't it?'

'Isn't it?' Jade smiled at them both. 'Don't worry about last night, Aiden. I was tired anyway.'

'You looked it. I was wondering if it would be OK if I took Fang home for a week or so. Just while I'm off.'

'Of course it is. I could do with freeing up some space. I've just agreed to take in another eight pups.'

'Oh, how cute. What kind?' Kate's eyes were shining with enthusiasm.

'Collie something,' Jade said as the phone started to ring again.

'Hi, Jade, it's Dawn. Sorry about yesterday. How did the home check go?'

Jade told her.

'I'll be over at lunchtime to give you a hand. You sound like you could do with it. Oh, and before I forget, my next-door neighbour's after a puppy for her grandchild. Do you have any in at the moment?'

Jade told her about the collie-crosses.

'Sounds perfect. I'll bring her with me to have a look round. See you in a bit.'

Jade disconnected and went out into the yard. Ahead of her, Kate and Aiden were standing by the cattery, deep in conversation. Small world indeed, she thought, wondering how long Aiden had been seeing Kate. It must have happened recently, or surely he'd have said something. Didn't that prove that miracles could happen? So maybe one would happen for her and Finn, although she had the horrid feeling they might need more than a miracle.

* * *

Dawn's neighbour, Sarah-Jane, who was plump and kindly and wore her glasses on a gold chain around her neck, came in with Dawn as she'd promised just before lunchtime and they headed off to the kennels.

Not very long later, they came back to tell Jade they'd found the perfect pup.

'He'll do us better than a collie-cross,' Sarah-Jane said, her eyes sparkling with excitement. 'They do a lot of chewing, collies, don't they?'

'All pups chew,' Jade said, thinking of Mickey, who was at the moment lying in the sun outside reception, looking like butter wouldn't melt in his mouth. 'Some of them never grow out of it.'

'This one's ready to go now, too. Dawn said we just need to have a home check, is that right?'

'Yes.' Jade realised with a jolt that she was talking about Tiny. She walked with the woman back up the yard to the main block.

'Are you really sure she'd like this one?' Jade said, bending to pick him up and resting her face against his soft baby fur. She loved the smell of puppy fur. Why couldn't she suppress the stupid and irrational feeling she had that if she let Tiny go, things would start to fall apart?

'Yes, he's the one.' Sarah-Jane beamed widely and Jade forced herself to smile back. She kissed Tiny's head and he blinked sleepily at her. 'I'll come and do a home check tomorrow night,' she promised.

39

Finn left his dad's about eleven, although both his father and
Dorinda had pressed him to stay longer. But, much as they made
him welcome, he still felt as though he were playing gooseberry –
and an uninvited gooseberry at that. He kissed them both
goodbye and promised he'd drive up and see them again soon.

Before he left Nottingham, Finn phoned Shona, deciding the
least he could do was to reassure her his father was not, as she'd
feared, at death's door.

'Pop in if you've got time, Finn. Stewart would love to see you.'

'And Andy?'

'He won't be back until three.'

Even so, now he was here, Finn hesitated outside the familiar
front door, not at all sure he wanted to re-awaken painful memories that he'd managed to put out of his mind. He'd brought four
framed sketches of the animals at Duck Pond Rescue, a present
for Stewart, and now he clutched the gift-wrapped package and
rang the doorbell.

'Hi, Finn.' Shona stood there for a moment, her blue eyes
anxious. Then she flicked back her blonde hair a little self-

consciously and smiled at him. 'Come in. I'm so glad your dad's all right. Sneaky old bugger, shacking up with a woman at his age and not saying a word about it.'

'Perhaps he thought no one would approve.' It felt odd being back in the familiar narrow hallway with its bare banisters and brown patterned wallpaper. It still all looked exactly the same, but changed somehow. It took him a few moments to realise the change was in himself. He was seeing it all through different eyes.

'Stewart,' Shona called up the stairs. 'Come and see who's here.'

A fair head appeared over the banisters. 'Finn!' Stewart came tearing down the stairs. At least there was no doubting his welcome.

'You haven't been to see me for ages. Why not?'

'I've been working a long way away,' Finn said, aware of Shona's anxious glance. 'It's a great place, it's a rescue centre for unwanted animals.'

'Like the ones on TV?'

'Just like those.' He handed Stewart the oblong package.

Finn and Shona watched as he ripped off the wrapping paper and studied each sketch, his head on one side. 'Are these all the animals that no one wants?'

'A few of them.'

'But they'll get good homes in the end? Families who'll look after them.'

'With a bit of luck. Yes.'

'We're a family again now, aren't we, Mum?' Stewart looked at his mother for confirmation, and she shifted in her chair. 'Yes, love, we are.'

'I'm glad. And I hear you've been looking after my dad too.'

'We've been fishing lots. I normally catch more than he does. He coughs so loudly he frightens all the fish away.'

'Does he now?'

'It's nice to see you, Finn.' Shona looked at him over her son's head. 'I'll make us a cuppa.'

He sat at the kitchen table, feeling out of place. 'And Andy's still all right, is he...?'

'He's still not drinking. He hasn't got a job, mind, no change there.'

'But you're managing OK?'

'Course.'

She looked happy. It didn't matter to her that Andy wasn't working. He could have done whatever he liked, with the possible exception of drinking, and she'd still have loved him. It shone out of her face. Finn realised he really *was* glad she was happy. She'd never felt about him the way she felt about Andy. He sipped his tea, surprised this didn't hurt.

'Will you stay in Wiltshire now then, Finn?'

'For a while longer, yes. Jade might not be able to afford me forever. It was meant to be a temporary arrangement.'

'She sounded nice. I suppose you'd have to be to run a place like that.'

'Yes, she is nice.'

Shona looked as though she'd have liked to say something else, but thought better of it. He refused a second cup of tea, anxious not to outstay his welcome, and not ready to meet Andy. He hugged Stewart goodbye and at the door he pecked Shona's cheek.

'Take care of yourself.'

'You too, Finn.'

'Thanks again for keeping an eye on Dad.'

'Obviously not a close enough one.' She laughed. 'I'm sorry I dragged you up here under false pretences.'

'I'm glad you did.'

For a lot of reasons, he thought as he drove away. Not so long ago he'd thought he loved Shona, but now he knew he'd never felt the same about her as he felt about Jade. It was a revelation.

He wanted to get back and talk to Jade. Get everything sorted out between them. After their meal at the pub the previous evening, he and his father had talked long into the night. Something that was almost unheard of in the McTaggart family, especially when the talk was about relationships.

He didn't know what sort of spell Dorinda had woven over his 'oh so reserved' old man, but as well as persuading him to give up smoking, which Finn had been trying to do for years, Ray seemed more open than Finn had ever seen him.

'I think you should stop mucking about, Finn, and tell Jade how you feel. Life's too short to faff about waiting for the right moment. She's a nice lassie. She's not going to hold some ancient misdemeanour against you.'

Finn desperately hoped his father was right. At least he'd got one thing clear in his mind. Being away from Jade had made him realise just how strong his feelings were. He couldn't stop thinking about the night they'd spent together. The way she'd been with him, so giving, so honest and uninhibited. But it wasn't just a physical thing; he knew that now. Seeing Shona had confirmed it. His feelings for Jade ran much deeper than that. He loved her and he'd never felt like this in his life.

To his intense relief, the unaccustomed exercise Dorinda had mentioned his father was taking had turned out to be long walks. She'd persuaded Ray to join her rambling club and Finn had met several members when they'd gone to the Cock and Bottle. Not that Finn was against his father having a few wild nights of passion, but he wasn't sure if Ray's heart was up to it.

All in all, it had been a weekend full of shocks. Starting with Dorinda and ending with the realisation he was in love with Jade.

And, in between, Ray's U-turn when it came to discussing matters of the heart. Finn wished now that he'd taken more advantage of it and asked Ray about his mother.

He'd been six years old when she'd walked out on them. It had been an ordinary Friday evening. He'd just gone to bed and she'd come up to tuck him in as she always did. He had a vivid memory of her leaning over him, her blonde hair tickling his face and her eyelashes all black and spidery. She'd stroked his forehead with a slender white hand, her fingers soft. Then she'd hugged him so tight he was half suffocated with her scent.

'Night, baby.'

'Night, Mum.'

Usually she turned out the light, but that evening she didn't. She just stood there looking down at him. Then she brushed something from her face and he realised she was crying. He'd never seen her cry before. For a moment he'd been so surprised he hadn't been able to speak. Then he'd said, his voice hesitant, 'What's the matter, Mum?'

'Nothing, poppet. I got something in my eye downstairs, that's all. Nothing for you to worry about.'

'Can't you get it out?'

'Yes, I expect I'll get it out in a minute. I just wanted to catch you before you fell asleep.'

He'd nodded, only partly reassured. 'Maybe Dad can help you get it out.'

'Maybe.'

In the morning, when he got up for breakfast, she was gone.

'She's staying with a friend for a few days,' Ray had told him. 'Nothing for you to worry about.'

'Did she get that thing out of her eye?'

His father looked at him, but Finn could tell he wasn't really listening. His father never said much anyway.

Finn couldn't remember how much time had gone by before he'd realised she wasn't coming back. Time had blurred in his mind. The one thing he could remember was that about the same time he'd read a fairy tale at school in which a beautiful princess got a piece of glass in her eye and it made her see the world differently. For a long time, he'd wondered if that was what had happened to his mother. She was a bit like a beautiful princess, but no one seemed to want to tell him. No one seemed to want to talk about his mother at all.

It wasn't until years later that he'd pieced together what had happened. There'd been a big age gap between his parents. Eleven years. The general consensus amongst his aunts, who weren't proper aunts but various neighbours who'd rallied around his father, was that poor Bridie had been too young to cope with the responsibility of having a child. She was still so much a child herself and had fled back to Ireland to her family, who'd never approved of her relationship with Ray anyway. This disclosure, which was said kindly and designed to make him feel better, had only made him feel more strongly that it was somehow his fault. If he hadn't been around, she'd never have left. If he could have somehow helped her to get that piece of glass from her eye that night, then maybe things would have been different.

A long time later he'd discovered his parents had never actually been married.

'She never wanted to marry me, lad,' his dad had said one drunken Christmas when Finn had been about fifteen. 'Her family never approved of me. Far too old – and the wrong religion. She never told them about you. She didn't dare.'

It explained why he'd never seen her again. And why his father had never tried to track her down.

'There'd have been no point. The family would have closed ranks if I'd gone over there. Anyway, I still had you.'

'But didn't you still love her, Dad?'

His father hadn't answered this. Even full of Christmas whisky, he hadn't been able to bring himself to talk about such things. He'd never married or lived with anyone else, although Finn did remember there being a few women around in his childhood. Some of them were kind to him, some indifferent. Finn didn't dare let himself like any of them too much in case they went away, like his mother had done.

He'd grown up craving the security he was sure love must bring, but not sure how to go about finding it, or even if he'd recognise it when it appeared. He never had any problems attracting girls, but as soon as they dropped hints about taking things further, he backed off. And it had been like this until now, he reflected as he drove past the 'Welcome to Wiltshire' sign. Jade had got inside his head, and inside his heart, too. Before he'd met her, he hadn't really known what love was.

At sunset, he stopped the car on the boundaries of Jade's land and got out, reluctant to finish his journey. What if she didn't feel the same? What if his father was wrong and he just ended up pushing her away from him by rushing her? Coward, he berated himself.

Dusk was stealing over the fields and he watched bats swooping out of the line of trees that bordered Duck Pond Rescue. He imagined Jade in the cottage, sitting in the little back room, going through the reams of paperwork she always seemed to have. Or maybe she'd gone out somewhere with Aiden, whom she'd obviously forgiven. No doubt the vet would have taken full advantage of his absence. His stomach churned at the thought. What on earth was the matter with him? He didn't even know if Aiden still had designs on Jade. He'd certainly seemed genuinely apologetic about hitting him. Much more bothered about it than Finn had been. Anyway, Jade rarely went out on Sundays.

Eventually, when the darkness had grown so deep the trees were just a blurred outline in front of his tired eyes, and the bats were just passing shadows, no more substantial, he decided, than his fears that Jade might not feel the same as he did, he got back in his car and drove the last few hundred yards. The gates were locked so he parked the car outside, got his bag from the back and, feeling oddly nervous, he let himself into the cottage.

Mickey came to greet him, but there was no one else about. Jade must be out somewhere.

He went into the lounge and sat in the armchair where he'd sat so many nights talking to Jade. Even though she wasn't there, the room didn't feel empty, but full of her presence. It was very peaceful. At his father's he'd had to get used to the traffic sounds all over again. He'd been surprised how difficult it had been to adjust to the constant buzz that was Nottingham. He closed his eyes, luxuriating in the silence. It was strange how quickly this place had begun to feel like home.

40

'He's back then,' Dawn remarked as she drew up outside Jade's cottage just after 9 p.m. She indicated the outline of Finn's Toyota parked on the verge outside. 'Couldn't have had that much to detain him in Nottingham.'

'No,' Jade said, feeling excitement tighten her stomach. It felt like he'd been gone forever. How had he got into her heart like this? How had she let him when she knew nothing could ever come of it?

'Go on, then,' Dawn prompted. 'If you don't mind me saying, you look worn out. You could probably do with a decent night's sleep.'

'I am a bit tired.' That was the understatement of the year. Jade felt shattered. Not just because of working flat out, but because she was so torn apart with wanting to go to bed with Finn again, and worrying about what would happen if she did.

'Thanks so much for coming to do that home check tonight,' Dawn added. 'Chloe's going to be thrilled to bits when she sees Tiny. I was worried for a while you were going to change your mind about them having him.'

'No, he's much better off with them than here. He'll make a lovely family pet. They can come and get him tomorrow. Any time after nine.' Jade got out of the car and stood in the darkness, gathering herself before she went in.

Her stomach was fluttering as she went into the lounge, which was also in darkness. Finn must be in bed. She didn't know whether to be relieved or disappointed. She was just reaching for the light switch when Finn said, 'Hi, Jade.'

She jumped and spun round to face him.

'Sorry – I didn't mean to startle you. I must've fallen asleep in the chair.' He stood up, his words slowing, and came across the room towards her. 'Is everything OK? I've missed you.'

'Everything's fine,' she said, looking into his tired eyes and knowing that now he was here, it was. 'You should be in bed.'

'Is that a proposition?'

'No.' She felt a contradictory clench of lust in her groin.

'What a shame. In that case, Jade, perhaps we could talk.'

'What about?'

She looked wary and Finn felt his resolve weakening, but only for an instant.

'Don't look so worried, it's nothing bad.' Taking her hand, he drew her on to the sofa beside him. He had no experience of this, no preparation; he'd never told anyone he loved them before. He hoped he wasn't going to cock it up. Every sense felt heightened. He could hear the beating of his heart, smell the apple-scented shampoo Jade used, and he could feel the warmth of her denim-clad knee against his. There was a mixture of emotions in her dark eyes and as he looked at her, Finn knew she was fighting her own internal battle. She was scared, too. They'd had similar upbringings in some ways. Both of them desperate for their mother's love and not having it. He'd been luckier than her because he'd had Ray, who he'd always known had loved him, in his gruff, down-to-earth way, and she'd had no one.

'I don't want to rush you, Jade, I just want you to know how I feel.'

Jade felt light-headed. This was what she wanted. This was what she'd wanted for a long time now. To hear him say he cared about her, to be able to tell him how she felt, but as she looked into his serious grey eyes, all she felt was a tearing pain. If being away from him these past forty-eight hours had taught her anything it was that she couldn't carry on lying to him. Couldn't let him bare his soul to her, knowing she hadn't been honest with him.

'Finn, wait a minute.' She put her hand on his arm and he hesitated. 'Before you say anything else, there are things you should know.'

'I know everything I need to know about you.' His eyes were soft.

'No, you don't.' She stood up abruptly. This would be easier if they weren't touching each other. She didn't want to feel his recoil. She paced to the window and looked out at the dark night.

It was months until Sarah's wedding day, but this couldn't wait. Every second she spent in Finn's company would make it harder to tell him the truth. And a great deal more painful when she did. Was she being utterly selfish? She wasn't sure any more. Betraying her best friend was something she'd sworn she'd never do, but living with this lie was worse.

'It's about Sarah,' she whispered, turning around at last to face him.

He stayed where he was, frowning slightly, his long legs stretched out in front of him. 'I thought we'd already sorted that out, Jade. It was a long time ago. I thought you understood that I wished it had never happened. And by the way she avoids me at every possible opportunity, I'd say she feels the same.'

'No, you don't understand.' She'd always known this wouldn't be easy, but it was ten times worse than she'd anticipated.

'Finn. That night that you and Sarah made love...'

'I wouldn't have called it that.'

Best to spit it out – just say the words she knew could never be taken back. The words that were going to end her relationship with him and very likely her friendship with Sarah, too.

'Sarah got pregnant that night, Finn. She got pregnant with Ben.'

For a moment, he didn't react. Then his face went very still. Jade swallowed and backed up against the window and folded her arms in a little gesture of self-defence.

'Are you saying that Ben's my son?' He still didn't get up, but she could see tension in every line of his body, from the straightness of his arms to the rigid planes of his face.

She nodded, and now he did get to his feet and he came slowly across towards her. Very self-contained, every movement controlled. When he was a step or so away, he put his hands on her arms. His touch was light and his voice was icy calm.

'How long have you known this, Jade?'

She looked into his eyes, wanting to lie. Wanting to say, 'Just a few days. Sarah told me when you were in Nottingham, which is why I'm telling you now.' Because then the lie wouldn't be so long lived, so treacherous.

'I've always known,' she whispered.

'I see.' He let go of her arms, went across the room, still at the same unhurried pace, and picked up his jacket and car keys.

'What are you going to do?'

'I should think that's pretty obvious.'

'You can't go round there. Ben doesn't know who his dad is.

And Callum – well, Callum thinks he left when he found out Sarah was pregnant.' So many lies, she thought. Lies that she'd helped to perpetuate. And she'd have given all that she owned for things to be different. Not to be the one standing here delivering the death blows.

'Well, maybe you'd better phone and warn her then, Jade.' His voice was clipped and he turned and looked at her, and for the first time she could see the icy fury in his face. 'What the fuck did you expect me to do?'

* * *

For a few moments after the door slammed behind him, she stayed where she was in the window. But when his taillights drew away and she knew it was real, she was galvanised into movement.

She hadn't thought Finn knew where Sarah and Callum lived, but then she realised she was being naïve. He could have seen it on Ben's school bag, or Ben could even have told him. She felt a twist of pain at the thought of Ben and the chaos this could bring into his safe little world. Oh, God, what had she done? She should have kept her mouth shut; she should have just told Finn she didn't want a relationship with him. Made him walk away.

She hadn't done that because she cared about him too much, she realised as she got out her phone to call Sarah and saw her hands were shaking. You couldn't lie to someone you cared about. Not forever. A decent person wouldn't have done it for this long.

* * *

Finn had a little trouble finding the road where Sarah lived, but no trouble at all finding the house because it was the only one with lights on at the front. It was 10.45 p.m. and the other residents of Arleston must be tucked up in bed – but Sarah was obviously prepared for him, he thought, slamming the car door and striding up the garden path.

She opened the door before he could ring the bell. Her face was white and her blonde hair all fuzzed up, as if she'd just got out of bed. Her tee-shirt was on inside out. And back to front too, by the look of it, the label sticking up at her throat.

She gestured silently towards the lounge door and he strode past her. He half expected Callum to be waiting in there, but there was no sign of him. He stood in the middle of an untidy room, letting his gaze travel over gilt-framed photographs of Sarah, Ben and Callum on the walls and on top of the television. The child he had never known was his, so clearly a part of someone else's life. The sofa was littered with soft toys. Sarah bent to move them, but he shook his head.

'I'm not stopping. You've spoken to Jade, I take it.'

She nodded. Her blue eyes were wide and afraid. 'What are you going to do?'

'It's more a case of what you're going to do,' he said, his voice quiet. 'I want Ben to know I'm his father. I want to be involved in his life. I've missed far too much of it already.'

'I can't.' She took a couple of small steps away from him. 'He thinks his dad's long gone and Callum thinks he did a runner.'

'Then you'd better find a way of telling them the truth. I've had enough lying to last me a lifetime. From you and from Jade.' He could hear the bitterness in his voice, but he couldn't hide it. He couldn't believe he'd spent so long playing softly softly with Jade, doing all he could to earn her trust, and she'd been deceiving him all this time.

'Finn, please – you have to give me some time. We're getting married.'

'You've had the best part of seven years already. I think that's plenty of time, don't you?' He strode across the room towards the door. 'Oh, and Sarah...' He paused and looked back at her. 'I shan't say anything to Ben because I think it should come from you. But that doesn't apply to Callum. Bear that in mind.'

He could hear her sobbing as he let himself out of the front door, but he was too angry to care.

41

Jade hardly slept that night. She kept hearing Sarah's stricken voice in her head.

'Why did you have to tell him, Jade? Why couldn't you have waited like you promised? What difference would another few months have made?'

She'd half expected Sarah to phone her back. Callum wasn't there, he was away on some sales trip, earning cash for a wedding that might now never happen. But the phone remained silent. Finn didn't come back either. Jade tortured herself with how he might be feeling. But however much she wished she'd kept quiet, she knew if she'd had to make the choice again, she'd still have told him.

This didn't make her feel any better. She'd managed to devastate both Finn and Sarah with a few sentences. She'd probably never see Finn again – well, she'd survive that; she'd have to. But she couldn't bear to lose Sarah and Ben too.

Jade got through the following morning on autopilot. She felt drained and numb and she didn't feel too brilliant physically, either. Her head kept spinning, lack of sleep probably – and her throat was on fire. She'd just popped into the cottage at lunch time to see if she could find some painkillers and a Lemsip when she heard the front door bang.

Thinking it was Dawn or one of the other volunteers, she called out that she was just coming, but when she turned, having finally found what she was looking for, Finn was standing in the kitchen doorway.

'I've come to get my things.' His voice was cold. 'I'm going to stay at the Red Lion for a while.'

She swallowed and regretted it. Her throat felt as though it were full of hot knives, and she didn't know whether it was the shock of seeing him, but Finn seemed to be standing at the wrong end of a telescope. Very distant and not really a part of her world. He came a few steps closer and she felt herself wobbling and grabbed hold of the table for support.

'Jade, are you all right? You look terrible.'

'Thanks very much.'

Now he was right beside her and she could see the strain in his face and smell the citrus maleness of him. She frowned. Before she could stop him, Finn rested a hand on her forehead. 'You're very hot. I'm going to take your temperature.'

'No, I'm fine. You get going.'

He ignored her and got the thermometer from the kitchen cupboard.

'I've got a sore throat, that's all.'

'It looks more like flu to me. Put this in your mouth and we'll see.'

She snatched it from his hands and did as he said, too weak to argue. His concern was worse than his anger and she wished she didn't feel so giddy. There were all sorts of coloured lights on the edges of her vision and hot and cold shivers were sliding up and down her back.

'You've got a temperature of 101,' Finn remarked. 'Hardly all right. I think you'd be better off in bed.'

There was no disputing that. She had a horrible feeling she would fall over if she didn't lie down soon. She moved to go past him and he stepped aside. Why did her legs feel so wobbly? It was a bit like being drunk. She hesitated and Finn, with an impatient shake of his head, put his arm around her waist. 'I'll help you upstairs,' he muttered. 'Because otherwise you aren't going to make it.'

'I don't need any help,' she snapped, but it wasn't true. She'd had summer flu like this once before – it had washed over her with the same ruthless speed and left her flat on her back for a week. God, she couldn't afford to be out of action for that long.

They took the stairs, step by wooden step, Finn's arm supporting her, but she still felt exhausted and breathless when they got to the top. She paused on the landing outside her bedroom door.

'I'll be fine now. You can let go of me.'

He let go, but only to open the door. Then he propelled her inside. 'Get in bed. I'll nip out and get you something from the pharmacist. Do you feel sick at all? Shall I get you a bucket?'

'No, I'm perfectly fine now,' she lied, and he frowned and shut the door. And then, suddenly, to Jade's very great dismay, she was sick all over the floor.

* * *

When she woke up, Finn was standing beside her bed, a glass of something opaque in his hands. Sleep hadn't been restful, but filled with nightmares, strange and garish and so vivid she wasn't sure which were reality and which were dreams. She glanced at the floor and decided she must have dreamed the vomiting bit. At least that was something.

He followed her gaze, but all he said was, 'Drink this. The pharmacist recommended it.'

She pushed herself up on the pillows, which seemed to take a lot more energy than the small movement warranted. Then she realised she wasn't wearing anything. So she hadn't dreamed it and he'd undressed her, too. Humiliated, she pulled the duvet up to her neck and glared at him.

'Your clothes are in the wash. You wouldn't have wanted to wake up in them, I can promise you.' She saw a flash of something in his eyes – wry humour. Perhaps after yesterday when she knew she'd hurt him beyond belief, he was enjoying seeing her discomfort.

'Drink this,' he said again, holding out the proffered glass.

She took it warily. 'How long have I been asleep?'

'A couple of hours.'

'My God, this tastes foul. I think I've got flu.'

'Yes.' He knelt beside the bed and she felt a snatch of pain because the last time he'd done that had been in such different circumstances. 'Can I get you anything else?'

'No, I'll be fine by tonight. You can go to the Red Lion.'

He raised his eyebrows. 'Much as I'd like to get out of here, Jade, I'm not that much of a bastard. I'm not leaving you in this state. Besides, you need me to look after the animals.'

'No, I don't. Dawn will help if I ask her.'

'Dawn's got a sore throat too. Which reminds me. The pharmacist recommended these pastilles as well. They'll help numb it a bit.'

'Thanks.' She took the packet from him, wishing fleetingly for something that would numb her heart, which she could feel breaking all over again. He was here, but he hated her, she could see it in his eyes and she couldn't blame him.

'I'm so sorry I didn't tell you about Ben before,' she whispered, putting down the glass and lying back down on the pillows. 'But it wasn't my secret to tell.'

'Not half as sorry as I am, I can assure you.'

* * *

It was four days before she felt well enough to get back on her feet. Sarah came to see her on her first day up.

'Florence Nightingale wouldn't let me in before,' she grumbled, coming into the back room where Jade was curled up on the sofa under a duvet. 'He said you weren't up to having visitors.'

'I wouldn't come too near,' Jade warned, gesturing Sarah towards Finn's armchair. 'You don't want to catch this, believe me. Or pass it on to Callum or Ben.'

'Callum's gone,' Sarah said quietly. 'I told him last night that the wedding's off and he's gone back to Scotland.'

'What do you mean, the wedding's off? Sarah, you can't do that. You love him.'

'I adore him, but he's going to hate me once I tell him about Finn. I couldn't bear him to hate me. I'd rather he just thought I'd changed my mind.' She blinked and Jade saw tears in her eyes. She wanted to cry too – she'd never been able to bear seeing Sarah upset. Before she could argue with her, Sarah came across and knelt in front of her.

'I've done nothing but think these past few days, Jade. I don't do it very often, do I – thinking? But you were right. I shouldn't have lied to everyone. Especially not to Ben – and I shouldn't have made you lie for me either. I put you in an impossible situation.'

'I had a choice,' Jade said, swallowing. It was a relief to be able to do it without pain.

'No, you didn't. You're my friend. You lied because I asked you to. Even though you knew it would mean the end for you and Finn. You love him, don't you?'

'I don't know.'

'Yes, you do. That's why you told him. I'd have done the same in your place. If someone had been keeping something from Callum, I'd have told him what it was.' She sighed and drummed her fingers on the arm of the sofa. 'Anyway, I've done what I can to put things right. I've had a long chat with Finn and I've agreed he can see Ben – have him some weekends if he wants, once we've made things official.

'I'm going to get his name put on the birth certificate. It's what he wants and it's only fair. All I have to do now is to tell Ben he's got a dad and a grandad, but I can't see him minding. He's always asking about Finn. We've already arranged that Finn is coming to the results of Ben's art competition at the school. It's in a couple of weeks.'

Jade blinked. The world had moved on without her in the last few days. 'I'm glad about Finn and Ben,' she murmured, suppressing the urge to hug Sarah because she really didn't want to give her flu. 'But I'm really sorry about Callum. You two are made for each other.'

Sarah shook her head. 'I should have done some thinking before, Jade, shouldn't I? Proper thinking, instead of just burying my head in the sand and hoping the problem would go away. Finn's going back to Nottingham to live, isn't he?'

Jade nodded, even though she hadn't known that. For the last few days, he'd looked after the animals and he'd looked after her, but they hadn't talked beyond trivia. Knowing he must be desperate to get away from her hurt badly. He would have to keep in touch with Sarah because he wanted to see Ben, she thought with a tug of pain. He'd probably forgive Sarah, in time, for lying to him. He would understand why she had; he was that sort of man. But he didn't have to forgive her.

* * *

Dogs were infinitely forgiving, Aiden thought as he watched Kate tickle Fang's tummy. They were in his lounge. Kate was sitting on the carpet and the little Jack Russell was lying on her back, loving the attention. Her scars had faded now and the hair had grown back, leaving barely a trace.

'She's really cute, isn't she?' Kate said. 'Are you going to call her Fang forever or change her name now she's a reformed character?'

'I suppose we ought to change it,' Aiden said thoughtfully. 'Got any ideas?'

'How about Lucky? She is, isn't she, considering that she had a death sentence hanging over her head when you first found her.'

'I suppose she is.' It was 7 p.m. and they had the French windows open to let in the last of the evening sun. Kate's hair gleamed gold in its light.

'It's all down to you,' she told him. 'If you hadn't persevered, she wouldn't be here.'

'To be honest, a lot of it's down to Jade. She was the one who took her in. I'm really glad she's feeling better. That flu was nasty. I've never known Jade to be ill before.'

'Was there ever anything between you two?' Kate asked idly, glancing up at him.

He knelt beside her on the carpet. 'Why? Would you mind?'

'No,' she said. 'Well, maybe a bit.'

'How much of a bit?'

'Stop teasing me, Aiden.'

'I'm sorry. And the answer's no, there's never been anything between us.'

'Truth?'

'OK, once I hoped there might be. But not any more. The truth, Kate, is that these last couple of weeks have been the happiest of my life.'

'Mine too.'

'Really?'

'Yes, really.' She stopped stroking Fang and reached out a hand to him so that her long hair fell forward. 'My only regret is that Gran's been living next to you all this time and we didn't meet sooner.'

He thought about the first time he'd seen her at Duck Pond Rescue when he'd been all screwed up with bitterness over Finn, and he shook his head. 'No sense regretting what's past. We'll just have to make up for lost time.' He caught her fingers and thought again how beautiful she was. And how amazing it was that she seemed to feel the same way about him as he did about her.

He'd never in a million years have thought that he'd be pleased he'd punched someone. Not that he was planning to repeat the experience. But if he hadn't hit Finn that day, he'd probably never have got talking to Emily. And he very likely wouldn't be sitting here now, feeling happier than he'd ever done in his life.

'Kate, I know this is really bad timing,' he said, squeezing her hand, 'but I might need to be really busy for a couple of weeks. My Uncle Seth works at a practice in the New Forest called Puddleduck Vets and they have a staffing crisis. The owner, Phoebe Dashwood, has a really bad flu. There seems to be loads of it around. Anyway, Uncle Seth has asked if I can help out. It would mean using up some of my leave to do it – I obviously can't work in two places at once – and I'd much rather be spending the time with you – but...'

'Of course you must go if they need you.' Her eyes were warm. 'It's lovely that you're prepared to do it. Maybe we could meet after work one evening in the New Forest. They have some great pubs in that neck of the woods, and it would be fun to go somewhere different.'

Once again, he marvelled at how lovely she was. 'I'd really like that,' he said.

42

'You've got to come, Auntie Jade. *Everyone's* coming and Miss Benson says I might win a prize.' Ben, who was painting a picture at Sarah's kitchen table, gazed across at her with Finn's eyes. The likeness between them caught at her heart and Jade knew she'd never again be able to look at Ben without seeing Finn. She swallowed down a bittersweet ache of longing.

Everyone meant Finn and Sarah, Jade guessed, and she hated the idea of trailing behind them like a spare part at Ben's school. But that was her problem, not Ben's.

'Of course I'll come, darling. When is it?'

'It's on Saturday afternoon,' Sarah said, coming back into the lounge with two mugs of coffee and meeting Jade's eyes over Ben's head. 'Are you sure you won't be too busy, Jade? Isn't that your busiest day?'

Sarah was trying to let her off the hook and she was grateful, but she didn't see why Ben should be disappointed to spare her feelings.

'I won't be too busy. Which painting have you entered?'

'The one of Ashley. Daddy Finn says it's the best.'

She blinked. It was hard to get used to him saying Daddy Finn, but the words tripped off his tongue as easily as he'd once said Daddy Callum. He'd barely mentioned Callum, Sarah had told her. Perhaps children of his age did adjust more easily to change. He'd accepted Sarah's explanation that she'd made a mistake about his father having run away and he'd seemed happy to accept that not all fathers lived with you. That probably applied to half his class, Jade reflected.

'I've got a Grandad Ray who lives in Nottingham and he's going to take me to see Robin Hood and he's going to teach me how to fire proper arrows,' Ben carried on happily.

'Is he, sweetheart?' She wondered what Ray made of it all. She guessed he'd be thrilled to bits, once he'd got over the shock. Finn was pleased. He hadn't said as much, he was barely speaking to her, but for some reason now that she didn't need to try and work out what he was thinking, it seemed that she usually could. He and Ben had renewed their friendship as if there had never been a gap.

Finn was still living with her – or rather he was living in the same house. But he was going back to Nottingham straight after the art competition.

Jade was worried about Sarah, though. She'd lost weight over the last couple of weeks. Her usual flippant manner had all but disappeared and although Jade had tried to get her to talk, she had said very little about Callum.

'If I talk about him, I'll fall apart,' she'd told Jade the previous night. 'And I can't afford to fall apart. It's not fair on Ben.'

* * *

The judging of the art competition was taking place in the assembly hall of Ben's school. Sarah, Finn and Jade wandered around, looking at dozens of paintings displayed on the walls and on several big green screens. The paintings were divided by age groups of the children. Ben had temporarily abandoned them to chat to some mates across the other side of the room.

They paused, yet again, to admire Ben's painting of Ashley trotting across the field. Ben had got the chestnut shine on Ashley's coat very close to the original and there was a sense of movement running through the picture.

'It's very hard to draw horses, but he's got the perspective just right,' said a voice from behind them, and they turned to see Miss Benson.

Sarah smiled at her. 'I'm so proud of him.'

'Do you paint?' Miss Benson went on. 'It often runs in families.'

'He gets it from his father,' Sarah explained, touching Finn's arm, and Jade saw pride leap into his eyes.

'I dabble a bit, that's all,' he murmured, flushing, and he and Sarah exchanged a 'proud parents' glance. Jade knew it was irrational and stupid, but their shared closeness made her feel as though someone had stuck a dagger into her heart.

'Well, I'll wish you good luck for later,' Miss Benson went on. 'He's up against some stiff competition, but I'd certainly give him a prize if it were up to me.'

'Are you all right, Jade?' Sarah glanced at her with anxious eyes. 'You look really stressed out.'

Jade realised Finn was looking at her, too, and avoiding his eyes, she said, 'I'm fine. A little hot, that's all.'

'We could go outside for a minute. It doesn't look as though the judging's going to be for a while.'

But just as Sarah spoke, a voice on the microphone followed by a screech of feedback told them to start taking seats at the front of the hall, as the results of the competition were about to be announced.

Ben ran across towards them. 'Miss Benson thinks I should sit on the end of a row in case I win a prize.' He frowned.

'Well, don't look so worried,' Sarah told him. 'I thought the idea of entering was to win a prize.'

'Yes, but if I don't, I'll feel stupid. I think I'll sit in the middle.'

Sarah and Finn exchanged glances, and they compromised and took the last four seats of a row, Ben on the third one between Finn and Sarah, so he'd only disturb them if he did have to get up.

As they waited for the rest of the seats to fill up, Jade wished she was anywhere but here. She scanned the faces of the other parents. Right at the back of the hall she saw a flash of red hair as someone sat down. Not Callum, surely? Before she could be sure, someone sat in front of him, blocking her view. She must be mistaken. Callum was in Scotland, six hundred miles away.

Ben won a prize, as Miss Benson had predicted. Not first prize, but runner up, which he was thrilled with. He ran back to them with the trophy, a silver-plated affair in the shape of an artist's palette, his face shining with excitement. Sarah hugged him, but he wriggled out of her grasp so he could show Finn the trophy. 'I wouldn't have winned it if you didn't help me.'

'Sure you would. You're really talented.' Finn hugged him too and Jade noticed Ben didn't pull away from his father. Their bond was apparent, even now. She saw Finn wiping something that looked suspiciously like tears from his eyes and she looked away, not wanting to intrude.

It was as they filed out of the main hall that Jade saw Sarah, who was walking ahead of her and Finn, come to a sudden halt.

'What is it?' she asked, catching up, and then she could see for herself.

Callum was standing by Sarah's car, his face serious, as he waited for them to reach him.

Finn glanced at Jade. 'Do you think we should disappear?'

'I think we should see what he wants first,' she murmured, worry coiling in her stomach. 'He doesn't look very happy, does he?'

'Hello, Daddy Callum,' Ben said, oblivious to the adults' tension. 'Did you see me winned a prize?'

'Yes, mate, I saw you.' Callum hunkered down to Ben's level and took the trophy from him and studied it. 'Congratulations – and may it be the first of many.' Then he glanced up at Sarah and added softly, 'I came because he phoned and asked me to.'

'You came all the way back from Scotland?' Sarah's face was apprehensive.

'Well, to be truthful, I was only halfway there. The camper van broke down. I left it in the Lake District and caught the train back.'

He handed the trophy to Ben and stood up. 'Ben told me there'd been a mistake about his dad running away. He said you'd found him.' He glanced sideways at Finn and then he looked back into Sarah's eyes. 'He also said he wasn't the kind of dad who lived with you. But the kind he'd just see at weekends. Is that true, Sarah?'

Sarah chewed her lip and nodded and wiped her face with the back of her hand.

Jade touched Finn's arm. 'I think we should leave them to it,' she whispered.

* * *

When they got back to the cottage, Finn had gone upstairs to pack and now his bags were piled up by the front door, ready for him to leave first thing tomorrow. Jade heard him going up and down the stairs and cried silently over the washing-up bowl, her tears plopping into the water. She was dreading him going, but she also knew she couldn't carry on like this. Living in the same house as him, but having him act like a polite stranger, was torture.

She wiped her eyes, splashed cold water on to her face and went into the lounge to do some paperwork. She'd barely begun when he came in, but instead of just saying goodnight and vanishing to bed, which was what he'd taken to doing lately, he sat in the chair opposite her.

'Do you think they'll get back together?' he asked idly.

'Yes, I think they will. They're besotted with each other. They'll have talked everything through and Callum will forgive her for sending him away and for lying to him about you.'

Finn raised his eyebrows. 'Sometimes we can't forgive until we understand what's going on.'

She stared at him. It was the first thing he'd said in days that was any more than polite conversation.

'What do you mean?'

'Sarah told me you didn't say anything to me about Ben because she'd made you promise you wouldn't.'

'That's right,' she said quietly, wondering where he was heading. 'Why else do you think I'd have kept it from you?'

'I want to know why you told me when you did. Was it because you didn't want us to become more involved? Did you tell me because you knew it was the one thing you could say to stop things going any further?'

Jade gasped. 'Of course not.'

He got up and came across the room and the sofa cushion dipped as he sat next to her. She glanced at him, torn between the desperate need to touch him and the fear that she'd be rejected if she did.

'Your timing was spectacular. Why then, Jade?'

'I...'

'You can't say it, can you?' His eyes held hers. 'You're afraid to let go, Jade, aren't you? You're terrified to love anyone in case you get hurt. I think you'd rather push me away than let me get close. In case I hurt you.'

She shook her head, but he carried on talking. 'You probably don't even realise it yourself. These things go back to childhood. You once told me you felt you came second in your mother's life.'

'I did.'

'I don't think it's as simple as that. Things are never black and white – but we think they are when we're children.'

'You don't understand. You can't. You weren't there.'

'I understand that she was a single parent and that she wanted you to have the things she never had so she worked hard so that you could. OK, maybe she was a little blinkered and she thought material things would make up for not spending time with you, but I'll bet if you'd ever told her how you felt, she'd have been amazed. Did you ever tell her how you felt?'

'No.'

He put his arms around her and she trembled beneath his touch. Something was tearing deep inside her. Something breaking and shattering and the pain was so deep that she wanted to die. She remembered how she'd thought that selling the hotels would help her to move on. How she'd thought that once they no longer existed neither would the pain she still carried within her. The agony of thinking she wasn't loved, because she wasn't worthy of it. But it hadn't worked. You couldn't wipe out memories, however hard you tried.

She covered her face with her hands, not wanting him to see, even though she knew it was too late to hide from him, far too late. 'The longest time I ever held Mum's hand was when she was dead,' she whispered through interlinked fingers. 'Every time I tried to touch her – even when she was ill, she shoved me away. She would never let me get close. Not even when she was dying, Finn.'

Very gently he pulled her hands away. 'You have to let it go. Look at me, Jade.' And because she had no choice, she looked into his eyes and his expression was so tender she wanted to weep.

'You're not the only one,' he went on gruffly. 'I'm the same, which is how I know about you. I'm going to tell you something I've never told anyone before. It's about my mother.'

He started to talk, haltingly at first, his eyes clouded with pain. He told her about the night his mother had come to his room to say goodbye. About the fairy tale where the princess had something bad in her eye and how he'd been sure the same thing had happened to his mother. How he'd always thought if he'd been able to help her get it out, she wouldn't have left him. He talked of the wall of silence his relatives had put up to protect him. About the terrible conflict he had between wanting love and being unsure that he really knew what it was. And although his words were sometimes rambling, the emotions were so eloquent that Jade wanted to cry her heart out with him.

When he finally lapsed into silence, she realised that her fingers were entwined in her lap and her shoulders were stiff with tension, because she wanted to hold Finn, to comfort him, and she couldn't, because if she touched him she'd be lost again. She knew he was right. She was afraid of love.

'The fairy tale you're talking about was called *The Snow Queen*,' she said, struggling for control. 'I remember it too. My mother used to read it to me in bed. It was to do with a magic mirror that reflected only bad things. And then one day it got broken and the glass smashed into a million pieces and it was said that if you got one of the pieces in your eye you would never see anything beautiful again. The whole world would become ugly and distorted.'

For a while she didn't think he'd heard her, but then he gave a deep sigh. 'Oh, Jade. All these years I've thought Mum had something in her eye, but it's been me, all along. I've been the one who hasn't been able to see anything clearly.'

'It's just a fairy tale,' she murmured.

'But aren't all fairy tales based on the tiniest grain of truth? I don't think I even knew what love was, until...' He looked at her and broke off. 'How do you feel about me, Jade? I need to know.'

His eyes were mesmerising. She didn't think she'd ever be able to look away. But she felt so exposed, so afraid. Emotions spun and churned inside her and all she knew was that she never wanted him to go. Never wanted him to stop holding her.

'Tell me, Jade.'

Still she couldn't speak and the room around them seemed to draw in, holding its breath, waiting for her answer.

'I can't bear the thought of spending a second away from you,' she whispered. 'I'm terrified of you leaving and I'm terrified of you staying. Is that love?'

'I think it is.' He smiled. That wry little smile she knew so well. Then he let go of her for long enough to hold his hands out in front of him and she could see his fingers trembling.

'I'm terrified too,' he said. 'For all the same reasons as you. And I'm not going anywhere. Unless you want me to go. Do you?'

43

Callum and Sarah arrived at the cottage early on Sunday afternoon.

'We've got some news,' Sarah said. 'And we wanted you to be the first to know. Apart from Ben, who we told last night. He's at Darren's now.' She grabbed Callum's hand and pulled him forward. 'We're back together. We've talked everything through and we're moving forward.'

'Is the wedding back on?' Jade asked cautiously.

'No.' Sarah glanced at Callum. 'We don't need a legal document to prove anything, Jade. We can always get married some time in the future, but there's no rush. He's here, that's all I care about. And he's forgiven me. And I know I don't deserve it. I don't deserve you either, do I?'

'Don't be ridiculous,' Jade replied. Ridiculous was one of her mother's words. She must drop it. She was going to have to drop a lot of things. The future had opened up before her, a yawning chasm filled with darkness and butterflies. Finn had a lot to answer for, asking her to jump into it. To make this leap of faith.

'I'm really pleased for you both. Finn's around somewhere. Shall I tell him?'

'Tell me what?' Finn said, coming through the door.

Jade told him and watched with some amusement as he shook Callum's hand and then couldn't decide whether to shake Sarah's too, or to kiss her cheek. In the end he did both.

'Obviously this doesn't affect your relationship with Ben,' Sarah said. 'You'll always be his dad and Ben has decided he'd like to call Callum – well, just Callum. He's old enough to understand what's happened.'

'Thank you,' Finn said.

'We're going to the Red Lion later for a wee celebratory jar,' Callum said. 'Would you like to join us?'

'We'd be glad to come.' Finn looked at Jade. 'Perhaps we ought to make it a double celebration.' As he spoke, he held out his hand towards Jade and she stepped closer to him and took it.

'We've decided to start dating,' Jade explained. 'Well, we've already tried living together and we like that a lot. There's nothing like doing things in the wrong order, is there?'

Sarah squealed with excitement and there were more hugs and then for a while they talked about some of the successes of Duck Pond Rescue, like Tiny the puppy, Ashley the frisky horse and Fang finding a home with Aiden.

'I've got a little bit of gossip about Aiden,' Sarah said. 'Apparently he's been seen getting up close and personal with a glamorous redhead.'

'That came from Mike in the Red Lion,' Callum said. 'So it might not be true.'

'It is true,' Jade said, pleased to be ahead of the curve for a change. 'He's seeing Kate, the nurse who's re-homing Ashley.'

* * *

After the two of them had left, Jade wandered up the yard to check everywhere was locked up and found to her relief that Ashley seemed to be more interested in the polos she'd bought him than in Rosanna. Maybe he was growing out of his tendencies!

Duck Pond Rescue was a far cry from the ramshackle collection of buildings it had been before Finn had arrived, she thought as she leant on the paddock railings. She couldn't have justified employing him for much longer, even if things hadn't turned out the way they had.

'What are you thinking?' he asked, coming to stand beside her.

She told him and he nodded. 'Mmmm. As we seem to have the place to ourselves for once, there's something I'd like to talk to you about.'

'Talk away.'

'Not here.'

He took her hand and led her up the yard and Jade thought about the first time she'd seen him here. It was only a few months since that wet February day. Yet it felt as though he'd been in her life forever.

They went past the dog-walking field, which looked pink in the September sun. There was a track around the outside worn down by dozens of walkers, but in the middle of the field, the grass grew long and wild. It may have been a trick of the light, but the feathery tops of the stems had the faintest of rosy tints, giving the impression of a field of pink grass. A scattering of bright poppies added to the illusion. It was like seeing the field through rose-tinted glasses, Jade thought. She knew there were thistles in the middle, but you couldn't see them from here. Perhaps there were always thistles in life, an irritating but essential part of the journey.

'I had a phone call from Mike this morning,' Finn said, pausing by the gate. 'He's got an art dealer staying at the pub who's interested in my work. He wants to meet me with a view to putting on an exhibition. I know it's early days, but I think I might be able to make a living out of painting, eventually.'

'That's brilliant. It's what you want to do, isn't it?'

'One of the things. I don't mind what I do for a living. People are more important than anything else. Do you know, I love this place almost as much as I love you. I thought I'd miss Nottingham, but I don't. So maybe it's true what they say about home being where the heart is.'

'Is that what you wanted to talk to me about?'

'Not exactly, no.' He swung a jean-clad leg over the five-bar gate. 'You'll have to humour me for a while, I'm building up to it.'

It wasn't until the sun was beginning to set and the field was bathed in honey-gold light that he pulled her into his arms.

He had a bit of trouble getting out the words. He skirted round what he wanted to say for a few minutes, talking about things like commitment and finding out the truth about your emotions.

Then, as the sun slipped below the line of trees, turning the field to a gloriously deep pink, he finally said, 'Oh, hell, Jade, I'm hopeless at this, but what I'm trying to say is, would you consider marrying me? Some day in the future when you're ready?'

'Is that your idea of a romantic proposal?' she teased, and he looked so affronted that the effort of keeping a straight face eluded her.

'Laugh at me, would you?' He pulled her down on to the grass and kissed her so thoroughly she had to pull away from him, breathless.

'Finn, we'll get arrested. And there are thistles.'

'I can't see any. It's your bloody field. Why shouldn't we make mad, passionate love in it if we want to?'

'Because the farmer's next door,' she pointed out, pulling away from him and thinking fleetingly of another long-ago field, not far from here. Of him and Sarah starting Ben, starting all of this. A shadow passed through her and she hesitated.

'I thought we were letting the past go, Jade.' He'd read her face, as always. 'But if you're still not sure of me, then I'll wait.'

'I don't want you to wait. I'd love to marry you, Finn. Any day in the future. Tomorrow, if you like.'

He looked so surprised she added, 'Did you seriously think I'd say no?'

'I hoped you wouldn't.' He propped himself on one elbow. 'I wasn't sure if you'd forgiven me yet for bullying you into admitting you loved me.'

'I have. Anyway, you're not the only one who needs forgiving around here. I lied to you for far too long. I'm so sorry.'

'We'll call it quits.' He kissed her again, and for a long while they forgot all about the farmer in the next field.

They decided to keep their big news to themselves for a while, though, because tonight was Sarah and Callum's celebration, and they didn't want to take anything away from them.

* * *

Much later, they sat in the Red Lion: Jade and Finn, and Sarah, Callum and Ben. At the bar, Mike was deep in conversation with the holidaying art dealer, who turned out to be a friend of the woman who'd bought the painting of the girl on the beach. 'He's practising his negotiating skills,' Finn told Jade. 'He keeps trying to persuade me I need an agent.'

'He'd make a good one. That's what he's best at – negotiating.'

'Who's for another drink, then?' Mike asked, coming across to them, smiling. 'This one's on the house.'

'We've all had far too much already,' Sarah said, clutching her head and rolling her eyes dramatically.

'I'll have one,' Ben said, who'd been cashing in on the fact they were all squiffy and had helped himself to a few sips of Finn's Guinness when no one was looking.

'But we can't turn down an offer like that,' Callum pointed out. 'It's never happened before and it might never come again.'

So the drinks came and they toasted Callum and Sarah yet again, and Ben's competition success and Finn's future career as an artist. And then, when each of them had just a sip or so left in their glasses, Finn stood up. 'I'd like to make one more toast.'

'Better be quick, mate,' Callum said, his glass poised at his lips.

Finn grinned, looked at Jade and raised his glass high. 'Here's to love and second chances.'

ACKNOWLEDGEMENTS

Thank you so much to Team Boldwood – you are amazing. Thank you to every single one of you who works so hard to bring my books to my readers in paperback, audio and digital.

As always, my special thanks go to my fabulous editor, Caroline Ridding, also to Cecily Blench, Jennifer Davies, and to Alice Moore for the gorgeous cover.

Thank you to Gordon Rawsthorne for being my first reader. And to Jan Wright who has been such a lovely friend since we first met through writing.

Thank you, perhaps most of all, for the huge support of my many readers – without whom it would be pretty pointless writing novels. I love reading your emails, tweets and Facebook comments. Please keep them coming.

ABOUT THE AUTHOR

Della Galton writes short stories, teaches writing groups and is Agony Aunt for Writers Forum Magazine. Her stories feature strong female friendship, quirky characters and very often the animals she loves. When she is not writing she enjoys walking her dogs around the beautiful Dorset countryside.

Sign up to Della Galton's mailing list for news, competitions and updates on future books.

Visit Della's website: www.dellagalton.co.uk

Follow Della on social media:

 facebook.com/DailyDella

x.com/DellaGalton

instagram.com/Dellagalton

bookbub.com/authors/della-galton

ALSO BY DELLA GALTON

The Bluebell Cliff Series

Sunshine Over Bluebell Cliff

Summer at Studland Bay

Shooting Stars Over Bluebell Cliff

Sunrise Over Pebble Bay

Confetti Over Bluebell Cliff

The Puddleduck Farm Series

Coming Home to Puddleduck Farm

Rainbows Over Puddleduck Farm

Love Blossoms at Puddleduck Farm

Living the Dream at Puddleduck Farm

Happy Ever After at Puddleduck Farm

The Duck Pond Cottage Series

A New Arrival at Duck Pond Cottage

LOVE NOTES

LOVE IN EVERY CHAPTER

WHERE ALL YOUR ROMANCE
DREAMS COME TRUE!

THE HOME OF BESTSELLING
ROMANCE AND WOMEN'S
FICTION

WARNING:
MAY CONTAIN SPICE

Boldwood

Boldwood Books is an award-winning fiction publishing company seeking out the best stories from around the world.

Find out more at www.boldwoodbooks.com

Join our reader community for brilliant books, competitions and offers!

Follow us
@BoldwoodBooks
@TheBoldBookClub

Sign up to our weekly deals newsletter

https://bit.ly/BoldwoodBNewsletter

Milton Keynes UK
Ingram Content Group UK Ltd.
UKHW042227120924
1621UKWH00007B/32

9 781835 185339